CARRIE VIXENHART

Carrie Vixenhart, Vixen Ink Books

Eye of Fire, The Wildes Witch Trilogy, Book 1

Editing by Andrea Hurst, Leanne Rabesa, Jamie Ryter, and Noah Sky

Cover Design by Sarah Hansen of Okay Creations

Author photo by Andria Lindquist

Kindle ASIN: B0DJK7RTR6

Paperback ISBN: 979-8-9915454-0-2

CONTENT NOTE

Please be advised that this book contains explicit content and dark elements that may be upsetting for some readers. For more details (including spoilers), please visit Vixenhart's website at vixenhart.com/books or scan the QR code below.

DEDICATION

For my daughters.
May you always discover the magic within.

EYE OF FIRE

Ophelia Wildes felt the weight of eyes dancing on her skin as she ran through the wooded labyrinth. She knew better than to run after dusk, when shadows no longer followed her. But she craved the soft dirt paths under her feet. She itched for the wind on her face as it whistled through the changing and falling leaves. Longed for the trickle of the ravine and the occasional splash of the natural pool. Running solo in the North Woods, under the blanket of night, allowed her to be alone with her spinning thoughts. It helped calm her always-racing mind, one of the few times she could outrun the memories clawing at the edge of consciousness.

Now, she was no longer alone. She could feel the unmistakable thrumming sensation that always came over her when peril was near. Vibrations had started in the tips of her fingers minutes earlier. The feeling had spread throughout her body, becoming impossible to ignore. Danger lurked in the woods, hunting her.

Slowing her run, she stopped near the Glenspan Arch, next

to a wrought-iron park bench. Mindlessly, she reached for the messy bun that secured her long midnight-black hair and gave it a hard tug. Ophelia was a lithe and graceful woman who could run a mile in just over five minutes, if necessary. And that speed might be needed tonight. Her yellow-green eyes were piercing and alert, and that shrewd stare recognized more than most. Scanning her surroundings, she realized the dark night had long settled into the late-September sky. Even with her usually perfect vision, it was difficult to see beyond an arm's length.

Reaching for the threat, trying to assess it, she pretended to stretch. With one foot propped on the park bench, she felt her calves pull taut and then adjusted to reach her hamstrings. Bending at the waist, both feet now planted firmly on the ground, she allowed her head to swivel slowly, letting her gaze sweep the darkness. Nothing. With a huff of air, she straightened.

The familiar tremors remained, intensifying and unnerving her. An internal alarm to alert her that something was very wrong. Long ago, she'd learned to listen to these warnings, even as she'd also learned to keep them to herself. She took a deep breath to steady her racing heart and scattered thoughts.

Wood splintered nearby.

Ophelia froze. The air stilled. There was no doubt now. That menacing presence might be behind her. *Was* it behind her? Her light blue leggings and white tank top against her tan skin made it impossible to blend into the night. She needed to get out of the park. Immediately.

Inhaling a gulp of air, she placed one foot in front of the other, ready to sprint toward home. But just as she lifted her back leg to run, she halted, nearly stumbling over her own feet.

For a breathless moment, she imagined she'd conjured it.

But she hadn't. A massive jet-black animal now blocked her path.

Blinking rapidly, Ophelia tried to compose herself, unable to process what she was seeing. Surely, this wild animal could hear her heart pounding wildly against the walls of her chest. She shut her eyes tight, forcing the world to vanish. When she looked again, and saw it still there, she slammed them closed once more.

An imposing, muscular black jaguar. In the middle of New York City.

No, this was just an episode. A typical episode, even if it had been a long time since she'd had one like this. She shook her head rapidly and squeezed her eyes closed once more. Ignoring her surroundings, she took a deep, shaky breath, reaching for the clarity drilled into her as a child.

Slowly lifting her gaze, she found the jaguar still there, standing a body's length away. Its nostrils flared as it breathed heavily and methodically, rigid and poised. Its ears were alert and pulled back with its huge paws staggered in a starting-line stance.

The jaguar didn't move. Waiting, it watched Ophelia with disconcerting intensity. She held still, matching its intensity, racking her brain for what to do when face-to-face with a jaguar. Vaguely, she recalled that the black jaguar is one of the rarest animals in the world. But that was all she could conjure right now; it wasn't as if she regularly needed this knowledge.

They studied each other for several long moments. Ophelia's sense of wrongness—and the vibrations coursing through her body—seemed to subside as her heart rate slowed. Which didn't make any sense. She should be scared. Very scared. The danger was undoubtedly in front of her.

Without warning, the jaguar bared its teeth, revealing long, sharp canines. It lunged forward. Squeezing every muscle,

Ophelia tensed her body, ready for the attack, hoping it would be swift and painless. But the jaguar didn't touch her. In three powerful leaps, it roared into the woods behind her.

An instant later, sounds of cruelty and violence filled the night air. Ophelia let out a deep breath and looked behind her, trying to make sense of what she was hearing. Another beast had been lurking in the woods. And judging from the sounds of the battle, something just as deadly and powerful as the jaguar had been right behind her. Tracking her.

She had the strange sensation that the jaguar was protecting her. Momentarily, she was torn between helping the animal or escaping while she could. Feeling the edge of sanity, she shook herself. No, no, she would not be helping a jaguar tonight. There wasn't much she could do about two predators fighting to the death. And if the jaguar lost, she didn't know what may come out of the woods to claim her.

Clearing the brief hesitation, she started sprinting faster than she had in years. Powerful legs carried her toward the edge of Central Park. If she made it to the busy part of the Upper West Side, revelers would still be out, even at this time of night. And she wanted to get to crowds—and safety—as quickly as possible.

Passing the Ramble on her left, she exited the running path to land on the hard surface of the road that surrounded the edge of the park. She sprinted even faster, allowing the wind to carry her as she crossed the last bridge to leave the seclusion behind her. When she finally reached a crosswalk, she bent at the waist to catch her breath, sucking air into her burning lungs. Several miles from the North Woods should be enough distance.

Straightening as her breath slowed, she found herself at the corner of a busy street. The vibrations had finally dimmed to a barely distinguishable thrum. The danger was behind her, almost over. But should she tell someone about the jaguar? Animal control? Anyone? No. She let the thought leave as quickly as it had arrived. That was a terrible idea. Strange things had been happening to Ophelia since she was a child, and she had learned long ago to keep the episodes to herself.

Just before the walk light turned, she heard a rustling sound behind her. Tensing, she waited, but the vibrations didn't return. No sense of any impending doom or danger. Still, she turned slowly, bracing herself.

Instead of a wild animal, she found a man sauntering from the park. She cocked her head to the side, unsure why she was staring but unable to look away. He had dark brown hair that kissed his shoulders, and his gaze was a deep, knowing green that met hers without flinching. Despite the distance between them, the man towered over her, which was hard to do, given her own tall frame. As her attention roamed over his body, her breath hitched. His clothes were formal, all black, but he looked downright indecent with how his muscles strained to stay contained.

The man neared her, his long, solid legs walking slowly and deliberately. Ophelia sucked in a breath and quickly looked away. Flushing, she felt a light pink stain her tanned cheeks as she glanced up, only to find his stare already waiting for her. As a New Yorker, she was accustomed to ignoring strangers, but there was something about this man that stirred her curiosity. It didn't hurt that he was striking, almost perfectly, eerily beautiful. But no, that wasn't why she was staring. She had the uncanny sensation that she had met him before. With a small smile pulling on his full lips, the stranger gave Ophelia a slow nod of greeting. He didn't speak, and she felt her curiosity grow at the same speed she felt her flush deepen.

The light turned, and he strolled away, toward the still-bustling restaurants and bars. His gait was confident, unhurried, stealthy. Ophelia tracked the subtle flex of muscle beneath his shirt, tense despite his deliberate pace, until he disappeared into a crowd. The trance was over as soon as he was out of sight. Cursing, she realized she might miss the light. She sprinted across the street, toward home.

Ophelia had long ago learned to live with the strange things that frequently happened to her. But even for her, it had been a particularly peculiar night. The jaguar. The other danger that lurked in the woods. Now, the man. She didn't need the distraction right now. Not when she was so close to finally finding her mother.

CHAPTER

TWO

With heavy steps, Ophelia trudged up the front stoop of the brownstone she shared with Uncle Elijah and his husband, Sebastian. It was dark out now, her residential street barely lit by lamps. The cold night air seeped into her bones. Despite a sudden shiver—from the adrenaline or cold, she didn't know—she paused to watch her uncles through the front bay windows. She dreaded another argument with Elijah. But that wasn't why she allowed herself to linger, concealed by the curved window.

Elijah was leaning over the old Formica countertop, his rotund stomach resting on the edge. It was his "happy belly," a term he used lovingly after testing his husband's repeated cooking experiments. He wore his well-worn wire-framed glasses. *"These are just fine,"* he would often say, seeing no point in buying new, more modern glasses when the old ones worked. His clothes were similarly utilitarian and cliché for a child psychologist, consisting of his typical uniform: a tweed jacket and corduroy pants that barely fit the large man.

Sebastian was the opposite of his husband. Where Elijah

was calm and thoughtful, Sebastian's short, lean body radiated an energy that was impossible to ignore as he bounced from one person to the other, doting on them. Tonight, he was wearing the apron Ophelia had gifted him during their first Father's Day together, just after he and Elijah had married. At eleven years old, she'd adored the pink apron with the phrase *Kiss the Cook but Leave the Buns Alone*. Now, fifteen years later, it was faded and frayed. But he still donned it like it was his most treasured possession, and she still felt that same warmth when she saw him wearing it.

Even now, she felt the corners of her mouth tug up into a grin as she watched them, savoring how happy they made each other. Elijah threw his head back in unheard laughter as Sebastian turned from the stove, steam rising from the pots and pans on the gas burners. With a spatula in his hand, he teased Elijah with it, making circles in the air and pretending he was too short to reach Elijah's mouth. Finally, the spatula landed on its target for a taste test.

Elijah rubbed his belly and leaned his head back, squeezing his eyes shut as he pretended it was the best thing he'd ever tasted. As Sebastian started to turn back to the stove, his mouth still curved with mischief, Elijah leaned over the counter, grasping at his husband. Elijah's dark brown hand engulfed Sebastian's smaller golden-brown one as their fingers tangled together. They leaned in for a brief kiss before Sebastian tugged away and turned back to the stove, adding more spices to the pot in front of him. Ophelia could practically hear him humming as he stirred the pot.

She needed to burn this image into her mind, not knowing when—or if—she would see them again after tomorrow. And knowing they were happy together was almost enough to make her forget the park. Almost. As dark thoughts skittered across her mind, the warmth drained from her face, and she let go of the deep sigh that had been lingering just beneath the surface.

Finally, pushing open the door, Ophelia felt the breeze pick up around her as she stepped quickly into the foyer. For a brief moment, she was enveloped by a second set of doors that led to their small living room. Sweat glistened and tingled on her exposed skin as the workout clothes stuck to her body. Her skin itched from the stark temperature change as she moved indoors. Kicking off her trainers and peeling off her socks, she padded through the second set of doors and into the cozy living room. The smell of garlic and tomatoes instantly invaded her senses.

The house was a mix of fading opulence and modest new-world updates, hallmarks of several owners over the last two hundred years. The living room featured original woodwork, ornate molding, parquet flooring, and floor-to-ceiling curved windows. A crystal and gilt bronze chandelier hung from the soaring ceiling. Vibrant art crowded the walls—one of Sebastian's additions after he moved in. Of course, Ophelia loved her home, with its character and odd layout with rooms like nested Russian dolls. But she would trade it all in an instant to have her mom back.

As she made her way into the room, the flames seemed to follow her until she stood next to the roaring fire. She stood awkwardly next to the lit fireplace, staring at it to avoid facing Elijah. As if sensing her reluctance, she heard Elijah's hesitant shuffling as he came into the room, no doubt thinking about their ongoing argument.

When she finally looked up at him, he closed the distance between them. "Come here," he said in his soothing baritone voice, pulling her into a crushing hug. He smelled like home, a mix of wood spice and the occasional cigar she knew he snuck in the evening. "You know I love you. No matter what."

She stood still at first, not sure how this would play out. Finally, she returned the hug, standing on her tiptoes to reach him, squeezing him back. "I know." After a few moments of embracing, she pulled back to take in his deep brown eyes and worry lines creasing the corners. "Love you, too." She peeked around him at the sound of a soft humming she knew by heart.

"Ophy, you're home just in time," Sebastian said, stopping mid-song. Only he and Ophelia's best friend, Alex, got to call her by that nickname. "Almost done with dinner. Hope you're hungry."

"For your food? Always." She wasn't hungry, still disturbed by the encounter in the park. And she couldn't shake the image of the man. Something about him had taken over her mind, invading her thoughts. Maybe it was just that he was attractive, but she didn't think so. He'd felt hauntingly recognizable and dangerous. A shiver ran through her again as his face crowded her mind.

With a wink, Sebastian handed Elijah a bottle of wine and two glasses before turning back to the stove, resuming his humming as he practically skipped away from them. Elijah poured a healthy glass for Ophelia and handed it to her. That was one thing they could agree about—their love of rosé year-round, despite Sebastian's objection that the wine should not be consumed after the summer days were over.

Ophelia plopped down in one of the oversized chairs across from the fireplace, curling into it with her long legs wrapped under her. As she took a deep breath and then a large gulp of wine, she extended her hand toward the blaze to feel that familiar calm. The flames stretched toward her. She wanted to forget the black jaguar and the man. She wanted life to be normal. But that had never been the case for her, and probably never would be.

Elijah sat down across from her in an identical chair,

staring at the fire. Regardless of the tension, they would always be family. Despite no blood relation, Elijah had taken on the role of dad with ease after Ophelia's mom—his best friend— had disappeared when Ophelia was six.

"How was your run?" he asked. Although his question was falsely nonchalant, his watchful gaze betrayed him as the creases deepened. These days, he was always worried about her. And she knew his worry ran deeper than a late-night jaunt through the park.

Reaching over to squeeze his large, soft hand, Ophelia gave him one of the false smiles she had perfected over the years. "It was exactly what I needed," she said. Even though he was the only person who knew the full extent of her episodes, she wouldn't tell him about the jaguar or the man. Not this time. He needed to think she could do this next part without him.

"The run should help with the flight tomorrow," he said, his words more a question than a statement.

"Maybe," she answered noncommittally, trying to avoid the subject.

He cast a quick glance behind them, then focused on Ophelia, leaning closer with his voice lowered to a near whisper. "Ophelia, I'm not trying to pressure you. But are you sure you're up for this? You know what can happen."

Ophelia snatched her hand away, her expression hardening. She was tired of this conversation. "I haven't had a bad episode in years," she said. As furious as she was, she whispered, leaning toward Elijah and not wanting Sebastian to hear.

"But you *have* had manifestations. They haven't completely stopped, despite all the running and yoga. Even one at an inopportune time could derail everything we've worked toward."

Ophelia knew he was right to be concerned. Her episodes had started immediately after her mom disappeared. She tried to explain the internal warnings to anyone who would listen, tried to tell people that she could sense danger or change. That she knew her mom wouldn't come back that day, or probably ever.

At first, Elijah didn't believe her. But then he witnessed it himself. She would warn him when something unexpected was about to occur. A stranger would knock on the door. They almost got hit by a car in a crosswalk. Smoke filled the room from a pan that had been forgotten on the stove. Ophelia's warnings happened so many times that Elijah had no choice but to believe her. And that had been only the beginning.

Elijah scooted to the edge of his seat, leaning forward even further until he was invading her space completely. He gripped her arms, and the air around them started to stir. Ophelia lowered her lashes, retreating into herself and forcing herself to calm down. She took a deep breath, as she'd learned to do to manage the occurrences. And then she exhaled it, feeling the air settle all around them.

Elijah looked at her pointedly. "*See?* I just want what's best for you. You know that. I want you safe."

"I know. I know. But I need to do this," Ophelia said, her jaw set in that stubborn way of hers.

He released her abruptly. Sinking into the chair, away from him, she glanced toward the kitchen as Sebastian returned to them.

Standing, she walked around the chair, staying clear of Elijah. "What's that smell?" she asked loudly, sniffing the air.

Joy sparkled across Sebastian's features, his face bright. "You'll see."

Elijah stood, following his husband back to the kitchen. "You know Sebastian. Always trying a new recipe."

With her glass in one hand, Ophelia grabbed the bottle of wine and padded into the quirky kitchen. Featuring rustic cabinets, old appliances, and a cozy built-in banquette with a dining table, the style clashed with the rest of the townhouse. But that was what she loved about it.

Sebastian stood at the stove again, piling the food onto serving trays. One of his many cookbooks was open on the counter next to him, pulled from the built-in sideboard that was overflowing with books and recipes. Fresh cooking stains splattered the pages.

Ophelia walked to him, pulling him into a side hug. As she bent to kiss the top of his balding head, still covered in a smattering of salt-and-pepper hair, she tried to sneak a piece of fish from the tray. Catching her, he playfully swatted her hand away. She wasn't deterred. Sebastian was never stern, with her or anyone else.

After she finally succeeded in sneaking a bite, she set the table with plates and forks as Sebastian brought the food to the table. The three of them took their respective places—Sebastian and Elijah on one side and Ophelia across from them on the other side.

"Thank you, Mr. Reyes," Elijah said as he gave his husband a quick kiss, just before he ate a hearty bite of the food.

"You're welcome, Mr. Chandler," Sebastian said, ducking his head, clearly pleased.

Their meeting had been fate. They had connected when Elijah was visiting Ophelia's elementary school for a parent-teacher conference. Sebastian was teaching a different fourth-grade class, but they ran into each other during the school's open house, instantly connecting over their love of World War II history. They still teased one another by using each other's last names, just as they had when they first met. Relief bloomed in her chest at the sight of them.

Turning his gaze to Ophelia, Sebastian's expression lifted. "Are you ready?" he asked.

"For?" She stared at him blankly.

"The trip?" he asked, concern creeping in.

Ophelia looked down quickly, avoiding his eyes before answering. "Oh. Yes. Sort of." She poked at the food, moving it around on the plate but not bringing it to her lips.

Sebastian's frown deepened. "What do you mean, sort of? You get to spend the next several weeks traversing Europe with your best friend," he said.

Distracted and still thinking about the jaguar and the man, Ophelia masked her thoughts with a practiced ease. She met her uncle's intense stare head-on. "Right. I'm just tired." Her voice was quiet, and she cleared her throat. "Of course. Of course, I'm thrilled for this last adventure with Alex before she heads to med school. And the break will be good for me."

She glanced at Elijah before lowering her attention to her plate. Her response was a typical half-truth. She had finished law school in May, a degree she had no intention of using, but had completed because she knew it would make Elijah happy.

It was the least she could do, given that he had become a child psychologist to help her in the first place. To help her control the episodes and learn how to manage them. But she'd spent one summer of law school at a nondescript soulless law firm in Manhattan, and she knew a desk job would never be for her.

Now her uncles thought she was headed to Europe on a trip with Alex. That was only partly true. They'd be together for the first two weeks, but then Alex would head home. And Ophelia would head to where her mother was last seen alive.

"It's just—it's just one of those times I wish my mom could be here. That's all." Ophelia focused on her plate, avoiding their gazes.

To her surprise, Elijah reached one of his hands across the table, turned up in invitation. "I miss her, too," he said, his voice soft. "But I know she would be proud of you. So proud of you. And she would want what's best for you. Just like us."

Ophelia stared at his hand for a long moment before finally taking it. She didn't want to start arguing again. Since childhood, Ophelia constantly thought of her mother, wondering where she was and what had happened to her. But as an adult, she'd become obsessed, researching the region where she'd disappeared and digging for clues. Just in case Celeste was still alive.

Changing the subject, Elijah caught her attention with his next question. "Any feelings about your trip?" His meaning was clear, at least to her. He wanted to know if she felt any impending danger. She couldn't tell him about the jaguar now. He would take it as a bad omen, and she didn't need any further resistance from him.

"I feel fine. I'm ready." She knew her uncle was being vague for Sebastian's sake, so she gave a similarly vague response. They'd never told anyone about the occurrences, not even Sebastian. The physical warnings were just the start. At first, items seemed to hang in the air before crashing to the ground. When she was particularly upset as a child, wind seemed to rush around her, disturbing an otherwise calm room. Fire gravitated toward her, flames licking in her direction when she was near. Waves gathered around her when she swam.

Ophelia hadn't understood. Elijah certainly hadn't understood. Then or now. But they had started to refer to these strange occurrences as "episodes." Concerned she would be taken away from him, they vowed to never tell anyone. Instead, he enrolled in graduate school and became a child psychologist. Convinced he could cure her, he studied paranormal reactions to childhood trauma, hunting for any scientific reason to explain what was happening to her.

Ophelia didn't buy it. She was certain that only her mother

could help. Although Elijah never found an explanation for the episodes, he found strategies to help her. When he noticed the symptoms subsided with physical activity, he encouraged her to run and exercise. It helped clear her mind. Sebastian had also unknowingly helped, as well, suggesting yoga. The yoga and running had certainly helped with the childhood tantrums. But she never really controlled the surges. She'd just learned to mask them.

"You're barely eating," Sebastian said, interrupting her thoughts as he piled more food onto her plate. As if adding more food on top of untouched food would force her to eat. "Everything okay?" he asked.

"Of course," Ophelia said, arranging her face into the same practiced calm. "I just have a lot to do tonight." She kept thinking about the jaguar and the man. Mostly the man.

"Have you decided where you're headed after Trieste?" Sebastian asked.

Deliberately looking away, Ophelia pretended to dig into the food before reaching for the wine and taking a deep drink. "Not exactly. Just east." That wasn't true. She knew exactly where she was headed—where her mom had last been seen alive in rural Slovenia.

"How long will you be gone?" Elijah asked.

Ophelia knew he was trying to sound neutral, but he wasn't succeeding. Judgment laced his words, mixed with worry. "I'm really not sure." She didn't want to make false promises, and she didn't know when or if she would be back. She didn't know what danger awaited.

"Are you sure you want to go through with this? What was the point of law school?" Elijah asked. Disagreement tinged the words, even as he tried to sound supportive.

Annoyance resurfaced as Ophelia met his stare, the fire waving in the hearth as it tried to stretch toward her. Forcing herself to stay calm—to avoid any episodes—she changed tactics, instead trying a reasonable tone. "We've talked about this. Over and over. What is the point of my twenties? And my mom's life insurance money? I think I deserve this. Deserve the chance to explore the world."

There was an edge to her voice, a warning that the conversation was over. They'd already talked about this countless times. Ophelia never wanted to go to law school, but she'd gone because Elijah pushed her. And now she was going to do what she really wanted. She was going to find out what happened to her mom. She needed to find out why her body had never been found. She was desperate to find the truth, even if it killed her. She stabbed at a piece of fish and forced it between her lips.

Elijah paused, seeming to collect his thoughts before he spoke. Now he was the voice of reason; his voice was lower, almost cajoling. "I know you miss your mother. Know you think that if you just find the answers you're looking for, everything will be better. Easier. But doing this won't bring her back. Or help explain everything that has happened. I know that's what you want most, but it might not be what you need."

He paused and then leveled her with an unflinching stare. "I know you think searching is the most important thing in life. But it may not bring you the answers you want." Everything about him seemed to beg her to reconsider.

Ophelia felt the air leave her body as she realized that he knew what she was doing. He knew this wasn't about finding herself. It was about finding her mother. Her shoulders sagged. "I know you're worried about me. But I'm going. I can take care of myself." Turning away from her uncles, Ophelia's stubborn jaw was angled down so they couldn't see the grief tightening her mouth. She and Elijah had kept secrets together since she was a child. And she knew it hurt him deeply that she wasn't including him in this one. But it was for his own good. She couldn't bear the thought of him getting hurt.

Sebastian finally spoke, easing the tension as he always did. "Ophy, we love you, and we trust you. We know you'll be safe. And I think a toast is in order." He hopped up from his seat, retrieving three glasses and champagne that had been chilling in the retro refrigerator. After pouring some for each of them, he held his glass in the air, a hopeful expression on his face until Ophelia and Elijah raised theirs.

"Our little girl is going on an adventure with her best friend. And she is going to find herself and what she needs in the process. I just know it." Addressing just Ophelia, he said, "We couldn't be prouder of you. You're making this world your own, despite everything you've been through. We'll always be here for you. Salud!" His eyes brimmed with tears that didn't spill over.

Ophelia cleared her throat, feeling a tickle of emotion that she didn't want to acknowledge. She wouldn't allow herself to cry, not now, or she might not have the courage to leave. "I love you both." She clinked her glass to meet Sebastian's, and they both looked at Elijah expectantly.

Finally, Elijah met Ophelia's expectant gaze. She could see the sadness swimming beneath his glasses. "You are our world, Ophelia. Life wouldn't be the same without you. Salud." His voice was soft as they all clinked their glasses together.

THREE

After she helped clear the table and wash the dishes, Ophelia escaped to her sanctuary on the third floor, her wineglass and a paranormal romance novel in hand. Technically, the house belonged to her. Elijah had purchased it for her with the insurance money after her mother was declared dead. Her uncles had volunteered to move out when she turned eighteen, but Ophelia couldn't imagine living alone in such a cavernous house. Plus, she knew she wouldn't stay put in one city for long. And she'd rather her uncles live in the house and fill it with their joy and love.

After ascending the stairs, Ophelia entered a small sitting area, filled to the brim with books. A wooden desk occupied the corner of the room, where she'd spent long nights studying during school. A red velvet wing-backed chair—a gift from Sebastian—was sitting haphazardly next to the fireplace to the left of the door. The armrest of the chair was faded and worn from where Ophelia usually sat for long periods reading, her legs draped over the arm sideways.

As she walked through the sitting area to her bedroom, she

dropped the book onto the full-size bed. All the furniture had belonged to her mom. On her way to the en suite bathroom, she stopped briefly to stare at a picture of her mother, which she'd placed on a chest of drawers just a few feet across from her bed.

The photo was taken just a few months before her mom disappeared. They'd been caught in a downpour on their way home from a museum, so Celeste had wrapped Ophelia next to her body and shared a long wool coat with her. Ophelia's face was hidden in the coat, with her little feet poking out in front of her mom. Ophelia couldn't remember who had taken the picture, but her mother smiled broadly and appeared more relaxed than she'd been in the last couple of months before her disappearance.

Tired of thinking about the past, Ophelia peeled off her leggings and tank top. She tugged the sports bra over her breasts, which always felt too large for her thin frame, and discarded the clothes in a pile next to her dresser. With the wineglass in hand, she tiptoed to the cold white and black hexagon tiles in the bathroom to start the water in the claw-foot tub.

As the basin filled with water, Ophelia found herself once again thinking about the man from the park. Shaking her head, Ophelia let loose a little laugh, surprised at her reaction to this complete stranger she hadn't even spoken to. She wasn't usually so easily distracted by men. Sure, she'd had lovers before. But she'd never formed a deep attachment to any one person and always found it difficult to maintain relationships.

She grabbed her earbuds and stepped into the bath with her glass of wine, sinking back into the curve of the tub and listening to her music at full blast, trying to forget about the odd events of the day. But as she started washing her body, she kept thinking about that gorgeous man. And when a particularly sexy song with a pulsing beat started blaring, she shrugged her shoulders and gave in.

After taking a swig of wine, Ophelia kept one hand on the glass, balanced on the edge of the tub, and eased the other hand below the water. Over her pebbled nipples, down her taut stomach, and still further down between her legs. And as she let her mind trace his body, her fingers—

"Ophy! Ophy!"

Ophelia gasped at the intrusion, a familiar singsong voice accompanied by muffled knocking on her bedroom door. The wineglass slipped. Standing abruptly, water sloshed over the rim as she tried to catch the glass. She reached for it, but it was slightly too far. For a moment, as her arm stretched forward, the glass seemed to be suspended in the air before it crashed to the tile floor, splintering into hundreds of pieces.

Startled, Ophelia stepped out of the tub and slipped on the water, glass crunching beneath her feet as she fell into the mirror adjacent to the tub. As glass shattered around her, she instantly felt sharp pain radiating up her arm. Raising her hand to her eyes, she inspected the deep gash forming on her palm.

She heard quickened steps through her bedroom, followed by loud knocking on her bathroom door. "Ophy, what is it?" Alex's familiar voice—raised an octave—asked.

"It-it's nothing," Ophelia said, trying to shake off the pain.

"I heard glass." Alex tried to open the door, but it was still locked. She jiggled the handle. "Let me in."

As water dripped down her body, Ophelia stretched for the plush robe hanging near the door. Wrapping it around her body, careful not to get blood on it, she stepped around the glass and opened the door to find her best friend waiting her expectantly. Ophelia held up her hand, blood dripping down her arm in long, dark streaks.

"That doesn't look like nothing," Alex said, her Type A personality in medical mode. She'd been working toward medical school for years, training as a nurse's aide and then an EMT. "Go sit down while I get the kit," Alex said, taking a hair tie off her wrist and pulling her long golden blonde hair into a high bun.

Not bothering to argue, Ophelia made her way to the bed, water droplets following her, as she plopped down. Alex emerged from the bathroom with a first aid kit and squatted in front of her friend, getting to work cleaning Ophelia's wounds. As she used tweezers to pluck glass, Ophelia watched her with curiosity. "You were meant for medicine, you know."

Ophelia knew that she was insecure about attending med school. Alexandra Harper had been underestimated her entire life. People read too much into her beauty, assuming she was dumb and ditsy. But she was a natural healer and had recently been accepted to medical school at Yale. Soon, they'd be on different paths after spending their childhood as inseparable best friends.

"I hope so," Alex said, frowning as she wiped the wound with antiseptic, eying her work. "The wound isn't as deep as I thought, and it has stopped bleeding already, which is... strange."

Holding out her hand for Alex to see, Ophelia said, "It's like nothing happened."

"That's so strange. I could have sworn we were headed to the ER for stitches," Alex said, features scrunching with the same clinical focus she'd had since high school biology.

As she gathered the supplies to put them away, Ophelia lifted her hand again, examining it. She couldn't get the image of the wineglass out of her mind, how it'd been suspended in the air. Worry leaked into her mind. Why were these episodes starting again? And so frequently? The jaguar, the man, the glass, and the hand. Ophelia closed her eyes and forced herself to breathe deeply, clenching her fist and bringing it to her chest.

"Ophy?" Alex asked.

Ophelia blinked her eyes open to find Alex's cerulean gaze staring at her with intensity, brows creased. "Everything okay?" Alex asked.

Ophelia forced a smile to her lips. "Of course," she said, a false chipper tone in her voice. She wouldn't allow these episodes to control her life. To take over and paralyze her. Not this time. Not like when she was a child.

Ophelia dressed quickly in black leggings and an oversized T-shirt. After running a brush through her hair, she grabbed her mom's bracelet, struggling with the clasp. The bracelet was thin, made of a platinum chain-link band, with an integrated charm in the middle of the bracelet in the shape of an eye, set with pavé sapphires as well as black and white diamonds. Her mom always wore the bracelet—at least she had before disappearing. Apparently, she'd forgotten the bracelet next to her bed the day she'd vanished. When Ophelia found it, she'd put it on and had seldom taken it off since. Somehow, it had survived her childhood and teen years.

Ophelia met Alex in the sitting room. They piled blankets and pillows in front of the fireplace, making themselves comfortable with a bottle of wine and a charcuterie board that Sebastian had prepared for them. Ophelia turned on the fireplace and lit candles in the room, turning down the overhead lights.

"Sebastian spoils us," Alex said.

"I know. I'm going to miss him. I'm glad he and Elijah have each other."

"We're all going to miss you," Alex said, her voice breaking slightly, and she leaned over to squeeze Ophelia's hand.

"You're going to be rocking med school, training to be the best surgeon in the world. You aren't going to have time to miss me," Ophelia said. She'd always had difficulty connecting with other people, but with Alex, it had mostly been effortless. She was grateful for Alex's friendship, even if they didn't always see eye to eye.

They sat in comfortable silence until Alex finally broke it. "Are you sure you have to go halfway around the world to find yourself?" she asked.

"I'm sure," answered Ophelia. "If I don't do this, I won't have another chance. I need the space to sort through the past." Ophelia hadn't told Alex everything, but she didn't need to. Alex knew Ophelia was leaving for her mother.

Ophelia changed the subject. "Something odd happened in the park tonight." She knew her voice sounded tentative, afraid of Alex's response.

"What do you mean?" Alex asked, turning from the fire to study Ophelia.

Hesitating, Ophelia almost stopped herself, afraid of her friend's response. Of the rejection. But she needed to talk to someone about the episode. And she couldn't tell Elijah because he would insist she skip the trip.

"While I was running in the North Woods—" Ophelia paused, gathering her courage. "I—I saw a jaguar," she said, glancing at Alex and then shifting her gaze back at the fireplace. She'd hoped her friend wouldn't dismiss her, but she instantly felt Alex tense. "I know that I couldn't have, but that's what it looked like to me," Ophelia said quickly, trying to take back her words.

She peeked at her friend again and then dropped her gaze, feeling her lips spread into a thin line. The expression on Alex's face made her stomach sink. She'd tried many times to tell Alex about the episodes. But Alex dismissed them as part of Ophelia's *"overactive imagination as the result of trauma from her mother's disappearance and presumed death."* Or something like that. At a certain point, Ophelia had stopped trying.

"It's just the stress, Ophy. Our minds can play tricks on us. A trauma response," she said. Alex's voice was gentle, like she was talking to a toddler, and she squeezed Ophelia's arm as she spoke.

Stifling a sigh, Ophelia rushed to dismiss her own words, trying again to take them back. "You're probably right. Of course. Of course, you're right." A quiet lull settled between them before Ophelia spoke again. "But after I left the park, I had a strange interaction with a man."

"You should have led with that," Alex said, perking up, always concerned about the fact that Ophelia didn't seem to get laid enough. "Do tell."

Ophelia laughed. "It was nothing. It's just, well, this man seemed so familiar to me."

"Was he hot?"

Ophelia rolled her eyes at her friend. "Well, yes. But that's not quite it. That's not what got my attention."

"Did you speak to him?"

"No."

"Ophy, speaking is typically the first step to meeting a man," Alex said, her voice teasing and back to the sing-song quality Ophelia recognized.

Ophelia scoffed. "I don't have time for relationships right now."

"Who said anything about a relationship?" Alex asked, wiggling her brows at Ophelia. "You've been single for years. I know exactly what you need."

"I have you. And my uncles. That's enough," Ophelia said.

"After three years of being cooped up studying, you need to let loose."

"That's what we'll do on our trip," Ophelia said, grinning at her friend as she eyed her sideways.

"I'm going to make you keep that promise," Alex said, a mischievous glint in her own eyes. "I intend to find a hot Italian lover before I'm buried in cadavers."

Ophelia groaned, fake gagging at her friend. "That's some sick humor, to put 'lover' and 'cadaver' in the same sentence."

They both started laughing. "Maybe so." Alex grinned. "We're going to have an unforgettable adventure," she said.

Ophelia didn't respond as she ignored the warning shudder that ran through her at Alex's words.

"You know what you owe me. It's time for another game," Ophelia said, changing the subject.

Alex groaned before starting to laugh. "No, you always beat me."

"I do not! Your dad taught both of us at the same time," Ophelia said, laughing because she knew she did always win. "Maybe you'll get lucky this time," she said. They both giggled as Ophelia arranged the chess set, knowing Alex would not be winning. Ophelia had a wicked sixth sense when it came to strategy games. They spent the rest of the night drinking wine and snacking on the treats Sebastian had brought them.

THE NEXT MORNING, Ophelia and Alex left early to attend a yoga class before their flight. Alex said that it would help with circulation on the long flight. Ophelia thought it would help calm her mind and suppress the episodes. She didn't want to have an incident in the middle of a flight.

Nearing the studio, Ophelia allowed the familiar sensation to come over her. It wasn't fear or danger—not like the episodes—but something much better. Intense calm. Tranquility, even. Stepping into the small space, Ophelia inhaled the ever-present smell of lavender and calendula, savoring the place that felt so much like home. It was tiny and tucked away on a quiet street. The single room fit just under ten people. Billowing white tapestries hung from the ceiling, casting shadows from the ambient light onto the light hardwood floors.

As they unrolled their yoga mats, Ophelia remembered the first time she'd come to this studio. Sebastian had practically dragged her, insisting that she attend with him, declaring that she was too volatile and needed another outlet for her outbursts and moods. *"Running is for exercising the body. Yoga is for the mind,"* he'd insisted over and over until she finally relented.

And from the moment she'd stepped into the studio, Ophelia knew she'd be back. It was one of the only places where she was able to block the outside world. Even if, as a moody teenager, she refused to admit that to Sebastian.

Everything about the owner, Mira, exuded peace and warmth, from her long black hair, usually braided down her back, to her flowing clothes. Faced with an angry Ophelia, Mira's gentle black eyes never returned the anger. Instead, she was soothing and taught Ophelia to regulate her emotions. And, unknowingly, Mira helped Ophelia control the incidents.

Over time, Ophelia learned to calm her mind with yoga and meditation. She'd sink deep into a pose and think only of her breathing and nothing else. Sometimes, she'd focus so deeply that Mira had to place a gentle hand on Ophelia's shoulder to let her know the class was over.

And eventually, the spells got better. They didn't stop completely, but Ophelia was able to avoid being consumed by them. With yoga and running, she had fewer episodes. And the outbursts virtually stopped.

But, this morning, Ophelia's mind roamed. She found herself unable to focus as Mira started class with a gentle meditation.

"Let's start class by sitting with our legs crossed and our palms flat over our hearts," Mira said, soft melodic music filling the room and invading Ophelia's senses. "Close your eyes. Take a deep breath in through your nose, and let it out through your mouth, releasing your mind and the outside world while you are in this room."

Ophelia methodically did as she was instructed, but she was having a hard time focusing, not really allowing the meditation to take over or her mind to empty. She kept thinking about the jaguar and the man. It'd been a long time since something so bizarre had happened to her. She'd thought she had a better handle on the episodes—maybe she was wrong. And she regretted trying to talk to Alex about it. The main sticking point in their relationship was Alex's disbelief of anything that didn't fit neatly within science.

"Let's all meet in a neutral tabletop pose, knees and hands touching the earth. Your hands under your shoulders and knees under hips," Mira said, leading the class. "Breathe in and push your navel downward as your tailbone presses up, creating a deep arch in your back as you lift your gaze forward. Now round your spine as you breathe out, looking behind you as you arch your back. Good. Now do three more on your own, at your own pace. Keep your breath steady and go at your own flow, breathing in and out slowly," Mira said, interrupting Ophelia's thoughts.

As her mind wandered, Ophelia followed the poses by memory without paying attention. It still seemed impossible that he'd emerged from the same path she'd just fled. Was that even possible? Surely, he would have seen the jaguar. Unless it was just her imagination. But hadn't she learned long ago that her episodes were real in some way? Even if the jaguar wasn't there, perhaps there was still a lesson to be learned.

Mira continued the class. "Walk your hands forward a half step, step one foot back and then the other, meeting in plank position. Good. Now bend your knees and lift your bottom to the sky, meeting in downward facing dog, stretching in an upside-down V. Good."

As Ophelia automatically made her way to the position, she wondered where the man was from. He'd seemed so familiar to her. Of course, it didn't hurt that he was so alluring. And attractive. And just flat-out hot. Maybe her attraction to the man was really why she couldn't stop thinking about him. She couldn't remember the last time she was so instantly aroused by another person. And she hadn't even talked to him.

Somehow sensing that her long-time student was not fully present, Mira stepped lightly over to Ophelia and placed a gentle hand on her upper back as Ophelia stretched in downward facing dog. The hand was immediately calming, forcing Ophelia to take deep breaths to focus.

Mira's touch was all Ophelia needed to ignore her racing mind for the rest of the yoga practice. The class flowed through several rounds of a sun salutation and ended sitting on their mats for the final meditation, ending just as they'd begun.

"Place your palms over your heart and take a deep breath," Mira said, her voice soft but firm. "In a gesture of gratitude, bow your heads as a sign of respect for this practice, for these ancient Eastern traditions, for your body, and for this meditation."

Ophelia bowed deeply, her mind finally at rest. As she lowered her head, she felt as if her seat were lifting, almost like she was floating in the air. She knew she wasn't. Of course, she wasn't. But that level of calm was how she always knew that the yoga had soothed her racing mind. She felt Mira's presence and two hands on her shoulders, grounding her so that she no longer felt like air separated her from the floor. Finally, she lifted her gaze, smiling up at her long-time instructor. Mira bowed to her student.

"Ophelia, I'm so glad you visited this morning. Did the practice help?" Mira asked.

"Always, Mira," Ophelia said.

"Your uncle says you're leaving?" Mira asked, her dark eyes were intense as she studied her student.

Ophelia faltered, casting her attention elsewhere before meeting Mira's face again. "I'm not sure when I'll be back."

"You will return when the time is right." Mira placed a golden brown hand on Ophelia's shoulder and squeezed. She seemed to hesitate before continuing. "Be careful on your travels, Ophelia. There is an entire world for you to uncover and understand. But you have everything you need inside. All you must do is listen." Mira turned and walked away, ending the conversation without waiting for a response.

Startled at Mira's intensity and strange words, Ophelia stared in the direction of her teacher until Alex interrupted her thoughts.

"Ready?" Alex asked.

Ophelia closed her eyes one more time, inhaling the smell of the studio, perhaps for the last time. Finally, she met her friend's gaze, clear-eyed and resolute. "Ready as I'll ever be."

FOUR

Ophelia and Alex walked the streets of Trieste, marveling at the eclectic architecture and trying to stave off jet lag. The flight had been uneventful, and they'd landed in the ancient city that morning. As the sea breeze whipped Ophelia's long dark hair around her face, she felt at peace. Taking a deep breath, she let the sun kiss her skin as she listened to the sound of the waves echoing around the seaport. Since arriving, she hadn't sensed any warnings. Nothing like the jaguar—and whatever else—that had lurked in Central Park.

The evening sky began to fade as they hiked up steep cobblestone streets and climbed a long staircase to the Castle of San Giusto. They'd purchased a cheap bottle of champagne from a market and brought plastic cups with them on the hike.

"Cheers," they said simultaneously as their makeshift champagne glasses met. They sipped on the golden liquid as they settled into a quiet spot on the terrace. The hilltop fortress offered panoramic views of the Adriatic Sea below as they watched the sun finally rock itself to sleep, settling into the water.

Ophelia took another deep drink that fizzled on her tongue and down her throat. "It feels like the end," she said, finally breaking the comfortable silence.

"Of?" Alex asked as she tore her gaze from the pink-and-orange-hued sky to study her best friend of nearly twenty years.

"Just—everything. Nothing will ever be the same," Ophelia said.

"Did you tell your uncles?" Alex mindlessly tucked a strand of hair behind her ear. A sign she was worried.

"No. I don't want them to worry about me. Sebastian brought us back to life after my mom disappeared. And I know Elijah would try to stop me. Discourage me from searching for her."

"Are you sure about this?" Alex asked, voice hesitant. "What if—what if you find nothing?"

"Then I'll end where I started. But I have to try. Try to find out what happened to her." Ophelia needed her friend to understand. To support her. She had lied to everyone about what she was really doing. She'd finally told Alex when they were on the flight so that at least someone in the world would know where she was. Of course, Alex had already guessed.

"I would try to discourage you, too, you know. But I know you won't listen. And I'm glad you finally told me," Alex said, placing her hand on top of Ophelia's and giving it a gentle squeeze. "I want you to find what you're seeking. Whatever that is."

"Thank you. For understanding. For not being mad that I lied." Ophelia turned her hand over to return the squeeze.

Alex let loose a small laugh before answering. "Oh, I'm

mad. You and your secrets. But at least you finally told me," she said, tipping the glass to her lips and emptying it.

They settled into silence until the moon peaked above them, the darkness urging them to make the steep trek to their hotel—where the next battle began.

"You need to borrow a dress," Alex said, wrinkling her nose at the outfit Ophelia was wearing.

"What's wrong with this?" Ophelia asked, glancing down at her leggings and sweater, smoothing her hands over the soft material. "I'm comfortable."

"More like boring. And uninviting."

Ophelia didn't stifle her snort as she rolled her eyes. "Aren't we strong, independent, smart women who don't need attention from men?"

"Yes, yes we are. But I told you. I intend to find a lover while I'm here. So put this on so you don't block me," she said, handing Ophelia a black minidress that was clearly two sizes too small.

Ophelia was significantly taller and bustier than Alex. Her breasts were only partially covered by the scoop neckline, and the spaghetti straps appeared to be for show because they did nothing to help the garment stay in place. The dress stopped several inches higher on her thighs than she would have liked. The stretchy fabric—what little there was—seemed to hug every curve. Vetoing Alex's stiletto heels, she opted for her black combat boots and a leather jacket to provide some coverage.

"I look ridiculous," Ophelia said under her breath, frowning as she surveyed herself in a full-length mirror, turning to assess her round, muscular ass, worried it wasn't covered.

Alex let out a long whistle. "You are absolutely hot," she said. Alex had opted for a midnight blue corset that made her pale skin appear almost translucent. She paired the corset with a short skirt the same color, paired with the stiletto heels Ophelia had refused to wear.

"You're absolutely radiant," Ophelia returned, meaning it.

"Two strong, independent, smart women. One of whom is ready to find a good lay. And one of whom really, really needs to get laid. Let's go." Alex's infectious grin caused both women to start laughing uncontrollably as they left the hotel room.

Making their way through the oldest part of Trieste, they walked a maze of narrow, cobblestone streets. When they stumbled upon an unassuming thick wooden door with soft music escaping under it, Alex turned to her friend with a genuine smile framing her face. "This is it. I read about this. One of the oldest bars in the region."

Ophelia almost groaned as she felt the unmistakable thrumming sensation, a warning. Not tonight, she thought to herself. Please, not tonight. Let me just have fun with my friend. *Without* the complication of an episode. Ophelia ignored the warning and forced a smile to her face. "Whatever you want."

They pushed their way into the bar and found a low-lit dining room filled with couples enjoying a late-night dinner. The room was quiet, and they couldn't work out where the sound outside had been coming from. Unsure, they stood in the doorway, moving from one foot to the other, until a smiling man greeted them silently. Instead of addressing them, he ushered them to the back of the dining room, where they found a flight of stairs leading to a lower level.

The steps were lined with white candles that flickered toward Ophelia as she walked down. At the bottom, they found themselves in an old basement lined by rock walls with low lighting. A bar was at one end of the room, near the stair-way, while a small dance floor occupied the middle of the room. Tables filled the rest of the space, surrounding the dance floor in a crescent moon shape.

The bar was half full of people mingling and enjoying cocktails. As the server seated them at a small bar-height wooden table next to a rock wall, Ophelia eased herself onto a barstool, trying to make sure her dress still covered the important parts. A candle burned in the middle of the table, periodically swaying toward her. She tried to ease her discomfort, ignoring the low pulse of warning as she leaned against the wall behind her.

As soon as they were seated, a server appeared, dressed in a white button-down shirt, black vest, and black pants. Without saying a word, he placed two chilled glasses in front of them, full of a reddish cocktail and a lemon wedge.

Ophelia and Alex exchanged a glance, shrugged their shoulders in unison, and clinked their glasses together before taking a large sip. The drink was bitter, but delicious, and tasted like citrus peels with a hint of orange and gin.

As she took a smaller sip, a shiver ran up her spine again. Scanning the room, she tried to identify any danger. She desperately wanted to ignore it, but she knew from experience that could be a bad idea. She was so tired of the episodes dictating her life, and she wanted to enjoy this time with her friend. Taking deeper drinks, they emptied their glasses. The server quietly and quickly delivered another round.

"When are you going to date again? It's time that you found someone," Alex said, her speech slowing as the alcohol settled into her stomach. Her high cheekbones were now tinted a rosy red.

Ophelia winced, remembering that disaster in her first year of law school. "Back to this again? Why are you more concerned about my love life than I am? I'm about to find out what happened to my dead mom. Seems like a bad time to start an online dating profile," Ophelia said dryly, one eyebrow raised at her friend. She wasn't sure why, but alcohol always took longer to work on her.

"Let me rephrase: You need to get laid. No one said anything about dating."

"I believe you did," Ophelia said with a wink. "But thank you for your interest in my sex life. I can always count on you to be a good friend." They both paused and then giggled, as drunk on the bar's atmosphere as the cocktails.

As they laughed, a group approached them—two men and a woman. One of the men addressed them in a language neither of them understood. When Ophelia and Alex stared at him blankly, he switched to English. "American?" he asked in a thick accent.

"Yes," Alex said, beaming and a little too eager. Ophelia rolled her eyes.

"May we stand here?" he asked, polite and formal. He was tall, with black hair that curled slightly at the ends and eyes so dark they almost disappeared in the low light. A broad chest strained against his fitted black T-shirt, and inked tattoos coiled up his arms, disappearing beneath the fabric.

"Of course," Alex responded enthusiastically, almost purring at him. "You can put your cocktails on our table."

The man flashed a smile in response. "My name is Marco," he said.

"Alexandra. And this is my friend, Ophelia."

Ophelia gave the man a tight smile and then gave her friend a knowing expression. It didn't seem like a good idea to invite a strange man to share the table. Alex ignored her.

Alex leaned over and whispered to Ophelia, "This one is mine. We'll find a different man for you." Ophelia glanced at Marco. He smirked, as if he'd heard Alex, although that would be impossible with the ambient noise in the room and Alex's whisper.

"All yours," Ophelia responded, smiling at her friend. Of course, Ophelia wanted her friend to have a carefree vacation, even if that wasn't an option for her.

As Alex and Marco chatted, Ophelia rested her spine against the stone wall, enjoying the momentary break in conversation and the warmth of the cocktail as it burned down her throat and into her chest. She had two more drinks, trying to catch up with Alex. The music became louder and started vibrating in the small space, transforming the bar from a quiet cocktail lounge to a dance club.

Ophelia swayed in her seat, feeling the music course through her body and trying to work up the courage to dance. Suddenly, she felt a strong, unmistakable warning that she could no longer ignore. It wasn't just the alcohol. Her spine stiffened, and her brows drew together as she scanned the room. Her eyes landed on the far corner of the bar. For a moment, Ophelia didn't recognize the man. Then, stunned, she realized she was looking at the stranger from the night in Central Park. Before he averted his gaze, Ophelia saw the green hue she would recognize anywhere.

"What is it?" Alex asked, cutting off her conversation with Marco mid-sentence. She stiffened beside Ophelia, every muscle drawn taut, until she tracked where Ophelia was looking. Then her expression eased. "Go talk to him," she said, poking Ophelia's thigh with her finger.

"Not a chance." Ophelia swatted at her friend's hand, afraid the movement would make her dress inch up even more.

"Come on, Ophelia. What do you have to lose?" Alex wiggled her brows in a suggestive manner and then shoved at her friend again.

At that moment, the bartender arrived with shots of

grappa. Marco explained it was a high-proof spirit made in northern Italy. Ophelia wasn't sure who had ordered them, and she didn't care. She tossed back her shot in one gulp, then grabbed Alex's glass and did the same before her friend could protest. The liquor scorched a path down her throat, heat blooming in her chest. Ignoring Alex's knowing glint, Ophelia slid off her seat before her courage dissolved.

Making her way through the crowd, she almost turned around several times. But the beat of the music vibrated through her, propelling her forward. He was perched on a barstool in a shadowed corner of the bar, his long muscular legs stretched out in front of him. And she was certain that he was watching her. That shoulder-length brown hair was swept neatly away from his face, and his full lips seemed to twitch as he pretended to ignore her.

Once she reached him, she asked the first thing on her mind. "Are you following me?" She almost cringed at herself. What a ridiculous question. But, through the haze of alcohol, she wondered if it really was ridiculous. What are the chances that she'd run into the same man halfway across the world?

Surprise flashed across his features as his eyebrows arched. Slowly, his expression settled once more into an unreadable mask. He considered her for a long moment before speaking. "Do you want me to be?" A trace of amusement flickered across his mouth, and he had a deep voice with a hint of an accent she couldn't place. And his answer made her shiver. Just like in New York, he was dressed in all black. The outfit was formal, but made indecent by his barely contained muscles.

"What's your name?" she asked, not sure where this boldness was coming from.

"Loukas." His response was clipped, as if he wanted the conversation to be over quickly. He angled that perfectly beautiful profile to the crowd, scanning it with focused intensity.

"Loukas." She said his name slowly, deliberately, twisting the word on her tongue.

He glanced at her briefly, before redirecting his attention to the crowd again. "Luka, for short," he said.

"Do you have a last name, Luka?" she asked.

He faced her again, those green orbs studying her before answering in that clipped tone. "Angelos."

"I think we've met before," she said. It was a challenge, she realized, to see if he would remember. She really wanted him to remember.

"I don't think so." His voice was dismissive, his gaze sweeping around the room.

Disappointment hit her as a knot twisted in her stomach. She would normally take the hint, but the grappa was hitting her hard. Was this the same man? Probably not. It couldn't be.

"Want to dance?" she asked, again blurting the question before she could think better of the request. She would have blushed at her forwardness, but her cheeks were already warm from the alcohol.

At her question, Luka finally stopped scanning the room and focused on her with an energy that made her skin prickle. She sucked in a breath, waiting for his response. After a long moment, he reached for her hand, grasping it firmly by the wrist. Rotating her palm to face up, he raised her hand to his mouth, so close she could feel his breath. "Maybe next time," he said before placing a soft kiss on the inside of her wrist, just below her mother's bracelet.

She shivered. His touch sparked through her like lightning, sending a jolt through her. She wanted to move closer to him, wanted him to touch other parts of her body. But what the hell was she thinking? She jerked her hand away, stunned at her reaction to him. And surprised by her disappointment at his rejection. Without saying another word, she pivoted abruptly, cutting through the crowd to her friend. Not giving Alex a chance to object, Ophelia grabbed her arm and dragged her to the dance floor.

Alex laughed, her cheeks that rosy hue. "Okay. Okay. You don't have to ask me twice." Marco followed, apparently unwilling to be parted from Alex. His eyes scanned the room in the same way Luka's had.

They joined the throng of bodies that had amassed on the small dance floor. Crowds pressed in on all sides, and she could sense the man staring at her. But she forced herself to ignore him as she and Alex swayed to the music, Marco never far behind. Ophelia started to lose herself as she moved in time to the beat. Marco and Alex drifted away from her as they danced together.

Ophelia danced alone until the music slowed to a song meant for two souls to collide. She spotted a man standing alone. He would do. But just as she was about to approach him, someone stepped in close behind her. She knew who it was without even looking. The heat of him curled around her. She shifted to find Luka, his focus locked on her, every inch of his presence humming with unspoken tension.

"Allow me," he said in his deep, husky voice. Without waiting for a response, he slowly traced his hand down her arm, starting at her shoulder until he reached her hand, interlacing his fingers in hers. He gently placed her other hand on his shoulder and then grabbed her waist with his free hand, drawing her closer until their forms met, slow dancing to the music.

"I thought you didn't want to dance with me," she said. She tried to ignore that almost every inch of her was touching him, making her feel like static all over.

"I didn't say that." He pressed more firmly on her lower back, somehow bringing them even closer together. Heat bloomed beneath her skin as they swayed together, their bodies held tightly as one.

Without thinking, Ophelia allowed her hand to fall from Luka's shoulder to his chest, her hand splayed to touch as much of him as possible. She ran her hand from his chest down to his abdomen and traced her way up again, feeling his firm body under her hand. Luka sucked in a breath at the contact, but he didn't stop her.

Emboldened, Ophelia stood on the tips of her toes and planted a soft kiss on each corner of his mouth. As he hardened against her, she didn't care that this man was a complete stranger. She wanted him. When he didn't move, she leaned in for another kiss, but he stopped her, holding her away from him.

"Not here," he said gruffly, almost angrily. Turning abruptly, he grabbed her hand and walked off the dance floor, Ophelia trailing behind him.

As they neared the table where she and Alex had been sitting, she found her friend close to Marco, their legs touching. As Ophelia grabbed her purse, she leaned in to whisper in her friend's ear. "I'm going with him, okay?"

"Okay. Don't head to the hotel room until you hear from me," Alex said. Ophelia knew Alex would call if anything was wrong. And she barely caught Alex's smug smile before Luka dragged her away.

Holding her hand tight, Luka led Ophelia up a narrow staircase that emptied into a shadowed alley behind the pub. As the noise faded behind them, he spun to face her, backing her gently into the rough brick. His arms rose, palms braced against the wall on either side of her face, caging her in.

For a moment, he simply looked at her—searching, assessing—before lowering his mouth to her ear. "Are you sure this is what you want?" he murmured, his breath grazing her skin like heat and static.

A shiver coursed through her. She didn't answer. Instead, she slid her hands up his chest, fingers splayed, until they reached the base of his neck. But before she could move lower, Luka caught her wrists in one firm grip and lifted them above her head, pinning her to the bricks with effortless control. Tipping her chin towards his face with his other hand, he said, "I think you might be drunk."

"Am not," Ophelia said, hiccuping. "Where are you staying? Take me there," she demanded. What was she thinking? The alcohol was hitting her hard and dulling her senses. But the command seemed like a better idea than asking Luka to have sex with her in the alley.

Without responding, he dropped her wrists and grabbed one of her hands, walking briskly toward the street and away from the bar. As they walked down alleys and side streets, he kept to the shadows, always concealing them. After walking several blocks, Luka stopped in front of large, oversized double doors. He pushed them open and stepped inside quickly, keeping Ophelia to his side and slightly behind him, as if afraid someone would see her. No one was in the ornate lobby as they quickly stepped into an old birdcage metal elevator. Luka kept his hand firmly intertwined in hers the entire time.

On the elevator, he dropped her hand, closed the old manual doors, and pressed the fourth-floor button. Once they were moving, he stepped away from her and leaned nonchalantly on the wall opposite her. The entire elevator ride, he stared at her, eyes roaming her body. She wanted him to touch her. And she knew he wanted that, too.

After the elevator stopped, he opened the doors, gesturing for Ophelia to step out. Once she had, he placed his hand on the small of her back, setting parts of her aflame as he led her to the end of the hallway where he opened the door, revealing a dimly lit flat. The apartment was both cozy and welcoming. A plush white couch was positioned in front of a fireplace that served as the center of the room. Books were stacked in mismatched piles near the hearth, their spines softened with use. Luka walked to the fire and started it, heating the room from the chill in the air. Ophelia eyed the fire as it roared to life, instantly feeling at home. He crossed the room to stand in front of her, not touching her.

Suddenly embarrassed at her boldness, Ophelia forced herself to meet Luka's eyes, who was staring at her intently.

What was she thinking? Standing here, in the middle of Trieste, with a stranger she had seen in New York just a few nights before? She shifted from one foot to the other, unsure what to do with her hands or how to stand. But at least she didn't feel danger. Not at this moment.

"I can take you back to your hotel, if you prefer," Luka said, answering her thoughts, his voice formal and full of restraint.

No, that wasn't what she wanted. She'd thought about this stranger since she had first seen him. And she was certain it was him, even if he didn't remember. She couldn't get him out of her mind, and now she wanted to get him out of her system. She crossed the room, heat building with each step.

"I'd like to stay," she said, hesitating, unsure if he wanted her to be there, "if that's okay with you."

"Are you sure?" he asked.

Ophelia nodded, wondering if Luka was regretting bringing her here. Apparently satisfied with her response, he bent his head to her and backed her toward the wall of the living room until she was pinned against it. With his hands on her hips, he planted soft kisses along her jawline, trailing lower until his teeth grazed her bottom lip. A gasp escaped her, and she tasted the curve of his smile. As she arched her back into him, he released his grip and cupped the sides of her neck, pulling her close for a kiss that was slow, reverent, and searching. But when she moved her hands to his hair, using her fingers to encourage him, the kiss turned aggressive. She pulled away first, breathless and alive with the passion of it.

They stared at each other for a beat before their mouths met again, full of need and longing. He reached his hands around her waist and slowly slid his hands down her ass, cupping her with both hands and lifting her up. Ophelia wrapped her legs around Luka's lower back as he pushed her against a wall. With her legs raised, the black minidress hiked up to reveal her black lace thong. Luka moved his mouth from her lips down to her neck, where he suckled and caressed every sensitive spot he could find. Her body responded as she ground her hips into him, feeling herself grow wet and wanting every part of him to touch her.

Using one hand to cup Ophelia's bottom, Luka's other hand trailed from her collarbone to her breasts. He circled her hard nipples through the thin dress, giving them a soft pinch. She gasped, arching her back into him as he trailed his hand down her stomach to between her legs, stroking her too briefly through the thong.

With her legs still wrapped around him, Luka carried Ophelia through a door next to the fireplace. He lowered her on top of the plush duvet that covered a large bed. Ophelia tried to sit up and reach the buttons on Luka's pants, but he pushed her back down, holding her down with one firm hand.

Swiftly, Luka unbuttoned his shirt and removed it before lowering himself to the bed, kissing Ophelia with reverence, his hardness pressing through his pants and between her thighs. A gasp escaped her again, as she felt herself grow wetter. She wanted him, deeply and without doubt.

"That's right," he said. "I want to hear more of those noises from you." His voice was husky and strained before turning to regret. "But."

"But?" Ophelia looked at him, confused.

"But you don't know me."

"And?" Ophelia asked. "I can make my own decisions," she said, feeling annoyed that this man would try to shame her.

"And I think you are drunk."

"Am not," she said, just before another hiccup escaped. Chagrined, she looked at him and then started giggling. "Fair point," she said.

He smiled at her and lay down on the bed next to her, no

longer touching her. He released a long breath. Oh, yes, he definitely wanted her, as well.

Sighing and sexually frustrated, she sat up on the bed. "I should go," she said.

Luka placed a hand on her back and stroked it in a lazy motion, moving up and down. "Go where, love? It's one o'clock in the morning. I'll take you back to your hotel if you'd like, but you could also stay the night."

Ophelia hesitated, suddenly self-conscious. But the jet lag and alcohol caught up with her as an involuntary yawn erupted from her mouth. She looked back at him. "Okay. I'll stay. Just for a bit."

Luka smiled at her again, pulling her back down on the bed next to him, her head lodged in the crook of his arm and a hand resting lazily on his chest. As he stroked her arm, she felt herself drifting toward sleep. But then Luka rolled away from her, leaving her empty in the absence of his body.

"Would you like something to drink?" he asked as he stood in one fluid, graceful movement.

"Water?"

Standing next to the bed, he held out his hand. "I want to show you something."

Hesitating, Ophelia looked at her dress, which had risen way too high now. She tugged on the hem, feeling ridiculous in the outfit Alex had forced on her. "Do you have something I can wear?" she asked.

He leaned down on the bed, brushing a chaste kiss across her lips. "I quite like the outfit you have on."

"I'm practically naked."

He grinned at her. "Exactly." As she rolled her eyes, he walked toward a wardrobe across from the bed. "But if you desire something more comfortable, allow me." She marveled at his bare back, the muscles rippling as he moved. He selected a green T-shirt and soft shorts for her, leaving them on the bed. "I'll be right outside as you get changed," he said.

Ophelia shivered at his absence and wondered once again what she was doing here. Changing quickly, she left Alex's dress bunched on the floor in his room. When she emerged, Luka stared at her intently.

"Your eyes are yellow, but the shirt brings out the specks of light brown and green," he said, reaching his hand out and brushing a piece of her dark hair from her face. "Gorgeous," he whispered, bending to kiss her again. Before she could drag him back to the bed and demand an orgasm, he took one of her hands and led her to the kitchen.

After handing her a glass of water and some aspirin, he motioned for her to follow him through glass double doors, out of the kitchen and onto a large terrace with a view of the sea. The crashing waves below were illuminated by the full moon overhead. The terrace was completely private, with large plants blocking any view from the sides. It was decorated with a large table and an outdoor fireplace.

Ophelia's eyes widened at the view. "Beautiful," she said.

"I love the peace of this terrace at night," Luka said, staring out at the water. "My family has been coming here for centuries."

Ophelia placed her empty glass on the table and walked to the edge, leaning over the concrete railing as she looked out at the sea. Closing her eyes, she smelled the salt air and listened to the waves crashing below.

Luka wrapped his hands around her waist, as if afraid she would fall below. Wanting to be closer to him, she turned to face him, her back pressed to the railing, his arms still around her. They looked at each other for a moment, and then Ophelia stood on her toes and started to kiss him. She could feel him grow hard, the pressure unmistakable between them. But he stopped her.

"Not tonight, Ophelia," he said with a sigh. He kissed the top of her head before swooping down and lifting her in his arms to carry her back inside.

Ophelia suppressed her own sigh as she rested her head on his chest. He walked back through the apartment and settled her under the thick duvet. Settling behind her, her back tucked into his chest, he brushed her hair with his fingers.

"Good night, Ophelia."

"Good night," she said with a sigh, ready for sleep.

But just as she drifted off, her mind snagged on something he'd said, her body trying to warn her.

CHAPTER

SIX

As the sun shone high through the windows, Ophelia realized she'd stayed much longer than she'd intended. In the bright light of the day, and without the benefit of grappa, Ophelia couldn't believe she'd come home with this man. This complete stranger. She had never done anything so…irresponsible. And she still had a feeling of unease that was growing stronger, that deep nagging tickling the back of her mind, telling her that something was wrong. Shaking herself, she scanned the room, only then noticing she was alone.

Following the smell of bacon, she found Luka standing over a pan of scrambled eggs, wearing a pair of gray sweatpants that sat low on his hips, revealing the muscular V of his abdomen. He looked up, expression unreadable, gaze snagging on hers before she could blink.

"Morning." His voice was gruffer than last night. "Er, afternoon, rather," he said, glancing out the window. "Coffee?"

"Um, sure, that'd be great." Caffeine would help her focus.

Maybe it would help her sort fact from fiction—or at least from what she was feeling.

She stayed quiet as she watched Luka fill the base of the moka pot with water, then add the grounds and set it on the stove. When it finished brewing, he handed her a small cup of strong, black espresso—just the way she liked it. As she took a sip and savored the taste with her eyes closed, awareness prickled at her skin. He was watching her.

"What?" she asked, cracking one eye open to meet the intensity of his stare, confirming her suspicion. She was acutely aware of every inch of herself under his gaze.

When he finally answered, his voice was hoarse. "I'm happy we got the chance to meet," he said.

Ophelia averted her gaze. In the sober daytime, his formal speech was downright odd at times. And she was confused by his intimacy, by his familiarity. But they'd just met. Hadn't they? The feeling of unease stirred, getting stronger. She didn't feel danger from him, but she knew something wasn't quite right.

"Breakfast?" He looked first at her and then outside. "Or really, early dinner?"

"You know, I should get going." She shifted from one foot to the other, uncomfortable, biting the inside of her cheek. This was supposed to be a one-night stand. A one-night stand with no sex, apparently. A little fun before she went searching for her dead mom. But her stomach rumbled, answering for her and eliciting an involuntary laugh from her lips.

"I'll feed you and then drive you back to your hotel."

"I can walk." Ophelia didn't like his presumptuousness. She was perfectly capable of getting herself back to the hotel. One night in his bed didn't mean he could control her.

"I don't mind driving you." His voice was insistent. She was definitely walking.

Ophelia watched Luka finish cooking the breakfast, marveling at the precision of his movements. He cut fruit faster than her eyes could follow and moved between tasks with unnatural speed. But as if sensing the discomfort that spread in her bones, he slowed his movements, taking two plates to the terrace and motioning for Ophelia to follow. He placed a plate of eggs, bacon, toast, and fruit in front of her, along with another espresso. After disappearing for a brief moment, he returned wearing a black T-shirt and carrying a sweatshirt and blanket for her. Gesturing for her to lift her arms, he placed the blanket on her lap and handed her the sweatshirt.

"It's chilly out here," he said.

"What about you?" she asked, confused that he wasn't wearing more clothes himself.

"I don't get cold easily," he said with a shrug. Ophelia knew a half-truth when she heard it. She had perfected that over the years. He was hiding something, and her growing worry started to deepen in her bones.

"Eat," he said, a command and not a request. "I can take you back after."

Despite despising the order, Ophelia's stomach growled in response. She was ravenous. And she needed time to assess this situation. She took a hearty bite of the eggs. "You're actually a good cook," she said between bites. "I wasn't expecting that. Where did you learn?" She needed to learn more about him.

"I've picked up tips here and there throughout my years," Luka said. Another evasion. Another odd phrasing of words. She could feel the humming getting stronger in her body, alerting her that something was wrong. She shot him a quick look before turning away, unease prickling beneath her skin. Why was an episode coming on now?

"How long are you in Trieste?" he asked after she had taken

a sip of the dark coffee, trying to turn the conversation away from himself. She knew that trick, as well.

"My friend, Alex, and I are here until…" Ophelia stopped herself, staring straight ahead before slapping her palm to her face. "Shit. I need to tell Alex where I am. She's going to be worried. Where's my purse?"

"I can get it for you." Luka stood to stop her, but she ignored him.

Without responding, she vaulted herself from the table and walked into the apartment, toward the small living room. Scanning the space, she glanced around the couch where she and Luka had entered the apartment. As her eyes wandered, across the room, they landed on her bag atop a desk in a small study next to the bedroom. She didn't remember putting it in there.

As she entered the study and reached for the purse, she saw a picture on the desk, stuck between stacks of paper, but sticking out enough that she recognized it. Would recognize it anywhere.

Sucking in air, she tried to steady her heart rate as she freed the picture. A picture of her with her mother, just before her mother disappeared. Trying to catch her breath, she gasped. With shaking hands, she swept the papers aside, revealing more pictures. Pictures of her running in Central Park. Pictures of her walking past her house. Pictures of her entering the yoga studio. Pictures of her laughing with Alex. Elijah. Sebastian. Mira. Her instincts were screaming now.

She didn't hear him enter the room. Didn't know he was there until he said her name softly. "Ophelia, please."

She flinched at the sound of his voice and met his gaze. "Who are you, and how do you know my name?" Her lips were pinched tight, her hands clenched into fists at her side. Furious, she ignored any feelings of danger.

She finally realized what had been bothering her. She had never told Luka her name. It wasn't her style to sleep at a man's house when he didn't even know her name, but he didn't seem to mind. And he hadn't asked her. Because he already knew.

"Let me explain." His voice was pleading with her as he took another step into the small room.

"Don't come any closer." She was having difficulty breathing. Starting to feel suffocated. The air stirred, papers fluttering around the desk and floor. "I knew someone was following me. Why?" she asked, crossing her arms over her chest. She moved to stand behind the desk, in front of a bookshelf.

"Because you are very important. More important than you know. A lot of people are looking for you. And have been, for quite some time," he said.

Feeling both chilled and feverish, Ophelia dropped her hands to her sides, fists clenched tight. She fought for control, for breath—but the storm inside only surged, rage blooming as the air thickened and lifted her hair like a warning. "What are you talking about?" she demanded.

"Ophelia, let me explain. You need to calm down," Luka said, his voice too smooth, too calculated. He edged closer.

"Don't tell me to calm down." The growl in her chest tore loose, dragging up a wild, spiraling fury she hadn't felt since childhood. She inhaled sharply, reaching for clarity, for quiet— but nothing came. Nothing worked.

"I didn't mean for it to happen like this," Luka said gently, inching forward. "I wanted to introduce myself so many times."

"You didn't mean what?" Her voice was raw now, breath coming too fast, hair lashing around her face like a live wire. "To follow me? To kiss me? To have me sleep in your bed? How long have you been stalking me?"

Her skin burned, cheeks flushed, sweat beading at her temples. She wasn't just yelling at him—she was furious at herself. She should have seen it. He'd been in New York just two nights ago. Of course it wasn't a coincidence that he'd turned up again in Trieste. And of course she shouldn't have drunk so much that she dulled every instinct that was supposed to protect her.

Luka gave a half-answer. "I have been looking for you for a very long time. There is a lot you don't understand."

"How long?" Refusing his half answer, she enunciated each word, feeling the anger raging inside her.

Luka didn't flinch, meeting her eyes. "Months. I found you in the spring. I didn't want to approach you. I wanted you to have a normal life."

"A normal life?" Ophelia started laughing a harsh, false cackle from deep in her throat. "There's nothing normal about my life." She wanted to scream, to let loose a frustration that had been buried deep within her and suppressed for a very long time. Nausea surged up her throat as she gasped like she'd surfaced from a deep water. The air continued to swirl and spin.

"Listen, Ophelia, why don't we sit outside in the fresh air, and I can try to explain everything." Luka had changed tactics, still trying to cajole and control her.

His tone, his voice. It all enraged her even more. Because she knew he was trying to manipulate her. The thrumming in her body had turned to a roar long ago and moved from her chest throughout the rest of her body. Air swirled more violently in the room, papers flying around them, the pressure building like a tornado. Suddenly, all the glass in the room began to shatter and rain down around them.

Quicker than Ophelia's eyes could process, Luka was at her side. Wrapping his arms around her as he backed her into the bookcase, his body enveloped hers as he took the brunt of the splintering shards.

As jagged fragments sprayed across the room, catching the light like weaponized crystal, Luka whispered to her, "Breathe in, Ophelia. Breathe out. Calm your mind. You've got this. You can manage your power."

Control began to return with each ragged breath, her energy spent. She hadn't had an episode like this since she'd started yoga. It'd been years.

"That's it. That's it. That's it," he said repeatedly as he coaxed her to relax, her face pressed against his chest.

At last, the air stilled, an eerie hush settling over the wreckage. Ophelia remained frozen, chest heaving from the effort, stunned by the force of what had just happened—by the fact that she'd let herself lose control. It wasn't until the warmth of Luka's arms registered that she shoved him back with sudden force, fury flaring in her veins.

"Get. Off. Of. Me." Her anger at him was palpable, coating the space around them. She shook out her hair, trying to dislodge the remaining debris.

Luka opened and closed his mouth several times, clearly struggling with what to do or say next. Scanning the room, he ran his hands through his hair in frustration, slivers falling from his hair like diamonds. As he turned away, Ophelia caught sight of the jagged shards embedded in his back— glinting like cruel ornaments. Luka gave no indication he even felt them.

CHAPTER

SEVEN

"Luka, I'm—I'm so sorry," Ophelia said, skipping over her words as she brought her hands up to her mouth.

Looking over his shoulder at the glass protruding from his back, Luka sighed, but he didn't seem concerned. "Don't worry. It doesn't hurt."

"How can that not *hurt*?" Ophelia asked, eyes wide as she pointed at the jagged shards.

"I told you. There are things you don't understand."

"So explain," she said, still fuming as she planted her hands on her hips.

"I will. I promise. But first, I need to take care of the door-man. I can hear him coming."

"You can't hear someone coming," she said, not even convinced of her own denial at this point.

"I can hear him on the way up. I will take care of him. After that, will you please help me remove these shards? I can feel smaller pieces embedded, and I don't want the skin to knit itself back together."

"No. No way. I'm not doing that. I'm taking you to the hospital."

"No hospital. You have to do it, Ophelia," Luka said, his eyes pleading with her.

"My friend would be better at this. But you probably already know that," Ophelia said, feeling herself growing angry all over again. She closed her eyes, wondering how she had ended up here.

"Ophelia, I need you to listen to me," he said, taking her by the shoulders to face him. "I know you are angry. I know you have questions. I know you've had questions your entire life. I can help you with some of that. But I'm asking you to help me. It will be much, much worse if my skin closes over the shards. I'm going to take care of the doorman while you consider my request."

His insistence caught Ophelia off guard. Before she could answer, he released her and stepped out of the room. She could hear him at the door, speaking in soothing tones. While he was gone, Ophelia texted Alex.

> Ophelia: Miss you. All is fine. How is the Italian? Meet for dinner?

She wasn't sure why she lied, but instinct told her she was protecting her friend. And the fact that Alex hadn't texted her was probably a good thing.

When Luka returned, she reluctantly grabbed scissors from the desk and followed him to the bedroom. As he stretched out on the bed, flat on his stomach, Ophelia searched the adjoining bathroom for supplies, grabbing a towel and a pair of tweezers. It was the best she could find.

"Aren't you scared I'll stab you?" she asked as she walked to the bed, gripping the scissors until her knuckles were white.

"No," he said simply. His face was turned toward her, and she saw his lips lift in an amused smile, which infuriated her.

"You should be. This is going to hurt," she said.

"I trust you," he said, closing his eyes as if to underscore the point and to further annoy her.

Ophelia scoffed. "Why?"

"I know you, Ophelia. I told you."

"That's not creepy at all," she muttered, her voice laced with sarcasm.

Luka ignored her comment. "You are going to see some things as you take the glass out. You may notice things that seem...impossible," he said.

"What things?" Using the scissors, Ophelia cut the remaining fragments of his shirt, removing it. She tried to be careful around the larger pieces, but she could see his muscles straining as she got closer to the wounds. So it did hurt, despite his insistence otherwise.

With his shirt gone, she didn't understand why there wasn't more blood. There should be blood. Lots of it. Why were there only a few trickles?

"Ophelia, I know what you have experienced. Growing up not understanding how you are different," Luka said.

Although she was trying to ignore him, she paused when he said that. "How could you know that?" Better to keep him talking while her fingers worked.

She braced one hand against his side and the other on a piece of glass. Cursing herself for agreeing to do this, she pulled with all her strength, freeing the largest shard. She placed it on the nightstand next to the bed and decided to work on the other large pieces. The skin was red and irritated, but it still wasn't bleeding. Odd.

"Ophelia, I know you didn't have a teacher. For your

powers, I mean. That you didn't understand them growing up."

He must be in shock, Ophelia thought, wondering how she'd managed to fall into bed with this strange man. Just her luck.

"You are a descendant of a powerful line of witches," Luka said, not even wincing as she worked.

"Is that right?" Ophelia asked as she kept working, picking up her pace. Great, he's out of his mind. She was alone in an apartment with a lunatic. A gorgeous lunatic, sure. And one she'd almost had sex with last night. She still didn't know why he'd been following her. Yet here she was, fingers slick with sweat, pulling splinters from a stranger. The skin almost looked like it was scabbing over, but that couldn't be possible. Not this soon after the injury.

"Your power is definitely fire. But oddly enough, it seems that you also command air. It's very unusual to control more than one element of magic, particularly in this century. Who is your father?" he asked.

As she jerked the last large piece out of his skin, he hissed. Good, that was meant to hurt. "It's not really any of your business." His question infuriated her. Mostly because she didn't know the answer and had always wondered. "My fathers are the men you photographed, as you must know." She remembered seeing pictures of Sebastian and Elijah and felt her anger rise again.

"I'm sor—" he started to say, but she interrupted him.

"Beyond that, I don't know," she said. "My mom disappeared before she could tell me. And my biological father never bothered to show up. My fathers—the men who raised me—were all I needed." She wasn't sure why she offered this second part. She never talked about her mom's death, and she didn't want him to pity her.

"I didn't mean—" he began, but she cut him off again.

"I have to pick the rest out with the tweezers, and I'm not sure what to do with the wounds from the large pieces I removed," she said, her tone short.

But as Ophelia bent her head again to work, her hair falling over her face and grazing him, she saw that his skin had already healed where she had taken out the large pieces. Afraid her mind was playing tricks on her, she traced lightly over the skin where the large shards had been. As he shivered at her touch, she jerked her hand back.

"I was trying to explain, Ophelia," Luka said, as he turned to look at her face. "I know this is confusing. There is more to this world than humans. It's unfair that no one taught you. I know it must have been bewildering growing up, not under-standing what was happening to you."

She stared at him, then at his skin again. The wounds had changed from an angry red to a light pink in front of her eyes. "Luka, it—it's already healing," she said.

Luka adjusted to grab one of her hands. "Ophelia, I need you to listen to me very carefully. If you don't take the tiny pieces out, my skin will close over them and then we'll have to open it up again," Luka said.

She didn't move, still frozen in disbelief.

"Ophelia, I'm sorry I have to ask you to do this, but you are the only one who can help. We don't have time to find someone else."

Ophelia jerked her hand away from him. "Face down," she ordered, starting to dig out the remaining fragments, one by one. She wanted out of this apartment, out of this city, and away from him. But she still didn't understand how or why he had started following her. Her curiosity was the only thing keeping her there.

"Keep talking," she demanded.

"You think magical things have just happened to you and that you've been alone in your journey. But the world is full of supernatural beings, just like you. There are other witches, like you, with different powers. There are also beings like me." He stopped talking as she continued to dig, waiting for her response.

"And what are you?" Ophelia asked the question as neutrally as possible. Her gut told her he believed every word, even if it sounded like madness to her.

"Ophelia, you needn't be frightened," Luka said.

"I'm not," she said. She thought he was insane. She just wanted to get away from him, as soon as possible. But she wasn't scared of him.

"My people have gone by many names. Empousai. Empusae. Lamia. Sasabonsam. Soucouyant. In your day, we are known as vampires. We usually refer to ourselves as the empusae," he said.

Ophelia laughed, a deep, hearty laugh, sure he was joking. Her laugh was cut short when he didn't join her. Now she was convinced that he was simply delusional. As soon as the rest was out, she was leaving.

"So, you drink blood to live, can only come out at night, and can read minds?" Ophelia was ready to get the fuck out of this place.

"Yes and no. I obviously have no issue with the sun. We had food on the terrace in full daylight. I do need to consume human blood to live at full strength, but animal blood will suffice. Beyond immortality, our gifts depend on our blood-lines. On when we were turned."

"And you die by a stake to the heart?" Ophelia asked, just to keep him talking as she removed the final pieces.

"No. Empusae can only be killed if our hearts are shattered or our heads severed."

"No doubt." Ophelia could feel the sarcasm building, but she tried to keep it out of her voice. Tried to pacify this man just long enough to leave. "And you are cold-blooded and have fangs?" she asked.

"No on the cold-blooded. That's a myth. Yes, we have fangs," he said matter-of-factly, as if not sensing her skepticism.

Not only had she spent the night with Luka, but she had also somehow allowed him to convince her to dig glass splinters out of his skin. She was kicking herself for not recognizing that he needed a very different kind of help. Elijah would be furious if he ever found out.

"It's all out." Ophelia ran her hand over his skin, inspecting her work. When he shivered again, she yanked her hand away, remembering too well how he'd reacted the first time. "And it's all healed." This was some kind of trick, something she couldn't explain. But the rest was complete bullshit.

Luka rolled over, revealing that chiseled chest. "Thank you. Do you have any questions? I have more to tell you," he said.

"No." She stood and stepped away from him, scanning the room and looking for her shoes. "Time for me to go."

Luka stared at her incredulously, his eyes wide with confusion. "You're going? We just started talking. You've only begun to understand who you are." He stood quickly, much faster than Ophelia expected for someone who'd just had shards lodged in his back.

"I'm absolutely leaving," Ophelia said as she spotted her combat boots on the floor and jerked them on. Glancing out the window, she saw the sun dipping low over the rooftops. Shit. It was late. She hoped Alex's night hadn't ended as poorly as hers.

"You can't leave," he said. His voice was soft but full of command.

"You aren't going to tell me what to do, Luka—or whatever your name is."

"Ophelia, please. I have more to tell you," he said.

"I'm sure you do." She turned away from him and grabbed her bag before heading to the apartment door. Luka was a few steps behind her.

"Stop following me," she said over her shoulder without slowing down.

Luka didn't respond until Ophelia reached the apartment door.

"I can't," he said. "I promised your mother that I would look after you."

CHAPTER

EIGHT

Ophelia faltered in her march to leave. Slowly, she turned to stare at Luka, hurt and confusion piercing through her.

He hesitated when his eyes landed on her face, but then he spoke in a rush. "I don't want to hurt you. I know you've been searching for answers. I've made sure you were safe. From afar. You seemed so happy, and I didn't want to disturb your life. But then I found out you were looking for her, and I knew you would be in danger if you didn't know. About who she was. About who you are. About what you can do." Luka's words spilled out of him, like he'd been waiting to say them for a long time. As if afraid she might leave before he could finish telling her.

"You didn't know my mother." Her voice was shaking, furious that he was poking at this wound. That he would pretend to know the very person she'd longed to know her entire life. "You couldn't have known her. You look too young."

"Celeste Wildes," he said softly. "Brown hair, lighter than yours, curlier. Eyes like melted earth. She lit up a room when she wanted to, but gods help you if she didn't. And she loved you. More than you know. And she always wore that bracelet," he said, gesturing at Ophelia's wrist.

Ophelia's gaze dropped to the bracelet, then lifted to Luka. Her brow furrowed, her lower lip trembled. "How?" The word cut like ice, sharp and cold. She didn't trust him, but she couldn't help herself. "How did you know her?" she asked, hating how raw her voice sounded.

"Ophelia, I shouldn't—" He started to walk toward her, stopping as she held up a hand, creating an invisible wall between them.

"No, don't come any closer." Alarm sounded in her voice, but she was getting this information. It was why she'd come here. "Tell me," she demanded, voice cracking. This was the closest she'd come to finding out more about her mom. Even if she didn't trust him. Even if she thought he was insane.

He sighed and perched on the arm of the sofa, his dark eyebrows pulled down in concentration as he seemed to make up his mind. "Your mother worked with me," he said.

"That's impossible. You aren't much older than me," Ophelia said.

"I am far older than you, Ophelia. I have been alive for hundreds of years."

Fantastic. More of his ramblings.

"I told you that you come from a long line of witches. Your mother was a fire witch, just like you," he said.

"No. She wasn't." Ophelia crossed her arms in front of her chest.

"She was. I know you don't believe me. But the only way for witches to pass power is through the female bloodline. That's why fire gravitates toward you. I saw it last night. I know you've noticed," he said.

Ophelia ignored his comment about her episodes. She

wouldn't be discussing that with him. "So how did you really know her?"

"Your mother was working with me and others, trying to make the world a better place. To keep powerful artifacts out of the hands of those who would abuse them. It was a big task," Luka said, a distant look in his eyes.

Ophelia's head was spinning. She must have said something about her mother last night. She'd had too much to drink, and she must've let it slip. She opened and closed her mouth, unable to speak at first. She decided to change tactics.

"If she was a fire witch, then why did she die?"

Luka's facial features softened, his expression shifting into something Ophelia recognized—and hated—immediately: pity.

"Supernaturals aren't invincible. That includes witches. I don't know what happened to her." His voice was gentle, like he was trying to ease the blow of bad news. "But I know the important things about your mother. I know she wanted you more than anything. She loved you. She wanted to protect you. She hid you from the other witches and supernaturals because she thought you wouldn't be safe with them. I'm starting to understand why," he said, staring at Ophelia thoughtfully.

Ophelia leaned against the door, a tightness in her chest and a heaviness in her body, unable to decide what to do. "I don't know who you are or what you want with me, but I'm leaving." She stepped into the hallway, her phone in hand. "And I'm taking your clothes," she said, ice lacing her words.

"Ophelia, stop. Please." He stood, reaching toward her. "We have a lot to discuss. People are looking for you. You aren't safe." Luka stepped toward her.

"Including from you?" All these years. All these years she had searched for the truth. About her episodes. About her mother's disappearance. And here was a man who claimed to hold all the answers. But he, too, had betrayed her. Tricked her and made her trust him.

Her throat tightened. The sting behind her eyes threatened to give her away, but she blinked it back, furious at herself for feeling anything. Not waiting for a response, she turned from him and stepped into the hall.

Ignoring the elevator, she made her way to a set of stairs. Running down them, taking two at a time, she exited through a door that led to a narrow alley. The passage was barely touched by moonlight. Shivering, she remembered that her jacket and purse were still in Luka's apartment. Shit. She would get those later. For now, she needed to think.

Alone, she allowed a single tear to drip down her cheek. Followed by another. And another. Wiping her face with the back of her hand, she wound her way through the alleys, allowing herself to get lost on the narrow streets as darkness seeped in around her.

Suddenly, Ophelia knew someone was following her. The familiar unease began spreading through her body. And it felt different this time—more dangerous. Malignant, even. Concerned, she whirled on the encroaching figure.

"Luk—" She stopped when she saw it wasn't Luka following her, but a man who screamed danger, like a pall of black smoke hovering in the darkest corners. Instinctively, she stepped away from him and into the brick wall of the narrow alley.

"Well, well. Who do we have here?" With preternatural speed, the man moved to stand inches from Ophelia. She closed her eyes and reopened them. Closed them. Opened them. This couldn't be real.

"I'll get a big reward for finding you," he said. This was real. He was still there, now taking deep breaths as he sniffed all around her. "Mmmm. You smell delicious. Perhaps a little taste. No one will know." With horror, she watched as the man opened his mouth, his two canine teeth extending beyond his bottom lip. He lowered his mouth to the pounding veins on her throat, scraping the fangs across her skin.

Tense, Ophelia felt her skin grow clammy as her body screamed at her to get out of there. Pushing against him with all her might, she shoved him into the opposite wall.

He quickly regained his strength, but his face contorted from amusement into shock. He wagged his finger at her. "You are strong for a witch."

Taking advantage of the momentary pause, she filled her lungs with air and sprinted down the alley, away from the vampire. Yes, vampire. There was no denying what Luka had tried to tell her now. And she needed to get away from this thing. This vampire. Empusae. Whatever it was called.

Racing down the cobblestone, she looked for an escape. At the end of the alley, she paused, trying to decide whether she should turn left or right. Panicking, she turned left.

It was a mistake. The alley ended. And the hesitation had cost her. As she tried to double back, she found the vampire right behind her. Stiffening, she moved backward until the cold brick wall pushed into her skin.

"You think you're faster than a vampire?" His unnatural laugh scraped down her spine, taunting her. The sound curdled in her ears. The vibrating sensation in her body wailed through her, a warning that she already very much understood. As he moved toward her, she pulled her arm back and punched him in the jaw as hard as she could. And then kicked up between his legs, the way Elijah had taught her as a child.

Before she could react, he struck her across the face with blinding speed. She doubled over, clutching her nose as warmth gushed between her fingers. When her vision steadied, crimson drops splattered the cobblestone. He kicked her leg hard, and something cracked. Pain screamed through her as she collapsed, knees scraping stone. Another brutal kick landed in her gut. She gasped, folding backward until the brick wall slammed into the back of her skull. Her head whiplashed. A trickle of red slid from the corner of her mouth.

As she tried to sit up, he crouched beside her and shoved her back down. One stubby finger raked across her cheek, then paused to collect the blood beading there. He popped it into his mouth, eyes fluttering in satisfaction. The sight of him tasting her made her gag. Bile surged, and she turned her head, retching helplessly.

Then something shifted. The moment her blood touched his tongue, his expression changed—surprise, then calculation. "Witch," he hissed. "You're hiding something. The Concilium will be very interested in this."

He leaned in again, tongue extending to lap at the blood still trailing from her lips. She shuddered, repulsed. His fangs descended, aiming for her throat. But he froze as a new voice shattered the night.

"I suggest you step away from her. Immediately."

She hadn't thought she'd ever be grateful to hear Luka's voice again. But the sound of it—cool, commanding—nearly broke her. There he stood, emerging from the shadows like a blade drawn in silence.

"And what will you do, *Gatto Nero*? You know the Alleanza won't let you touch me. Did you think you could keep her to yourself?"

Luka said nothing. Instead, he lunged at his prey. He was stronger and faster than the vampire he pinned against the alley wall. Ripping into his throat, Luka bit deeply. The moment the vampire's blood hit his tongue, Luka froze. A flicker of something unreadable crossed his face—recognition, maybe, or awe. Then, with a guttural sound low in his throat, he made his choice. In one swift, brutal motion, he wrenched the vampire's head from his body and let it fall to the ground.

Ophelia tried to move away from them, to crawl on her hands and knees to get away. But she started retching, falling to the ground when she could no longer support her own weight.

Luka rushed to her side. "Ophelia, are you okay?"

"No. I'm. Not. Okay," she said between heaves. When she finally stopped, Luka lifted her by the waist, helping her stand.

"Is anything broken?" he asked as she wobbled on her feet, inspecting her body for wounds. As she started to sway, Luka didn't give her a chance to object as he swept her into his arms and held her close to his chest.

The movement made her gasp as every part of her body ached. Her skin drained of color, and her head started to spin. "Something's wrong. Really wrong."

The sound of distant church bells roused Ophelia. She peeled open her scratchy eyes, her head pounding and her mouth dry as chalk. As the room came into focus, she realized she was back in Luka's apartment. In his bed, naked, with a thin sheet covering her. He sat in a chair beside her, leaning forward, his head in his hands.

"Luka." Her voice came out raspy as she croaked his name.

His eyes snapped up to meet hers, relief washing over his face. Wordlessly, he handed her a glass of water. She drank it all before handing it back to him and raising an eyebrow, waiting for an explanation.

"I suspect a collapsed lung. Perhaps some brain swelling." He seemed to carefully consider his next words. "I had to give you some of my blood. To help you heal," he said.

Ophelia shrank deeper into the bed, pulling the sheet higher and fidgeting with the hem. "Will I turn into a vampire?" she asked. A cold, clammy horror spread through her.

He hesitated, averting his eyes and looking at the floor before answering. "You will not change," he said.

Relieved, Ophelia blew out a loud breath. "Okay. Okay." She arched a brow, glancing down at her barely covered form. "And giving me blood required me to be naked?"

Luka cleared his throat, covering his mouth with a hand. Ophelia wondered if vampires could blush. "Your clothes were destroyed. I thought you'd be more comfortable waking up without blood on you." He reached forward, his fingers brushing her cheek.

She flinched and turned her face away.

Luka jerked his hand back and stilled, studying her Ophelia intently. "Are you scared of me now?" he asked.

Crossing her arms over her chest, she stared at the ceiling, nails digging into her biceps. "No." Maybe a little. And she had too many questions she refused to ask. "But I don't want you to touch me. Ever again. I will never forget, or forgive, what you've done. How you misled me." She couldn't erase the image of him killing that vampire.

"Okay," Luka said quietly. "I'll respect your wishes."

An awkward pause lingered before Ophelia changed the subject. "Why did that man—er, vampire—attack me?" she asked, correcting herself mid-sentence.

"Ophelia," he said, voice heavy, "We have a lot to discuss about the supernatural world. And I promise I will answer all your questions. But first, we need to get out of Trieste as soon as possible. The city is no longer safe for you."

"I'm not going anywhere with you. You owe me answers. Why have you been following me? Why did that man—vampire—attack me? Why am I in danger? What is the All—whatever that vampire said?" Her questions tumbled out. But she left one unspoken, lingering in the air. *Why did my mother ask you to protect me?*

Luka raked his fingers through his hair. "Ophelia, please let me get you to safety. And then we talk."

"No." Her eyes narrowed, jaw set. "Apparently, people have lied to me my entire life. That stops now."

He leaned back in the chair, fingers digging into his thighs, frustration shadowing his features. "Are you always this stubborn?"

She didn't bother to respond.

"Fine," he said. "The supernaturals—witches, vampires, fae—have an alliance. The Alleanza, or Alliance, governs peace in Trieste and requires neutrality here. No violence between supernaturals is allowed here. But I killed that vampire. It doesn't matter that he attacked you. His punishment would've been proportional. Not death. Now I have to get you out."

Ophelia's eyes widened. "You mean *you* need to leave. Not me." She sat up quickly, the sheet falling to her lap. She didn't bother to cover herself, but her head spun, and she nearly toppled forward. "I have to get to Alex. She could be in danger."

Luka moved fast, placing pillows behind her without touching her. "I took care of Alex," he said quietly.

"I took care of Alex," he said, so quietly she almost missed it.

But she hadn't, and she jerked her head up sharply. "What do you mean, you *took care of her*?"

"A friend is keeping her safe," he said, his tone exasperated as he glanced at the ceiling.

"What friend?" she demanded, arms crossed over her chest. He seemed accustomed to control, and she wouldn't give him that.

"Me," said a new voice from the doorway. A petite woman stepped in, commanding the space despite barely being five-foot-two. Tattoos curled along every inch of visible skin. She wore leather everything—thigh-high boots, a trench coat. A gleaming lip ring caught the light.

Ophelia yanked the sheet up.

"Brisa," Luka acknowledged, nodding his head.

"Your friend is on a plane back to the States," Brisa said with a smirk. "She thinks you fell for some dark-haired man and decided to travel with him to Greece. A little magic helped her see it my way." Boredom dripped from her voice.

Ophelia scowled, her lips twisting. "Alex wouldn't believe that. She's too smart. And she's going to be worried about me," she said.

"Well, she believes it now. She was in danger because of you. So are you. Time to go," Brisa said, inspecting her nails.

"She's not safe anywhere. I need to get to her," Ophelia said.

"She'll be fine. She's being watched," Luka added.

"By who?" Ophelia asked.

He hesitated. "Marco. The empusae from the bar. He's loyal."

"Are. You. Serious?" Ophelia asked, her mouth falling open.

"When I realized you were in Trieste, I added security. Marco is loyal to me and will keep her safe."

"Is this what vampires do? Follow women, seduce them?" Anger surged. She stood, shoulders back and chest out. When Luka cleared his throat, looking at her pointedly, she suddenly remembered that she wasn't wearing any clothes. Hastily, she reached back for the sheet, wrapping it around herself.

"Don't worry," Brisa said dryly, not bothering to look away. "I'm not into my cousin."

As Luka draped a robe over Ophelia, she turned to Brisa. "Cousin?" she asked.

"My dad is your mom's half-brother. They have the same

father," Brisa said, examining her nails again. "We played together as kids, when you visited Spain with your mother."

Ophelia couldn't remember any of it. And she didn't think she had family left. But she wanted answers.

Luka cut in. "How are you feeling? You shouldn't be up yet," he said.

She waved him off. "I want—*need*—answers."

"We can talk when—" Luka started to answer.

"We don't have time for this shit," Brisa interrupted. "You're coddling her."

"Brisa, stay out of it," Luka said, a warning in his voice.

"You don't order me around, vamp. We work as a team?" Brisa's eyes flashed as air stirred around them.

Power crackled in the room. Ophelia felt it radiating from Brisa. She had episodes, too? But that wasn't important right now. "Neither of you will be ordering me around, controlling me, or telling me where to go," Ophelia said. "I'm leaving."

"You want answers?" Brisa asked, sighing. "You are one of the last witches of your ancestral line. One of the strongest lines of fire witches to exist. Everyone wants you. The vamps, witches, probably the fae. Everyone. They believe you can help them find a lost amulet. They'll hurt people you love to get to you. Until you're captured." Her voice was harsh and to the point.

Ophelia considered Brisa's words, looking at her for a long time before turning her gaze on Luka. "And is that what you want, as well? To use me?" she asked, not knowing what to do, whether to flee or stay for answers.

Brisa sighed loudly. "No, we're stuck babysitting you because your mom threatened us if we didn't. We hope you'll help us eventually, once you understand. Is that answer enough? We need to get moving." Brisa was done talking. That was clear.

She scanned them for lies. But found none. She didn't feel any of the internal warnings. Nothing to indicate that she should fear these two people. And for years, she'd longed to know her family. Longed to know her mom. Wanted to know why her father had not come for her when she was left alone and why she had the episodes. And she was almost certain this woman—her cousin—could help her.

"Fine. I'll go with *you*," Ophelia said, pointing at Brisa.

Brisa stood her ground, hands firmly on her hips now and legs spread in a strong stance. She didn't flinch. "That's not the way this works, cousin. We work as a team. He's coming with us, like it or not. Your petty argument does not trump safety. He's powerful, and you're untrained. I'll take his skills over your infantile powers. But yes, I'll answer your questions as soon as we get to safety. You've been kept in the dark for too long. I've never approved." A look passed between Luka and Brisa, and Ophelia knew this was not the first time they had discussed her. Luka stayed quiet, letting the two women talk. If Ophelia had hurt his feelings, he didn't let it show.

Ophelia sighed, crossing her arms over her chest. "Fine, I'll go with both of you." As much as she distrusted Luka, she knew he was powerful. He'd shown that when he killed the vampire. And she did want to get out of this alive.

"Excellent suggestion," Brisa said, as if leaving with them had been Ophelia's idea all along. She clapped her hands together. "I'm glad you're over the tantrum. I brought your clothes from the hotel." She gestured to the corner of the room at Ophelia's luggage. "Get dressed."

When Luka and Brisa didn't make a move to leave, Ophelia raised an eyebrow at them. "Privacy?"

Luka left quickly, but Brisa didn't budge. "It's nothing I haven't seen." She rolled her eyes and turned slowly. "Him either, I take it," Brisa muttered under her breath.

Ophelia couldn't help but laugh, a rich, real laugh. "Do you ever filter the words that come out of your mouth?"

"Not usually."

Ophelia hauled her suitcase on top of Luka's bed. Removing the robe, she dressed quickly in a pair of jeans and a white sweater. She found her combat boots next to the bed and realized Luka must have cleaned them for her because they were spotless. Not a drop of blood on them.

"Done."

Brisa circled her cousin, staring. "You look just like Celeste," she said.

Ophelia's eyes widened slightly. She was about to ask more when Luka called out.

They joined him in the living room. "We have a problem. Time to go," he said.

As they left the apartment, they opted for the stairs Ophelia had used earlier in the evening. Instead of stopping at the alley door, they descended to the lowest level, to a door with a small window that revealed an underground garage where two men were searching cars. Looking for them, she assumed.

Luka and Brisa exchanged a look, one Ophelia recognized must have come from years of working together. Luka whispered in Ophelia's ear, his lips almost touching her. "Stay here. We'll be right back."

He vanished into the shadows, but Brisa sashayed toward the two men, no fear in her steps. Ophelia stared, her mouth agape.

"Careful, witch," one of the men said to Brisa. "Don't come any closer. We just want the other witch, and then you can be on your way." As his teeth extended, Ophelia jerked back, despite the protection of the door. They were vampires, she realized. Empusae. Not men. This could not be real.

"Ah, you don't want to play with me?" Brisa asked, faux disappointment in her voice as the air picked up around her. With impossible speed, one of the vampires rushed toward her. But he was stopped as the air gathered around them, invisible shackles holding him back. He pushed against the wind, straining, but he couldn't budge. As Brisa lifted her hands, the man lifted with them, suspended in the air. The air rushed down his throat, gagging him until he lost consciousness. Brisa then lowered her hands, dropping him into a heap on the ground.

At the same time Brisa was fighting the first vampire, Luka had snuck through the shadows to surprise the other vampire, snapping his neck in one swift movement.

Brisa came back to Ophelia, opened the door, and pulled on her arm. "Come on, cousin, we need to go." Ophelia stood immobile until Brisa half dragged her toward a car. Luka was already in the driver's seat and behind the wheel, starting the engine.

"Are—are they dead?" Ophelia asked as they stepped around the men. She was afraid of the answer, but she had to ask.

"Like all vampires. Dead hearts," Brisa said. "But no, we didn't kill them in the way you mean. They'll wake up in a couple of hours with pounding headaches."

Brisa and Ophelia slid into the back seat of the four-door Ferrari as Luka put it into gear and sped toward the exit ramp. As they left the garage, he scanned their surroundings, his eyes flashing with concentration.

Ophelia expected to be stopped. To be taken. Her body was tense as she held her breath, waiting for resistance and a fight.

"The others have been taken care of already," Luka said, understanding her worry.

She caught him looking at her in the rearview mirror. She

held his gaze for a moment, but then looked away, not wanting to see his green eyes. She leaned her head back on the headrest and breathed deeply. As the adrenaline of the night disappeared, she fell asleep to the hum of the car as it sped out of Trieste.

CHAPTER

TEN

The tires crunched over gravel, announcing their arrival. Groggy and disoriented, Ophelia sighed heavily and pinched the bridge of her nose. She checked her watch, surprised to see that it was almost six in the morning. Her nap wasn't as short as she'd thought. They'd been in the car for hours.

Annoyed that she hadn't demanded answers during the drive, she glanced to her left and found a sleeping, unbothered Brisa, slumped in the seat next to her. Studying her cousin's face, Ophelia saw hints of her mother in the brown hair and golden skin.

Shaking her head, trying to clear the cobwebs from her mind, Ophelia turned to look out the window and realized they were no longer in a city or on a main highway. They were now driving down a long road framed on both sides by lush green trees.

"Where are we?" she asked, directing her question to the front of the car. Her voice was still hoarse from sleep.

Luka glanced in the rearview mirror, meeting her eyes. "My home. You're safe here," he said.

Ophelia stifled a retort. Her mouth opened and closed. How dare he talk about her protection when he was the reason she was in this position? She narrowed her eyes but said nothing. Safety had not been her concern. Of course, she *was* worried about Alex. But this was the closest she had come to learning about her mother in years. And she had been promised answers.

Luka averted his eyes from the rage that was building in hers. She followed his gaze down the long driveway. As they cleared the trees, she openly gaped when his home came into view. Home wasn't quite the right word. It could only be described as a fortified castle, surrounded by a twenty-foot-tall stone wall.

Luka steered the car through a tall wrought-iron gate, and the rest of the building came into view. It appeared to be straight from the 1500s—a stone-covered rectangular castle with four cylindrical towers, one at each corner, where guards could be stationed to watch the estate from all sides.

As Luka piloted the car up a half-moon drive, he brought it to a smooth stop beside a grand set of stairs that swept up to the castle's entrance. Before he could move, Ophelia pushed open her own door. Dammit, she didn't need him to do everything. She stepped out, stretched her arms overhead, and rose onto her toes to work out the stiffness in her legs. The breeze caught her hair, and she inhaled deeply: brine and salt. They were near the sea.

Ophelia watched as Brisa let out a ridiculously long yawn and slid across the backseat to stand next to her cousin. The top of her head didn't even reach Ophelia's shoulders.

Amusement danced in his eyes as he smirked at Brisa. "Get your beauty rest?" he asked.

"Like a baby, vamp. Thanks for asking. I'm sorry you weren't able to get a nap in your coffin," Brisa responded.

As Luka barked a laugh, Ophelia caught sight of them in her periphery, a gnawing sensation blooming in her gut. Why did *he*—a vampire—get to have a relationship with her cousin, when she'd been denied that chance? She also noticed that Luka had driven the entire trip without a single pause, not even a hair out of place. Her stomach turned. She quickly shifted her focus, looking away when she sensed him watching her, his expression taut with unspoken thought.

At the top of the stairs, one of the oversized double doors swung open. A tall, broad-shouldered man bounded down the steps. His sweeping grin couldn't fully mask the deep worry etched into his features—brows drawn, shoulders tense. The tension only eased when he reached Brisa, pulling her into a bear hug. "So glad you're safe." Then, turning toward Ophelia, he added, "All of you." He let Brisa go and stepped in front of Ophelia. "I'm Marcello. Mo. Your uncle."

Another family member she didn't know about. Unsure how to respond, she studied her uncle. He also resembled her mother, but his brown curly hair was cut close to the scalp. "Oh. It's—it's nice to meet you," she finally said. For so long, she didn't think she had any family. Now, in the space of a day, she'd met a cousin and an uncle.

"We met when you were a toddler, when you and your mother visited our home. I'm sorry it has been so long," Mo said.

Regret laced his words, and she believed him. But she didn't know how to respond. So much of her life—and her family—was still a blank. Should she hug him? Shake his hand? Instead, she stuffed her hands into her jean pockets and stared at the gravel, shifting her weight from one foot to the other.

As if sensing her discomfort, Luka stepped in, saving her from having to reply. "Ophelia must be exhausted from the trip. I'm taking her inside to rest," he said.

"We'll have time to catch up later," Mo said, placing a warm, solid hand on her shoulder but keeping a respectful distance. "It's good to see you, Ophelia," he said, his voice gentle and sincere.

Luka moved without hesitation, no longer bothering to conceal his unnatural speed. He circled the car, retrieved her suitcase from the trunk, and stopped beside her with it in hand—waiting. She exhaled heavily, the weight of the past twenty-four hours settling into her bones. What she needed most was sleep, and space to absorb everything she'd just learned. This was why she'd come. To uncover the truth about her mother.

Just before climbing the stairs, Luka spoke to Brisa. "Same place as always."

Brisa rolled her eyes and crossed her arms. "Obviously. I've already decorated."

Ophelia took note—Brisa had clearly spent a lot of time here. Enough to have a designated space. One she'd made her own. But the thought slipped away under the fog of exhaustion. With slow, heavy steps, she followed Luka up the stairs, through the grand entryway, and down a long corridor.

The house unfolded around a central courtyard bursting with vibrant blooms, a sleek infinity pool, and a sprawling patio anchored by a long dining table. Floor-to-ceiling windows lined the hallway, offering uninterrupted views of the secluded, well-guarded oasis. Morning sunlight streamed through the glass, bathing the corridor in golden warmth as they walked.

"I guess you really don't have to worry about sunlight?" Ophelia blurted out, curiosity about vampire lore besting her.

A smirk tugged at his mouth as he tilted his head in her

direction. "Actually, I sparkle in the sunlight. Can't you see?" He wiggled his brows, teasing. "But no, it doesn't bother us. We can stay in the sunlight without issue. I think an ancient empusae leader created that myth so our enemies would think we couldn't attack during the day."

He moved easily through the corridor, his posture looser, less guarded. He seemed at ease here—more himself. She wasn't sure how to feel about that. Questions burned on her tongue, but so did hesitation. A yawn escaped before she could stop it, and when he chuckled softly in response, she covered her mouth, sheepish. "Sorry," she muttered. "Don't you need sleep?"

"Not as much as humans. The empusae can go days without sleeping, but we do eventually need some," he answered.

Stopping in front of a thick wooden door, Luka pushed it open and gestured for her to step inside. She found a warm, inviting space, anchored by an oversized bed layered in plush white pillows and soft linens. The entire area felt like Luka. It even carried his scent: pine and night-blooming jasmine. This was clearly his bedroom. She opened her mouth to protest, but he cut her off.

"I'll be in the suite next door," he said quickly, setting her bag down beside the fireplace opposite the bed. "I just don't want you far in case we need to leave quickly. I'm not staying here, obviously."

Ophelia bit back her objections, too tired to argue and willing to let this one go. Besides, she understood the subtext. They were safe for now, but Luka wasn't taking any chances. As much as she resented him, she didn't want to face another supernatural attack either. The memory of the last one made her shudder.

"Why are people after me?" she asked suddenly. "You must

know. Or at least suspect. I deserve the truth." She crossed her arms over her chest, squaring her shoulders, determined to face him without flinching.

"Ophelia—" Luka's voice carried a note of fatigue, as if he was already bracing for the fight. He walked over, leaned against the edge of the bedframe, and pressed his thumbs to his temples.

"No. Stop trying to put me off," she said, following him and planting herself in front of him, hands on her hips, refusing to let him look away. "I'm sick of people lying to me. I've been kept in the dark my entire life. I didn't even know about Brisa and Mo. Do you know what it's like to not know who you are? To feel like something vital is missing? I want the truth. I deserve the truth." She hated how close her voice came to begging. But she needed answers.

Luka's expression shifted, less guarded now, more human. He ran a hand through his hair, stepping closer until he stood just inches away. His gaze lingered on her, searching for something she couldn't name. "Okay. Okay." He started to raise a hand to her shoulder, then thought better of it and dropped it to his side. "You're right. But why don't you get more comfortable?" He nodded toward a nearby door. "That leads to a private bath. I'll bring something to eat. Then we'll talk. I promise."

Ophelia caught sight of herself in a floor-length mirror next to the fireplace and winced. It had been a rough night of sleeping in the car. Without answering, she walked to the bathroom and locked herself in. She heard Luka leave as the heavy wooden door closed behind him. Leaning against the counter, she inhaled deeply and exhaled slowly, over and over, trying to calm herself the way she had learned to do over the years. A tightness had formed in her chest, and her head was spinning with everything she'd discovered in the last twenty-four hours. Supernaturals? Witches? Vampires? Family? It was a lot to take in. And she still felt lost, like she was missing a piece of the puzzle.

Finally feeling herself relax with each deep breath, she took in the bathroom. It had a large soaking tub, an oversized shower enclosed in glass, and marble countertops that gleamed under soft light. She studied the shower and decided the steam might help clear her mind, staying under the hot spray longer than she intended.

When she finally stepped out, dressed in soft leggings and a cropped T-shirt, her hair damp and skin flushed from the heat, she found Luka sitting cross-legged on the floor by the fire. One arm rested casually over his knee, his head bowed, face buried in his hands. He looked deceptively peaceful, almost boyish. But she knew better now. She knew how easily that calm could splinter.

As she drew closer, she caught the scent of soap and something darker, familiar. He'd showered too, changed into lounge pants and a fitted T-shirt that clung to him in all the ways that made it hard not to notice. Damn. He might be infuriating, but he was still unfairly attractive.

She settled beside him, careful to leave space between them. Reaching toward the fire, she watched in quiet awe as the flames leaned in her direction, dancing closer like they recognized her. At least now she had some sense of why, even if the full truth still eluded her.

Luka handed her a mug. The tea was unexpectedly good: soothing, floral, with a hint of something sweet and earthy. Chamomile and passionflower, she guessed. As she sipped, she lifted a brow, silently urging him to begin.

This time, he didn't hedge. "I told you your mother was a witch. That she was searching for answers. But the story doesn't start there," he said.

He paused, and Ophelia clenched her jaw to keep from rushing him. Every nerve in her body buzzed with impatience. Why did he have to speak so damn slowly? "The vampires, the witches, the fae—"

"The fae?" Ophelia's eyebrows scrunched in confusion, remembering that Brisa had mentioned them before. She wondered what other supernaturals existed that she had yet to learn about.

"Ancient supernatural warriors who are also known for healing abilities. They originated from Scandinavia," Luka answered her question quickly and then continued with his story. "For centuries, supernaturals—especially the witches and empusae—have been hunting for the Lunula Amulet."

"You mentioned ancient artifacts. Is that what you mean?" Ophelia asked, unclear how this amulet had anything to do with her.

"The Lunula Amulet was forged centuries ago, with the cooperation of all supernatural races and with the blessing of Pax, the Goddess of Peace."

"I'm assuming the Lunula Amulet features a moon in some way?" Ophelia guessed.

Luka stood quickly and went to a table next to the bed, pulling a pad of paper and a pencil from under a stack of books. She wondered what he liked to read. Probably not smut, like her. When he returned, he sat closer to her. She tried to hold her breath to avoid inhaling his scent. She was unsuccessful.

He placed the paper in front of them, starting to draw as he explained. "There are no known photographs of the amulet. But the stories have been passed down for generations. It is an upside-down crescent moon, made of gold. It contains three rare gems in the middle of the moon—a black diamond, a blood diamond, and a colorless diamond. A gem for each supernatural being that helped create it and imbued it with their magic. The combined magic is very powerful. The human or supernatural who wields the Lunula Amulet can control the actions of any other supernatural being. Or human." He paused, giving Ophelia time to ask questions.

"What do you mean by *control*?" Ophelia asked.

"Legends are often wrong about the powers of each supernatural being. In modern stories, humans have described vampires as being able to glamour a person or use compulsion to force a human or other supernatural to take certain actions. We believe this myth started because some vampires had control of the Lunula Amulet centuries ago."

"And the amulet can be used for this power of compulsion?" Ophelia asked.

Luka gave a short nod. "The Lunula Amulet hasn't been used in centuries, but legend says that whoever wears it can control the minds of others. Entire armies could be forced to obey a single will. That's the danger—it doesn't just influence, it compels. With that kind of power, any of us could be made to use our gifts for evil. No one should have that kind of control," he said.

"But I don't understand why something like that was created. And with the blessing of all supernatural beings, as you call them?" Ophelia asked. She wasn't sure these words would ever feel natural on her tongue.

Luka rose with effortless grace and moved from the fire to the bed. He climbed on, settling against the headboard with his legs stretched out in front of him.

"The amulet was forged during a time of great unrest. The supernaturals were fighting and slaughtering each other, and they were all ruled by evil creatures. At that time, the only thing that mattered to some supernaturals was obtaining more and more power. And humans were in danger of being enslaved. A faction of supernatural beings from all sides wanted peace, and they brokered a deal with Pax. If she helped them forge the amulet, they promised to use the amulet for peace," he said.

"I'm sure that worked out well." Ophelia didn't hide her sarcasm. "And did peace come?" she asked, even though she could guess the answer.

Luka's lips spread into what could only be described as a grimace. "For a time. For almost eight hundred years. The amulet was used to fight chaos, controlling the evil supernaturals and eradicating them. And once peace came, the amulet was placed into a secure vault in the Concilium's headquarters—at that time, in Rome. It could only be used with permission from a representative of each supernatural race."

"Concilium?" Ophelia asked.

"It's the head council of the empusae. Each supernatural has a governing body, and the Concilium is ours," Luka answered.

"I take it something happened to the amulet—and to that agreement?" Ophelia asked, turning back to the drawing.

"Alaric happened. He was an arrogant warlock with minimal talent, but he wanted to rule. Starting around the year 400, Alaric began plotting ways to attack the Roman Empire, which was controlled by the empusae at the time. Over and over he tried, until he finally got lucky and succeeded. He pilfered the jewels and treasures—including the Lunula Amulet. He left Rome, and no one knows what happened after that, other than that he died at some point. And supernaturals have been searching for over a thousand years for Alaric's treasure and the amulet."

"So what does this have to do with me?" Ophelia asked.

"With you, we aren't sure," Luka admitted. "We think it may have to do with your ability to control fire, which is now a rare power."

"And my mom?"

"Before she disappeared, she was working with me to find the Lunula Amulet. So that it doesn't fall into the wrong hands," Luka said.

"Is that common? For supernaturals to cooperate like that?" Ophelia asked.

"It's extremely rare. But like the supernaturals who helped form the amulet, several of us decided to work together because we all believe in peace. In a better world. We were with a few other supernaturals, including Mo, when your mother developed a lead." Luka closed his eyes for a minute, as if trying to ward off a bad memory. "And then she disappeared. We truly tried, but we found nothing. And she had left instructions in case this ever happened. If she disappeared, she insisted that you be kept away from the supernatural world. Away from other witches, even. She didn't want anyone to know about you. She wanted you safe. We respected her wishes, for nearly twenty years," Luka said.

"What changed?" she asked.

"We still have many sources. I heard rumors that other supernaturals were looking for you. Somehow they'd found out about you. As soon as learned that, I began following you. To protect you." He lifted his head sharply, urgency in his voice. "I swear I haven't been following you your whole life. Not until I knew others were after you. I didn't even see you in person until that night in Central Park."

Ophelia didn't respond. She wasn't sure why it mattered so much to him that she believed that part.

"I think—" He hesitated, dragging a hand through his hair. "I think you're connected to the amulet. We just don't know how yet. Your uncle is still trying to piece it together."

Ophelia rose and crossed to the bed, settling on the far side from Luka. He tracked her movements with quiet intensity, but didn't speak. She stretched out stiffly and let her head sink into the pillow, casting a sidelong glance in his direction. As angry as she was, she couldn't deny the relief of finally having some answers. When she allowed herself to soften, Luka exhaled—a low, weary sound—and she noticed how pale he'd become, the strain etched in his features.

He hadn't slept in over a day, she guessed. Still, she asked, "Tell me about her. Please."

"Of course," Luka said, shifting to lie beside her, their bodies separated by inches and miles of unspoken things. "She resembled you. Just as stubborn. Just as brilliant. Brave to the point of recklessness. She hated leaving you behind when we chased down leads, but she always said she was doing it for you—to make the world better."

"Luka, do you think she is really dead?" It was a question that Ophelia had wanted to ask since she learned that Luka knew her mom. But she was scared of what his answer would be.

Luka rolled onto his back, eyes fixed on the ceiling as he draped the back of his hand across his forehead. "For a while, I couldn't accept it. She was so powerful. But it's been nearly twenty years. If she were alive, I don't think she would have stayed away from you this long."

Ophelia's mouth tightened, a frown tugging at the corners as disappointment settled over her like a stone. "That's not what I wanted to hear," she murmured, her voice flat with defeat.

"I know," he said softly. "I'm sorry."

Silence stretched between them. Sleep tugged at her, and her lids grew heavy. Luka shifted and gently pulled a blanket over her. "Sleep now, love. I promise I'll try to give you answers later, even if they are hard truths."

Ophelia felt Luka start to move away. In the haze of

drowsiness, she reached for his hand, lacing her fingers through his. She didn't know why. She just needed the steadiness of it. She was still furious with him. But he also felt like home, and right now, she needed that more than anger. And she realized she hadn't had an episode all day. Tomorrow was another day. But for now, she wanted him near. Luka settled beside her, careful not to edge closer.

ELEVEN

Ophelia jolted awake, heart hammering. Someone was watching her. Her eyes flew open, only to land on Brisa perched casually on the edge of the bed. Relief swept through her in a shaky exhale.

"Rise and shine," Brisa said, giving her leg a lazy poke. "You've been out for nearly twenty-four hours. Time to move. Training waits for no witch."

"My what?" Ophelia pulled the covers over her head, feeling grumpy, groggy, and tired of people telling her what to do and where to go. And not for the first time, she thought that her cousin was more than a little odd. But she liked her that way.

"Most witches spend their entire lives learning to control their powers and develop any latent skills. You have years to make up, and we don't have much time. Also, Luka wants to train you to defend yourself after what happened the other night," Brisa said. She paused, a smirk on her thin lips. "I like being odd. And I think I like you, too." Brisa jerked the blanket off Ophelia, dropping it to the floor.

Sitting up quickly, Ophelia stared at her cousin, shock tightening her features. "What did you just say?"

Brisa pretended to study her green sparkling nails—a different color than yesterday. Apparently, she'd taken the time to repaint them. "Oh, didn't I mention that I can read minds?" she asked.

Ophelia groaned and pressed her hands over her face. "No. No, you definitely didn't mention that."

"It's one of the rare gifts that some witches have, along with their elemental powers."

"Their what? Does this mean you've been reading my mind this entire time?" Ophelia was horrified. She didn't want others to know her thoughts, and she had no idea what they had revealed.

"I usually tune people out," Brisa said.

"Wait, I thought vampires could read minds."

"You know about as much as a newborn." As usual, Brisa did not mince words. She crossed her arms over her chest. "Vampires are mostly useless, other than being strong, fast, and nearly immortal. But that's about it. Thousands of years ago, witches commanded many different talents and skills, but most of the magic faded beyond the basic elemental powers."

After a lifetime of no answers, Ophelia wanted to soak in the knowledge. "What about spells? Other types of magic? Potions?"

"Some witches can still use spells. Potions, yes, if you are taught. I used a potion to make your friend a little more...cooperative. And some of the lucky witches have other skills. We think you may, as well—somehow you can sense danger or upcoming change." Brisa poked her cousin again, this time more vigorously. "Up, up so we can start dissecting you." Brisa walked toward the door, motioning for Ophelia to follow her.

As Brisa disappeared from the room, Ophelia quickly

hopped out of bed, brushed her teeth, and pulled her long hair into a ponytail. For just a moment, she allowed herself to wonder where Luka was and when he'd left the room. But she pushed the thought out of her mind and left to find her cousin. And to start her training. The thought made her smile.

Walking down the long, ornate corridor, she followed the sound of voices. She found Luka standing in the kitchen, staring out the open glass doors to where Brisa and Mo were having breakfast at the long table in the courtyard.

As she walked up behind him, he turned to face her, appearing rested, his face no longer pale.

"Good morning." His voice was formal again, and his gaze searched her face. She could detect some uncertainty in his words. And she wondered what had shaken his cool confidence.

"It's you," Brisa called loudly from the courtyard. "It's all about you."

Ophelia rolled her shoulders as Luka regarded her with unspoken questions.

"Ignore her," Ophelia said out loud. *Get out of my head, Brisa,* Ophelia thought, hoping her cousin was listening long enough to hear the command. She had to admit that it would be helpful to have a mind reader to decipher this enigma of a man.

"Would you like some breakfast?" Luka asked.

Ophelia was starving. She hadn't eaten since the day before, but she didn't want Luka to serve her. She had been independent her entire life, and that wasn't about to change. "I'll just grab something myself." Without waiting for a response, she opened the refrigerator to her left.

"Wai—"

Luka tried to warn her, but he was too late. The refrigerator was stocked full of bags. Blood bags. Grimacing, Ophelia closed the door. Turning to face Luka, she tried to ignore the thought of him drinking blood. Of him tasting the other vampire's blood before ripping his head off.

"Wrong refrigerator," Luka said with an expression on his face that Ophelia couldn't read. He pointed to another refrigerator on the opposite side of the room. "Human food is in there."

"So, you drink out of blood bags?" Ophelia asked, unable to stifle her curiosity.

"Yes, usually." His words were slow and laced with discomfort. He was clearly reticent to discuss his eating habits. At least with her.

"Is that why you look better? Less pale?" Ophelia asked.

Luka glanced at her in surprise, one brow raised. "Lack of blood causes us to weaken. Lose control," he said.

"Do you bite people?" she asked.

"Not usually. It's forbidden by the Council, except in rare cases," he said.

"What rare cases?" she asked.

"Defense of your life." He paused. "Or if the person wants you to bite them. To bind you to them."

"Have you ever bitten me?" she asked.

His face changed instantly, now obviously angry at her question as he moved slowly toward her. So slowly that she knew his pace was deliberate. He was capable of much greater speed. She took a step away from him, backing up until she hit the counter and was forced to stop. When he was close enough to whisper in her ear, he braced his hands on the counter, on either side of her hips, never touching her. "I will never bite you. Unless you ask me to. And then, with pleasure."

Ophelia shivered at his words. "I won't." Her words were rushed and sounded false even to her own ears. She wasn't sure if she was scared of him or just scared of what she wanted him to do to her. And he knew it. He backed away, his green eyes smoky with emotion that Ophelia couldn't read. He turned away from her, adjusted his shirt, and ran a hand through his hair.

They didn't say another word to each other. And they were saved by Brisa yelling at them to hurry up. Ophelia stepped around Luka, grabbed a banana that she spotted on the counter, and strolled out to the courtyard. The sun hit her face, and she took a deep breath, smelling the salt in the air and feeling the breeze on her face. Brisa and Marcello sat at the outdoor table. Ancient leather-bound books, cracked from age, were stacked high. Some of them were in languages Ophelia didn't recognize. Ophelia planted herself between Brisa and Marcello. No chance that Luka could sit next to her.

"How far are we from the sea?" she asked no one in particular.

"Not far," Luka replied, stepping into the courtyard and taking the seat across the table from her. Dammit, now she couldn't avoid facing him as she ate.

"You can see the sea from the top of the watch." He pointed to one of the cylindrical towers at the corner of the estate. "That tower faces east to the Ionian Sea."

"Where exactly are we?" she asked.

"On the southeastern tip of Italy," Luka responded.

Surprised, Ophelia tilted her head toward where he pointed. She hadn't realized they were this far from Trieste. "So, what's the goal here?" she asked, skipping pleasantries and doing her best to ignore Luka. "Mo, you're trying to find out why so many people are after me?"

"Exactly," Marcello said, nodding. "Brisa may have given you the basics, but there's much more to understand. Consider this your first real history lesson. Luka, would you do the honors?"

Ophelia tensed, resisting the urge to groan. Great...now she had to meet his gaze again.

Luka met her gaze, all business now. Whatever tension had sparked in the kitchen was gone, replaced by cool authority. "The empusae are descended from the goddess Hecate and the spirit Mormo," he began. "Zeus—whom you might recognize as the king of the gods—was furious when he discovered Hecate had fallen in love with a female spirit. She was one of his favored goddesses, and he forbade the relationship. But Hecate defied him, and from that union, Empusa was born. As punishment, Zeus cursed Empusa and all her descendants to crave blood to survive. That's how the empusae came to be."

"So...gods and goddesses are real?" Ophelia asked, eyebrows raised.

"Not quite as they're portrayed in modern mythology," Marcello replied. "They were powerful immortals, yes—but flawed, like the rest of us. Human, supernatural...divine. It all blurs."

"You said Zeus *made* the first empusae. How are they made now?" she asked, turning her attention back to him.

Marcello exchanged a glance with Luka before answering. "Some of the most ancient vampires are true descendants of Empusa. The rest are created the way you've likely heard: a human is drained to the brink of death, then given vampire blood just before their final heartbeat. But making new vampires is forbidden now, by decree of the Alliance. Too many vampires would tip the balance. Worse, other supernaturals can't be turned, so it's a power only vampires possess."

Ophelia glanced toward Luka, tempted to press him for more. But thought better of it and pivoted. "And what about witches?"

Brisa jumped in before anyone else could. "We're also descended from Hecate," she said, lifting her chin. "She ruled magic, spells, and could command air, earth, and water. She had a fling with Aeetes, a sun god who wielded fire. Their daughter, Circe, inherited all of it. And now she's the matriarch of every modern witch. In the beginning, her bloodline carried all elemental powers, but over time those abilities diluted. Most witches today are born with only one elemental gift."

"And what about you two?" Ophelia asked, her gaze shifting between Brisa and Mo. "What are your powers?"

Brisa answered first. "I'm an air witch. You saw me use air to control the vampires in Trieste." She shot Ophelia a knowing grin. "And today you learned about my extra gift...I can read minds."

"Witch powers are passed through the matriarchal bloodlines," Mo added. "That's why your mother and I have different abilities. My mother was a land witch, which means I have command of the earth."

To demonstrate, he lowered his hands to the ground on either side of him. The dirt began to shift, swirling beneath his fingers. With a small push of his palms, the soil turned over and shot toward a nearby flower bush. The plant withered and died instantly, the earth swallowing the brittle stems and scattered petals until nothing remained.

"That—that was amazing," Ophelia breathed, her mouth falling open. A rush of anticipation filled her. She wanted— needed—to understand her powers.

"I also have another gift," Mo said, his tone modest but tinged with quiet pride. "I can speak and read any language— past or present. We don't know why or how the ability developed. But perhaps it's tied to the earth. All people come from it, after all. That connection might allow me to understand them, no matter the language."

He took a bite of toast, as if it were the most natural thing in the world.

"Can other earth witches do that?" Ophelia asked.

"Not that I've heard of," he said. "But the ability has been useful. I can decipher ancient texts, even those in languages that no longer exist." He gestured to the leather-bound volumes stacked in front of him. "I've been reading everything I can from around the time of Alaric's crusade. Luka was kind enough to smuggle texts from the Council's headquarters in San Marino."

Ophelia frowned. "I thought the Council seat was in Rome?"

"It was," Luka said. "But after Alaric sacked the city, everything changed. Rome hadn't been breached in more than eight centuries. Once it fell, the vampires realized their secrets weren't safe. Other supernaturals saw them as vulnerable. Attacks became more frequent. The Council had no choice but to relocate. San Marino is fortified—surrounded by walls—and the vampires built three castles there, one for each Council member. They've remained ever since. No one's breached the city since the 400s."

Ophelia sat back, trying to take it all in. The world she thought she knew was vanishing, replaced by something ancient and dangerous. "So...what now?"

"We want to help you access your fire witch powers," Mo said gently. "As far as we know, you're the last. You deserve to know your history. I never agreed with keeping you in the dark —but I respected your mother's wishes. Until those choices put your life in danger."

When Ophelia didn't respond, he continued, "We don't know exactly why the Council is after you. Maybe they want control over the last fire witch. Or maybe it's something more. But we're hoping you'll help us destroy the Lunula Amulet using your power."

"Why me?" she asked.

"The amulet was forged with the help of four witches—one from each element—along with a fae and a vampire. To destroy it, we'll need the same. We're still searching for a water witch, but it's a delicate task," Mo explained.

"Ophelia also commands air," Luka said quietly, glancing at her as if unsure how she'd take the revelation.

"What?" Brisa and Marcello said at once, both turning to Luka with wide eyes.

"It's true," Luka confirmed. "She summoned air by accident in Trieste. And she's strong. The pressure shattered the glass in my study."

Ophelia noted that Luka was leaving out a lot of what happened.

"That's impossible," Brisa said. "No witch has commanded more than one element since the early days of Circe and her direct descendants."

"She might also have a form of foresight, something instinctive. But it's uncontrolled. She has an ability to sense impending danger."

Mo's brow tightened, his expression distant. "I'll have to research this further. It's rare—almost unheard of—but some of the oldest accounts speak of witches who could see beyond the present."

"I can't predict the future," Ophelia said, quick to correct Mo. Her stomach was in knots, and she felt that she would be sick. She was finally getting answers, but now it seemed that she would be out of place with the witches, as well. She didn't know if she would ever feel at home.

Sensing her discomfort, Mo tried to reassure her. "There is nothing wrong with you, Ophelia. All witches have powers that manifest in different ways. We just need to study what you can do. So we can help you control it."

"We keep this to ourselves for now," Luka said. "The

Council is already after Ophelia. We don't want to expose her even more."

Everyone seemed to agree, but when no one spoke, Luka took control. "Brisa, time for Ophelia's first lesson."

"With pleasure." Brisa turned to Ophelia with a wicked grin. "Ready to learn, cousin?"

CHAPTER

TWELVE

Brisa led Ophelia to the infinity pool at the center of the courtyard and forced her to stand at the edge, near the deep end. "We should be next to water, just in case," Brisa said as she backed away from Ophelia, smirking.

"In case of what?" Ophelia asked, narrowing her eyes. Her brows pinched as she watched Brisa with the same wariness she might reserve for a prank about to detonate.

Without answering, Brisa raised her arms, spreading them wide as if embracing an invisible giant. Ophelia felt the air pick up around them as her hair began swirling and flowers began swaying. Suddenly, without warning, Brisa moved her arms quickly together, her hands meeting as her fingers pointed at Ophelia.

It was as if Brisa had taken all the air around her and hurled it toward Ophelia, hitting her. Hard. For a moment, she teetered on the edge of the pool, trying to withstand the wall of air forcing her back. Her strength lasted just a few seconds before her feet flew out from underneath her, causing her to land on the surface of the pool. As she sank, she allowed herself to be momentarily suspended, stunned by the welcoming cool water. Sinking to the bottom of the pool, she used her feet to push herself up, kicking until she emerged, sputtering.

"What the hell, Brisa?" Ophelia asked as she hung on to the side of the pool, coughing as the water worked its way out of her lungs.

"Well, I'm impressed." Brisa studied her fingers, picking at something invisible, as if she were anything but impressed.

"With what? You just sent me to the bottom of the pool in two seconds." Ophelia could hear Mo chuckling. She glanced quickly at the table and saw that Luka was trying to hide a smile, as well. Traitors.

"You are strong, but not much stronger than a witchling. Hop out. We'll go again."

"What? I'm freezing. Surely, there is a better way to do this."

"Stop whining. The pool is heated by the rich centuries-old vamp. And if you use your power, you'll be very warm, very quickly."

"But how do I do that?" Ophelia asked as she climbed out of the water. She flopped onto her stomach and rolled onto her back, breathing heavily. Her clothes were sticking to her and dripping water onto the pavement that framed the pool.

"How do you walk?" Brisa asked. She stood over Ophelia, hands planted firmly on her hips, her impatience radiating in the sharp set of her jaw.

"What do you mean?" Ophelia asked, savoring this moment of finally getting answers about her episodes.

"Your powers will come to you. Right now, you are unfocused and untested. You've never been trained. You've never seen anyone practice magic either. In the same way a baby learns to sit up and then crawl and eventually walk, your powers will also come to you. We just have to figure out what triggers them."

When Ophelia didn't answer or sit up, Brisa used her magic to force Ophelia to stand.

"Hey! Stop that!" Ophelia said. She felt wind curl beneath her body as she was lifted off the ground, floating until she was on her feet again.

"I don't have all day," Brisa said. And then, once again, without warning, Brisa collected the air around her and flung it at Ophelia. Ophelia grounded her feet, trying to root herself against the invisible pressure. But the air felt like Brisa was shoving Ophelia's shoulders with all her might. Ophelia's effort to stand against Brisa's power lasted less than ten seconds before she was forced back into the pool.

As Ophelia broke the surface of the water again, Brisa gave her words of encouragement in the only way Brisa knew how. "You held your ground for about five seconds longer this time. Slightly better than a witchling. But you are trying to use physical strength. You need to focus on your mental strength. Your powers."

Refusing to let Brisa force her to stand, Ophelia moved quickly out of the water and stood on her own, facing her cousin. "Again," Ophelia demanded, defiant.

Brisa tilted her head to the side and glanced at Ophelia, considering her for a moment. "As you wish," she said.

This time, Brisa kept her arms at her sides before lifting them overhead in a fluid arc. The gesture summoned a surge of air that swept beneath Ophelia and lifted her off the ground, weightless and startled. She twisted midair, trying to wrest herself free, but Brisa released her without warning, sending her plunging into the pool like a tossed coin.

"Like I said," Brisa called as Ophelia swam to the edge, breathless and sputtering, "you're relying on muscle. But this isn't about brute force. It's about strategy. Instinct. You were ready for a frontal attack, so I changed the angle. In a real fight, no one comes at you the same way twice. You have to think on your feet...and with your magic."

They repeated the sequence more times than Ophelia could count. Brisa manipulated the air from above, behind, from her blind side. Each time she sent Ophelia into the water in new, unpredictable ways. And each time, Ophelia climbed out quickly, dripping and determined, more focused than before.

She tried to force her powers to rise, willing them into action. But they refused. For years, they had surged forward without permission, out of control and uninvited. Now, when she needed them most, they held back, elusive and silent, like a secret she couldn't quite remember.

As Ophelia came up for air and out of the water, hoisting herself out of the pool for what felt like the hundredth time, she glared at her cousin. "How helpful is it to launch me into the water over and over? How is that teaching me?"

"How else will you learn?" Brisa asked.

As Brisa started to rant about the value of their lesson, Ophelia was distracted when she spotted Luka at an outdoor fireplace near the edge of the large courtyard. While Brisa droned on, Ophelia watched Luka add wood to the brick fireplace. Lighting dry pieces of tinder wood, he glanced at her out of the corner of his eyes as the fire roared to life. Ophelia felt something inside her stir. She had an idea.

She interrupted Brisa's speech. "Again," she demanded.

Brisa smirked at her, almost gleeful, but Ophelia ignored it. As Brisa began to build air around herself, Ophelia didn't focus on her cousin. She didn't try to take a stance to withstand the air coming toward her. Instead, she closed her eyes. She breathed deeply and focused on her inner strength, like she'd learned to do years ago in yoga. She thought about the flames that Luka had brought to life. With her eyes still closed, she felt her mind reach for those flames. She felt the air around her grow still and warm.

After several moments, when Ophelia still didn't feel Brisa's powerful air forcing her back, she blinked open her eyes. To her amazement, she found a line of fire streaming from the fireplace toward her, suspended in the air. When it reached her, the flames wrapped around her body in loose swirls, protecting her from Brisa's magic but not touching her. Awestruck, she lifted a hand to the flames. But the movement caused her to lose her concentration. The fire dropped to the ground, engulfing the courtyard where it landed.

Brisa moved quickly to douse the out-of-control blaze. With her power, she lifted water over the pool's edge to drench the flames. Mo—who'd been observing the lesson from the table as he read—stepped toward them, unhurriedly. He used his power to turn over the dirt, smothering the flames before they could reach Ophelia and Brisa.

Ophelia stood still for a very long moment, as Brisa and Mo stared at her, expressionless. Finally, Ophelia started to laugh, a deep and genuine laugh.

Brisa clapped slowly. "How exciting. You almost torched the vamp's estate," Brisa said in her typical deadpan tone.

"Oh, shit. Sorry about that," Ophelia said, tilting her head to find Luka. He was still standing near the fireplace, a smile spread on his lips, his arms crossed over his broad chest in an unworried stance.

"If destroying my garden means you learn how to control your power..." His voice trailed off.

He opened a cabinet near the fireplace, grabbed a large blanket, and walked briskly to where Ophelia and Brisa were standing. He wrapped the blanket around Ophelia's shoulders.

"Brisa didn't go easy on you."

"Thanks," Ophelia said, twisting her head from him so that she could hide her expression. She had been shivering, standing in dripping wet clothes that were plastered to her body. And he'd noticed. But she didn't want her tangled feelings for Luka to overshadow the thrill of her breakthrough.

"Well, now we know you can control your air power," Brisa said.

"Didn't I use fire to bring the flames to me?"

"No, I don't think so. The flames are drawn to you, probably because of that power. But you used the air to bring the fire over, rather than creating your own." Brisa seemed to consider her next words. "How did it feel?"

"What do you mean?" Ophelia asked.

"I mean, how did it feel to control your power? How did you do it? What did you do? Anger didn't seem to be working, no matter how many times I dunked you into the pool."

"I just relaxed. I stopped trying to react to you. I tried to think inwardly about what I wanted to happen, not what I was anticipating."

"So provoking you didn't work," Brisa said, to no one in particular. "The power came from within."

"Anger *can* motivate her to use her powers," Luka said.

"How?" Brisa asked.

"Her temper," Luka said, pausing with his eyebrows lifted, "can produce results."

"Hello, I'm right here," Ophelia said. "That's a rare occurrence these days. That hasn't happened to me in years."

"What do you mean?"

"When I was younger, after my mom disappeared—died," Ophelia corrected herself, "I had episodes." She found it hard to talk about that time in her life.

"What do you mean by *episodes*?" Mo asked.

"That's what my uncle Elijah and I called them. I could

sense danger. He didn't believe me at first, but it happened so many times he didn't have a choice. There was more, as well. I had tantrums."

"Can you tell me about the tantrums?" Mo asked. Together, they walked toward the courtyard table. Sitting down close to the fire, Ophelia pulled the blanket tighter around her.

"They started when my mom disappeared. I was so angry at the world for my mom being gone. And I was confused. Chairs would turn over, glass would break, candles would start burning in our apartment—the list goes on."

"And what did you do to control these—" Mo paused to consider his words, "these episodes, as you call them?" His voice was soft but probing.

Unable to face Brisa or Luka, Ophelia kept her attention fixed on Mo, anchoring herself in his steady presence. For once, Brisa didn't fire off a sarcastic remark. And Luka quietly rose from the table and disappeared into the kitchen. The soft clatter of the kettle, the rhythmic slice of a knife, became a kind of background hum. She knew he could still hear every word. But he was giving her space. And for that, she was quietly grateful.

Drawing from the place where old memories lived half-buried, Ophelia exhaled slowly. "When my uncle Elijah finally believed me—when he saw it with his own eyes—he trained to become a child psychologist. He read everything he could find. Scientific journals. Parenting guides. Therapy manuals. Tried experiments, hypnosis, everything short of magic. But nothing worked." Her gaze dropped to her hands. They rested in her lap, still damp from training, the fingers curling slightly inward.

"There was never anything wrong with you," Mo said gently.

A pause. Then: "I hadn't hurt anyone until Trieste," she

murmured, voice fraying at the edges. "Until I hurt Luka." The shame was sharp. Her anger, her magic, her lack of control—none of it felt redeemable. She stayed curled in on herself, unwilling to let them see the guilt etched across her features.

Silence stretched between them until Brisa broke it. "After a few hundred years, I promise that vamp had it coming."

A laugh slipped from Ophelia, unbidden and shaky. It hit something inside her like relief and grief tangled together.

"He's fine, right? Not a mark on him." Brisa's tone sharpened. "We were raised better. You shouldn't have been left in the dark, not like that. No training. No guidance. Not when your powers were starting to rise."

The heat in Brisa's voice wasn't for Ophelia. It was for the people who had failed her. Ophelia felt that truth settle into her chest.

"It's true," Luka said as he returned, a tray balanced in his hands. He moved without fanfare, placing it on the table and passing out mugs. When he handed Ophelia hers—a steaming cup of green tea—his touch lingered for just a moment. "I should have told you everything. From the beginning."

She wrapped her hands around the mug, the warmth a balm against the chill that hadn't quite left her skin. His meaning wasn't lost on her. He should have been honest before the kiss. Before the night she trusted him. Before the betrayal that still throbbed between them.

But for now, she said nothing. Just brought the tea to her lips and let the steam wash over her face.

"But what did you ultimately do, to control the episodes?" Mo asked, prompting Ophelia as he repeated his original question.

She took a deep drink of the tea and then answered the question. "Elijah eventually realized that sports and any exercise seemed to dampen the episodes, even if they didn't completely stop them. When Uncle Sebastian came into our lives, I still had some tantrums. And, frankly, I was a brat. When I was thirteen, he suggested yoga to help with my mind. And he was right. With my yoga instructor, I learned to go inward and meditate, which helped control the episodes. Sebastian was honestly a gift for us. Brought Elijah and me back to life. He's been a light in our lives."

Ophelia caught a glance exchanged between Luka and Mo. She was about to ask them about it when Brisa cut in. "It's a good thing you found yoga when you did, and that it helped," Brisa said. "Most witches begin developing full magical strength when they are going through puberty. If you hadn't started, you might have hurt someone."

Her stomach growled low and loud, and Ophelia realized she was famished from the lesson. She reached for one of the sandwiches Luka had brought out. Full of vegetables, hummus, and other flavors she couldn't identify. It was delicious.

"Thanks for this," she said to Luka, motioning with the sandwich.

"Luka always spoils us," Mo said.

"I guess he does," Brisa said, as she used air to ruffle Luka's hair.

"Brisa," Luka said, a warning in his voice. They all laughed, and Ophelia thought—not for the first time—that these three really knew and respected each other. She wanted to ask about her mother, but it didn't seem like the right time. They had talked about the past enough for now.

After their brief break, Ophelia practiced all afternoon with Brisa. Now that Brisa knew that anger didn't help, she stopped throwing Ophelia into the pool every chance she got. But they stayed near the water because Ophelia kept setting the courtyard on fire. Repeatedly. She wasn't able to make her own fire, but she used her air power to bring it from the fireplace. Brisa had used the water from the pool to douse the fires, and Mo stayed nearby to extinguish any remaining flames.

At the end of the day, Ophelia bristled at herself for causing such destruction to Luka's courtyard. The place had been luscious and gorgeous just that morning and now was charred beyond recognition—because of her.

"Your gardener will be very curious how this happened," Ophelia said to Luka as they surveyed the damage at the end of the night.

"No one told you?" Luka asked Ophelia as he turned to look at Brisa behind him, his brow furrowed in annoyance.

"But that would ruin the fun," Brisa said, coming to stand next to them.

"Brisa, you should have told her so that she wouldn't worry," Mo said, chiding his daughter. "Ophelia, witchcraft isn't just for fighting or defense. We can make beauty, as well."

Mo lowered himself to the ground and plunged his hands into the soil. Ophelia watched as he concentrated, his eyes closed. To Ophelia's surprise, the lush green grass came back, and bountiful flowers bloomed all around them. Once the garden was transformed into the beauty it had been that morning, Brisa helped her father stand. The work had obviously taken a toll on him as he stumbled to sit at the table.

"Are you okay?" Ophelia asked.

"You noticed that you were hungry after practicing your craft?" Mo asked. "Your metabolism burns constantly while you are using elemental magic. Witches get exhausted when using full strength," he said.

Once again, Ophelia felt terrible that her witchling skills had caused Mo to expend so much energy fixing her mistakes.

"Not to worry," Mo said. "You deserve to learn, and this is

the perfect place to do it, out of sight from other supernaturals. I'm happy to teach you. To help you. We are family."

Exhausted, Ophelia could barely keep her eyes open that evening. Although Luka had tried to ply her with food, she could only eat a few bites. She excused herself early and collapsed into the bed. But before she fell asleep, Ophelia realized that she was both relieved and oddly disappointed that Luka did not join her.

CHAPTER

THIRTEEN

Luka sat on the edge of the bed, shaking Ophelia's shoulder. "Time for training."

She ignored him, not caring that she was wearing a barely-there crop top and underwear. Or that she'd kicked the blanket off at some point. Because she felt drained, like rocks were weighing her down. The edges of her body ached and screamed.

"Brisa isn't even up at this ungodly hour," she said, realizing it was still dark out.

"The gods have nothing to do with it. Nor Brisa. Your training will be with me." She felt his hand disappear, disappointing her. And that feeling confused her. She decided to ignore it. Yes, she'd ignore it. Managing to squint at him through eyes that felt like they'd been polished with sandpaper, she said, "You? Teaching magic?" She lifted slightly, resting on her elbows and forearms.

He chuckled, his hand resting on the bed next to her exposed abdomen. "No, love. Never." The warmth of his body shifted as he stood and moved toward the door with preternatural speed. How had she never noticed that he was so clearly not human?

Irritated by his term of endearment, her lips pressed into a thin line. She kept meaning to ask him not to call her that. But instead, she asked, "Then what?"

He paused at the door, voice serious. "Yesterday you learned how to use your mind. Today, I want to teach you how to defend yourself."

"Isn't that why I'm learning to control my magic?" She flopped back onto the bed with a dramatic huff. The blanket slipped lower on her hips. "I'd rather be in bed all day."

His gaze raked down her body, lips curving into that same infuriating smile he'd worn the night they met. Involuntarily, her nipples tightened beneath the thin fabric of her shirt. Fine. She could admit that he still affected her. Lit a slow, simmering heat beneath her skin. Even if it made her want to scream.

"Mmmm. Well, while that is tempting," he said, "there may—no, likely will—be a day when magic isn't available to you. You need both mental and physical strength for what is to come."

"And you'll help me with the physical, I take it?" She raised one brow, dry skepticism sharpening her gaze. "I think you've done enough in that department."

Luka didn't answer. His expression sharpened, a flicker of something unreadable passing over his face as he opened the door. "I'll meet you outside in ten minutes. Put on some clothes you don't care about. Something you'd run in."

Surprised at his unrelenting and inflexible tone, Ophelia watched him from the safety of the bed until he disappeared behind the closed door. Eventually, curiosity spurred her into movement. Even before she knew about supernaturals, she'd used physical activity to calm her episodes. Her power. Now that she recognized the signs, she realized it had always been raging against her. Wanting to be used, to get out of her. And now she needed to know how using the magic with physical exercise would make her feel.

She put on the only pair of running clothes she'd packed—long black leggings and a halter tank top Alex had gifted for her birthday. Shit—Alex. They hadn't been in contact in days. And where the hell was her phone? Promising herself that she would call Alex as soon as training with Luka was over, Ophelia left her room in a hurry.

Walking through the kitchen, she found a smoothie on the counter next to an oversized plate of scrambled eggs and fresh bread. She spotted Luka in the courtyard and walked toward him with the food.

"It has been twelve minutes. You were supposed to be out in ten." His lips were pursed with displeasure.

When had this side of Luka materialized? Like a child, Ophelia stuck her tongue out at him.

Luka didn't change his expression. "I'm serious. I need you focused."

"Luka," Ophelia said, trying not to lose her temper with him, "you have changed my entire life in less than a week. Introduced me to a world of...supernaturals. I have come with you willingly. I think two more minutes won't kill me." She sat down across from him with a huff, practically dropping the plate of eggs and the smoothie in front of her, feeling her anger bubbling to the surface.

After a long moment of a silent standoff between the two, Luka let out a deep breath before finally responding. "It could." Ophelia stiffened. He was worried about her. "I don't want you to be defenseless again, like you were against the empusae in Trieste. I can help you with that. If you'll let me," he said.

Not knowing how to respond, Ophelia opted for silence, lifting the smoothie to her lips to fill the space between them.

Abruptly, Luka changed topics, not letting the unspoken words stretch too long. "The smoothie has extra vitamins and nutrients to help with your magic hangover." He handed her a mug of steaming black coffee that she hadn't noticed before.

"My what?" she asked, setting the smoothie down and wrapping her hands around the mug, savoring its warmth.

"Your body feels lethargic. Every muscle aches," he said, not asking, just fact.

"How did you know?" she asked.

"That's the magic regenerating. You worked really hard yesterday, learning how to control those muscles. But it's new to you. Eventually, using magic will be second nature and you won't experience these whole-body aches each time. But for now, you need proper nutrients to recover."

"Is this witch knowledge something you have collected in your vampire repertoire?" she asked.

"I've been around for a while," he said, noncommittal, not really answering.

"No." Ophelia set her jaw, refusing to accept his evasive answer. Sitting taller in her chair, she locked onto his gaze and held it.

"No, what?" he asked, tilting his head to the side and fixing his gaze on her, meeting the challenge.

"If you want me to start trusting you, stop with the half-truths. Just answer the question. Honestly."

He leaned back in his chair and crossed his arms over his chest as he avoided her gaze. "I'm not accustomed—" he said, before stopping himself and meeting her eyes again. "I learned a long time ago to keep things to myself—information, thoughts, feelings. All of it. I had to learn to survive after I became an empusae, and that has meant not sharing until it was useful to do so. But," he paused again, shifting in his seat, "I understand what you're saying. I understand what you're asking. And I'll try. Because I want your trust. More than you can know."

Ophelia waited, feeling deep in her bones that there was so much more he wasn't telling her. She didn't need vibrations for that. It wasn't danger, but something was missing. An answer to a question she hadn't asked yet. But she felt some relief flood her. It was a start, but to what, she didn't know.

"For now, I'll tell you that I'm hundreds of years old. I became a vampire against my will. I was made and not born—a human. And perhaps someday, when we have more time, I will tell you that story. But to answer your question now, I have gathered information over the centuries, including from witches. I have seen witches try to control their power, and I know how much of a toll it takes on a witch's body. Also, I spoke with Mo last night, and he suggested that I make your smoothie with specific herbs to help heal the aches caused by the magic," he said in a stilted tone. Glancing at his watch, he bristled. "Eat up. We have work to do," he said.

Luka's stern schoolteacher voice was back. It was kind of hot. But Ophelia knew it wasn't the time to pry into his past, intrigued as she was by what he'd said. He'd been human? She wanted to know more, but she drank the smoothie quickly and ate all she could of the eggs. To her surprise, her body felt better almost instantly.

"First, a run." Luka's face told her that the exercise regimen wasn't up for discussion.

As she stood, she groaned playfully. Why was she still giving him a hard time? His lies were no different than all the other lies she'd been told her entire life. But she actually liked him. Enjoyed spending time with him. Enjoyed seeing him interact with Mo and Brisa. Felt comfortable with him in so many ways. Maybe her developing feelings for him made his lies hurt her more deeply.

For now, though, they would run. And she was so ready to feel that burn in her chest, the ache in her calves, and the wind in her face. They walked to the front of the estate and stretched at the top of the stairs in front of the double doors.

"Where to?" she asked. She knew she couldn't beat a vampire, but she was too competitive not to give it her best shot.

"Let's run down to the sea and back up."

Ophelia grinned. She loved the water. She started sprinting down the long driveway, getting a head start on Luka.

"Pace yourself," he said, easily catching up with her and meeting her speed. "You have a long day of training."

Ignoring him, she pushed harder as she felt him glance at her sideways, matching her speed yet again.

"You're fast," he said.

"For a human, yes."

"Not a human." He smiled to himself but kept his eyes focused ahead.

About halfway down the long driveway, they veered onto a path that wound through the trees. The forest was quiet, peaceful. It reminded Ophelia of her runs through the wooded trails in Central Park. As her thoughts began to wander, she risked a glance at Luka. He looked entirely at ease, not a hair out of place, and not a drop of sweat on his lean, infuriatingly perfect body.

"I know you don't need much sleep, but do you ever get tired?" Sweat was already glistening on her body, trickling between her breasts.

"I can." At first, he seemed to want to stop there, before

forcing himself to give more than the partial answer he had offered. "It's not tired in the way you mean. It's a fatigue from blood hunger. And the more power we exert, the more we need blood. The longer we wait, the less control we have," he said.

"Have you ever lost control?" Ophelia asked.

Something about Luka's face made her regret the question. "I have," he said simply.

She decided not to explore his reaction. "What happens when you lose control?" she asked.

"An empusae should never let himself get to that point," he said.

"But if he does?" she pressed.

"He could drain someone. Kill them from the bloodlust."

"Interesting." Her breathing started to pick up. She didn't want Luka to see her struggling with this pace, so she kept on pushing.

"Is it?" he asked.

"Of course. A few days ago, I didn't know about supernaturals. I thought vampires were a myth in pop culture. Now I'm kicking a vamp's ass."

He glanced at her, gave her a wicked grin, and then pushed them to run faster. Ophelia internally cursed herself for taunting him, but she met his speed.

"It must have been confusing not growing up around your kind. Not knowing who you were," he said.

Her instinct was to brush off the comment, but she couldn't ask for honesty without returning it. "Incredibly confusing," she said finally, as she also tried to focus on her breathing. "My uncle loved me. But he was always trying to fix me."

"There's absolutely nothing about you that needs to be fixed," Luka said, so softly she almost didn't hear him.

Ophelia kept her gaze on the road ahead, refusing to turn

toward him. He'd said it like a passing thought, but it hit her with weight. She wasn't ready to let him see how much it meant. After a long pause, she replied, her voice low. "He just doesn't understand the supernatural world. You know he isn't really my uncle. He was my mom's best friend growing up. He did the best he could. But it helps knowing I'm not some anomaly to be controlled. That I don't need to be fixed. Just trained. Guided. That I have…" She hesitated, swallowing the last word. "Power." Even now, it felt strange to claim it as something good.

They ran in silence until the trees broke open at a cliff's edge. Ophelia bent forward, bracing her hands on her knees and pulling deep breaths into her chest. Luka stood beside her, maddeningly composed. Of course. Damn vamps. Straightening up, she took in the view. White-capped waves slammed into jagged rocks far below, the sea a wild force crashing against the base of the cliff.

"Ready to head back?" she asked, finally turning to Luka. His attention was already fixed on her, unreadable.

"Not yet. We go down," he said, nodding toward the base of the bluff, "and then back up."

"You're joking." Her voice flattened as she scanned the drop again. The cliffside was a mess of slippery rock and tangled moss, like nature's own obstacle course…one she had no interest in attempting. "How far down is that?"

"Does it matter?" he asked.

"It matters to my legs. And my face," she said, arching a brow full of warning. "And how exactly are we getting down there?"

"There are two ways—the fast way and the slow way. Your choice." Luka peeled off his shirt and shoes, stripped to just his running shorts. Before she could protest—or appreciate the full effect of his wet, shirtless audacity—he backed up several steps and sprinted forward, diving off the edge in one clean, fluid motion.

Ophelia gasped. His body sliced through the air, disappearing into the waves far below. Then, a beat later, he surfaced, cocky as ever, motioning for her to follow.

"Shit. Shit. Shit," she said.

She hated heights. Hated being shown up even more. Stripping quickly, she tossed aside her top, shoes, and leggings, left only in a sports bra and the least embarrassing underwear she could have hoped for in the moment. No frills, thank the gods.

With a deep breath, she backed up, ran hard, and launched herself into the air. For one second—maybe two—she felt suspended, held aloft like her magic might catch her. But gravity had other plans. She plunged into the sea with all the elegance of a sack of potatoes, the water rushing up to meet her.

Cold, fast, and punishing. She went under, saltwater stinging her nose and throat, current battering her from all sides. Miraculously, she missed the rocks and broke the surface, coughing.

Luka was already waiting. She swam to meet him, scowling.

"Excellent jump," he said, dry as bone.

She wasn't sure if she wanted to strangle him or kiss him. Possibly both.

"Now we climb to the top."

Ophelia followed his gesture to the cliff face, where jagged edges gave way to smooth, wet stone. Moss clung to the surface like a warning.

"You're joking."

"Nope. You first." He gestured again, water dripping from his impossibly still-perfect face. His expression held no apology. And damn him—the green in his eyes did seem brighter down here.

"Absolutely not," she said, shaking her head at him as she trod water. She could not do this. She would not do this. What if she fell?

"How else will we get back up?" Luka asked. When Ophelia didn't respond, still wondering if someone could rescue them, Luka shook his head and repeated himself. "You first. I didn't think you'd give up so easily." He tsked, baiting her competitive side. And it almost worked.

Swimming in circles, she searched for another way. No beaches were within sight, and the water was too strong to fight, constantly shoving her toward the looming cliff. He was right. This was the only way out, unless she chose to stay in the water and drown. She whipped her head toward him, her glare sharp and unyielding. "Absolutely not. I'm practically naked. And I'm dripping wet. You first."

He shook his head. "It's not up for discussion. If I fall, I won't die. You could."

He had a point.

"And no magic," he added.

Hoping her eyes could pierce straight through him, she swam to a boulder jutting from the sea. With half her body still submerged, she reached for the cliff's edge. But her fingers kept slipping. Frustrated, she shot him another look before sinking back into the water. "I'm not sure I can do this." She hated admitting it to him. Absolutely hated it. "Of course, you can. You do everything you set your mind to, and this will be no different. Take a deep breath and focus, Ophelia."

His confidence in her helped. Breathing deeply, she cleared her mind. *I can do this. I can do this.* She repeated it over and over until she believed it.

Finally, she managed to grab a firm edge of the cliffside,

and she pulled with all her might. One leg and one hand at a time, she climbed. And climbed. And climbed. Her muscles strained, her back beginning to cramp. But she kept climbing. And she blocked from her mind that she was wearing soaking wet underwear that left nothing to the imagination.

Tracing her steps and placing his hands and feet where she had, Luka followed. As she breathed heavily from exertion, she heard no noise from him. Damn vampire.

As they neared the top, Ophelia started to get excited, proud of herself that she had climbed the face of a bluff, dripping wet, in nothing but her underwear. But the overconfidence cost her. She reached too high in her eagerness, missing the crevice in the rock. Instead, her hand hit smooth stone, and she couldn't find a place to grip. Her fingers slipped as she palmed the rock. As her muscles strained and ached from holding on with just one hand, she started to panic, her legs flailing. It was too late. Her whole body started slipping, and she felt herself claw at empty air. The side of her body hit the rock wall, and she screamed as she felt the air rush around her.

But just when she thought she would crash on the jagged rocks below, Luka grabbed her by the arm. He gripped the cliff's side with his feet and left hand, holding her right forearm with his right hand as she dangled in the air.

Ophelia's stomach dropped, a scream clawing its way up her throat. Panic surged—sharp, breathless, absolute. She was going to fall. She was going to die. She'd never get the answers she needed. Never learn what had really happened to her mother.

"Ophelia. Focus on me." Luka's voice cut through the spiral, low and commanding. Her eyes locked onto his, finding that impossible green, a tether in the chaos.

"Breathe in. Breathe out. That's it. I've got you," he said, voice steady as stone. He kept talking her down, his tone coaxing and calm, until her vision stopped swimming and her thoughts sharpened just enough to think. "I'm going to lift you so you can grip the ledge again. Trust me."

She swallowed hard, throat raw, and gave a tight nod. "Okay." The word barely made it past her lips. If she hurt him —if her panic caused them both to fall—she'd never forgive herself. Even if this had been his reckless idea to begin with. With fluid strength, Luka pulled her up to his side, positioning her so she could find a hold in the rock. His arm wrapped around her waist, anchoring her to him.

"Now take a deep breath and start again," he said, giving her a brief, reassuring squeeze before releasing her.

Her muscles screamed in protest. She shut her eyes, exhaled hard, then shook herself free of the fear fogging her mind. Bit by bit, she hauled herself upward, the final stretch of the cliff a blur of pain and determination. When her fingers finally grasped solid ground, she dragged herself over the edge and collapsed onto her back, chest heaving, limbs trembling with exhaustion.

Luka stood above her, unreadable. He didn't look winded. Of course he didn't. He gave her barely a minute to breathe before saying, "Good job. Time to run back."

Groaning loudly, Ophelia didn't even care that she was splayed out on the ground, barely covered. "Remind me. What is the point of this?"

"I told you. It's physical training."

"I've had physical training. This is something very different."

"Respectfully, I don't think you've ever trained with an empusae."

She let loose a laugh that started deep in her belly as she rolled over onto her hands and knees, trying to stand but only managing to flop back down on her ass. "That's true, Luka.

That's very true. As far as I know, I've never trained with a vampire."

With her clothes in his hand, he sat down next to her. "Supernatural training will push you to your limits. And you'll be better for it." He knocked his knees against hers. "You've done extremely well, love." Giving her a few more seconds of rest, he stood and offered his hand to help her stand. She quickly pulled her running clothes on over her underwear, which had dried as they climbed the side of the cliff. Curiously, she watched him out of the corner of her eye as he pulled on his own clothes.

This time, Luka paced her, pushing her to keep up with him. As exhausted as she was, her competitive streak would not allow her to fall behind. And he seemed to know it as he kept up the unrelenting pace.

Finally, the estate came into view. She was ecstatic, ready for a break. A nap. Rest. Maybe wine. But then they made their way to the courtyard, and she saw the table of knives and other weapons next to the pool. She stopped, refusing to budge. "What's this?" she asked.

Luka looked from the table and back to her. "I'm teaching you how to defend yourself," he said.

Standing with her hands on her hips and legs spread slightly apart, Ophelia realized she was not, in fact, having wine or a nap. "For what? A medieval duel? And what did we just do?" she asked.

"The warmup," Luka said, shrugging his shoulders and walking to the table to palm some of the weapons.

"That was the warmup?" Ophelia asked incredulously.

"I told you. People are after you. You need to learn to defend yourself. If—when—you are attacked again, you may be exhausted. Out of energy. You will need to dig deep. To find the strength to defend yourself, and keep going," Luka said. His voice was patient but unrelenting.

Mo and Brisa had come out to the courtyard to watch. "Trust him," Brisa said. "He's old as dirt, so he's seen a few fights. Plus, he trained me."

Ophelia didn't respond. Truthfully, she was impressed with Brisa and how she'd handled herself with the vampires in Trieste. Sighing deeply, she nodded her agreement to Luka. "Let's go." Her voice conveyed anything but happiness at this development.

Luka nodded once at her and then started his lesson immediately. "Physical combat is all about timing, balance, and momentum," Luka said. "You are already fast, but you will never be faster than a full empusae—or stronger. You'll need to learn to compensate for that."

"Okay, how?"

"When a person comes at you, you need to use all of your senses. Don't just react. Instead, anticipate where they are going. Brisa, why don't you help demonstrate?"

"I'd be happy to kick your ass, vamp," Brisa said, a challenge in her eyes. Licking her lips as she stepped toward him, she removed her black leather trench coat, revealing leather leggings and a leather crop top. As she backed up to stand near Mo, Ophelia wondered if Brisa was cosplaying.

"Cousin, you don't like my clothes?" Brisa said.

"Get out of my head," Ophelia responded.

Luka ignored their exchange. "No magic," he said.

"I don't need magic to kick your a—"

As Brisa started to taunt Luka, he used the distraction to strike. He sped forward, knocking her flat on her back and landing on top of her. Cursing colorfully, she didn't allow him to best her. Instead, she used the momentum of being thrown onto the ground to buck him off. As she rolled away from his grasp, she quickly kneed him in the groin.

Luka didn't flinch. His gaze intent and focused, he advanced on her. But Brisa stood still, not taking her eyes off of him, until he was about to strike. Just as he neared her, she swept low with one extended leg. Although he didn't trip like a human would, he still had to readjust his stance.

Using the second of advantage that she gained, Brisa launched herself toward the table and grabbed a knife in each hand. When he approached her, she slashed at him—unrelentingly, forcing Luka to retreat. As he avoided her slashes, Ophelia realized that he was purposefully leading Brisa toward the pergola. At the last moment, he ducked, causing Brisa to slam the knives into the decorative wood, trapping them.

Luka rounded behind Brisa and kicked her in the back of the knees, causing her to fall forward. At first, Ophelia thought Luka had won, but Brisa allowed her body to keep moving, pivoting herself to roll away from him as she fell. She landed near the outdoor fireplace, grabbing an iron poker. Luka lunged at her, his teeth at her throat, but the poker held to his heart. It was a draw.

Absolutely awed, Ophelia wanted to clap. Although her cousin was small, she had held her own against a very old and very powerful vampire. Ophelia wanted to be able to do that. To be able to defend herself if—when—she was attacked again. She could admit that, even if she wouldn't say it out loud.

"Not bad for a witch," Luka said, amusement softening his features as he looked down at Brisa. "I taught you well."

"Not bad for un gatto and a braggart," Brisa said, laughing as she dropped the poker at her side. Her chest rose and fell from exertion, but Luka looked unbothered—not a drop of sweat, not even winded. He extended a hand to help her up.

Still laughing, Ophelia furrowed her brow. "Gatto? I've heard that before. That vampire in Trieste said it. What does it mean?"

"Cat," Brisa replied, lips curling. "Don't you know?"

Ophelia's amusement faded. The realization slid into her gut like cold water. She turned—slowly, deliberately—to face Luka. "Know what?" she asked, though deep down, she already did.

FOURTEEN

"Brisa." Luka's voice was sharp, an edge to it as he stared at Brisa, not meeting Ophelia's gaze. "We are still teaching Ophelia about the supernatural world. Let's take it slow."

His reluctance made Ophelia want to press him, to understand what he was trying to hide. Angling her body toward him, she blocked out her cousin and uncle. "Luka, what does she mean?" she asked, wanting him to answer, not Brisa.

Discomfort was etched across his body as he crossed his arms. She heard Brisa and Mo disappear into the house, leaving her and Luka alone in the courtyard.

After several long moments, Luka lifted his gaze through long lashes, his green eyes finally meeting Ophelia's. His shoulders sagged, resigned. "I can become a cat, Ophelia."

She tilted her head to the side, watching him intently. "That was you. In the park." It wasn't a question.

"It was." He looked down. "I'm sorry I didn't tell you."

"I thought I was seeing things. Having an...episode." Her gaze drifted toward the horizon as she folded her arms tightly over her chest. There was nothing to see, but everything to feel. The more she learned, the clearer it became: she had never been crazy. Never imagined things. And that truth was almost as destabilizing as the lies.

"I know. I know. I'm sorry." He reached out and touched her upper arm, his fingers barely pressing into her skin. Still, his touch made her shiver. "I should have told you sooner. But…"

She turned to face him, placing her hand over his. "But what?"

He took a breath, looked down at their hands, and then back up. "I told you I was made, not born. What I didn't say is that I was made by one of Empusa's direct descendants. I don't even know how long ago anymore." He paused. "But her blood was so powerful, I inherited magic usually only found in born empusae. I'm an outlier. Most haven't wielded shapeshifting magic in centuries. That's why the empusae fear me. And hate me."

She studied his face, seeing the pain etched into his features. She understood it. She'd been treated like an anomaly too. Her mind had been poked and prodded by her uncle. Even if Elijah had meant well, it had hurt to be treated like a freak. Her heart ached for Luka.

Tentatively, she asked another question. She stepped closer, placing her hand on his chest, instinctively trying to offer comfort. "Can you only become a black jaguar?"

He lowered his eyes to her hand, placing his over it, fingers curling around hers. He sighed, the sound heavy but warm. "I can become almost anything that breathes."

"What does that mean? I want you to trust me, too," she said, unsure why that was important. But she didn't want him to keep secrets any longer.

Luka sighed and shifted from one foot to the other in a way

that seemed almost too human-like for a vampire. He brought his free hand to her other arm, stroking up and down. She could tell this was for his own comfort, not for hers, so she didn't shrink from him.

"Do you remember what I taught you about the empusae? That we and the witches are descendants of Hecate? We think some kind of magic causes the empusae to exist. The early ones had other powers, like the shapeshifting. Just as witch magic has faded, so too has empusae magic. But some of us—very few—retain those powers." He shrugged as he said this, as if trying to dismiss what made him so beautifully different. He softly stroked her arm and started to circle his thumb over the hand that was on his chest. She didn't make him stop.

"Why were you there?" she asked.

"Where?" His eyebrows furrowed until recognition relaxed the features of his face. "Ah. Why was I in the park?"

Ophelia nodded her head, not taking her eyes off him.

"I started watching you when I found out you were being hunted. Someone was tracking you in New York. I wasn't sure who. I still don't know. But I had to shift to protect you."

"I thought I was hallucinating. Why did you reveal yourself to me?"

"I know. I'm sorry." He turned his head, letting his words trail off. When he turned back to face her, he lifted the hand covering hers to rest it on her cheek.

"Luka," she said, shaking her head. His hand fell, brushing her arm instead. "Do you know what it's like? To grow up without a mother? With episodes that made my uncle think something was wrong with me? That I needed treatment? And then to see a jaguar in the middle of New York?"

"I'm sorry, Ophelia. If I could take it all back, I would. I've never agreed with—" He stopped, turning his head toward the courtyard, still lightly stroking her arms.

She knew what he meant. Her mother's choice to hide the supernatural world. But she wasn't ready to face that yet. So instead, she asked for something else. "I want to see."

"See what?" His arms stilled. He looked at her sharply.

"You. Shifting."

He exhaled and squeezed her arms before stepping back. "Okay. For you, yes."

He pulled off his shirt. She turned to avert her eyes as he reached for his shorts, but he stopped her.

"Ophelia, watch. I want you to see." His voice was gentle, vulnerable.

As she turned her head back, he nodded at her, his eyes nervous as he stood nude in front of her. Suddenly, she felt magic stir in the air. Transfixed, she watched as his lips and teeth transformed from his beautiful human features into the maw of a jaguar. Ophelia felt the shift as magic filled his body. Wind churned, the ancient power at work. Ophelia's eyes stung, but she didn't close them. Suddenly, the rest of his body rapidly morphed into the black jaguar she'd seen in the park.

Standing still, Ophelia felt none of the danger she'd felt in the park. No vibrations coursed through her. She admired the creature standing before her. His body was at least six feet long, with a two-foot-long tail and massive paws. Rosette patterns of his body peeked out from under the dark fur. And how had she never realized that the jaguar in the park had Luka's emerald eyes? He was still there, just in a different form. As he breathed deeply, the air swirled around her legs, lifting dust with each exhale.

Timidly she stepped forward, not scared for her safety, but unsure if she could, or should, touch him. If he'd want her to. When she was inches from him, she reached out her hand, hovering it just above the top of his head. He nuzzled into her and made a deep sound in his throat as she rubbed and scratched his head. Ophelia let out a soft laugh of pure delight as Luka Angelos seemingly purred at her touch. She ran her hand down his back as he rubbed against her legs and hips. She could feel the muscular power of this jaguar body. Safe— that's what it made her feel. She didn't feel a hint of danger, no warnings stirring deeply in her belly.

"You're incredible," Ophelia said as she walked the length of him, touching his tail. Rounding his body, she kept her hand on his back the entire time. Finally, she stood in front of him again. "Thank you for showing me." She looked into his eyes, wanting him to see her gratitude for this moment, for him being vulnerable despite his obvious reluctance.

Backing away from her, he stretched into a low bow before letting out a loud roar as he ran and disappeared out of the courtyard and into the trees. Ophelia watched him leave and stared at the empty space long after he was gone, confused by his initial reluctance and then his disappearance.

After several moments, she heard someone behind her and instinctively knew it was her cousin. Ophelia was learning to recognize the magic around her, and somehow she knew when a witch or vampire was nearby.

As usual, Brisa did not mince words. "You should know that he has never done that for anyone."

Turning to face her cousin, Ophelia felt her eyebrows drawn together in a question. "What do you mean?"

"He refuses to shapeshift for others, especially vampires. They're afraid of his ability, so they taunt him. Test him. They've tried to control him for centuries, and he refuses to be a puppet." Brisa crossed her arms over her chest, her eyes narrowed at her cousin.

Her heart sinking, Ophelia realized what her demand had meant for Luka.

"Shifting also takes a lot of magic. He will be exhausted this evening. He'll need a lot of blood," Brisa said.

Brisa didn't stop there, and Ophelia could feel a warning coming. "You may be my cousin, but I have a long history with Luka. I met him as a child, when our parents started working with him. He has saved my life on more than one occasion. His feelings for you...are complicated. I don't want that to be his undoing." Brisa turned and walked away before Ophelia could answer.

"I care about him, too," Ophelia said to the wind, her voice soft, afraid others would hear.

WHEN LUKA DIDN'T RETURN RIGHT AWAY, Ophelia paced her bedroom, worried about him. She tried to read. She went for a run, hoping to see him. Finally, she tried to practice calling her magic with Brisa.

"Focus, cousin. This is worse than a witchling. You've gone backward in your training," Brisa said after another failed attempt at summoning fire. "I know you've got a kitty-cat on your mind, but come on."

Ophelia stuck out her tongue like a child. In response, Brisa flicked her hand, using enough of her power to knock Ophelia on her ass. Perhaps this was what it would have been like to grow up with a sibling.

"Teamwork," Mo called from a nearby table, where he was reading a book written in ancient Greek. Although he was chastising them, he chuckled when he spoke.

"She started it," they answered in unison, causing both of them to start laughing again, as Brisa stood over Ophelia, who was now lying flat on her back.

"Well, what do we have here?" Luka asked, emerging from the shadows.

Ophelia twisted to see him, scanning his face. He looked pale, but his eyes were steady.

"Having a hard time focusing?" he asked, his voice gruff.

"A bit." She looked up at him expectantly, shielding her eyes from the sun with her hand, unsure of what to do next.

"I want to show you something," he said, extending a hand to her, which she took without hesitation. As he effortlessly brought her to her feet, he laced their fingers.

"The lesson isn't over," Brisa warned, crossing her arms over her chest, a pout on her lips.

"I think this will help with her lessons," Luka said, the discussion over before it began as he led Ophelia to a small stone door hidden in a tower. Vines curled up its side. The door creaked and groaned as Luka pushed it open, revealing winding stairs that led only up. They began climbing, winding round and round, until they reached the top. There, the stairs emptied into a large sunlit room facing the ocean. The windows filled the space with light and wind, and Ophelia breathed deeply as the smell of saltwater hit her nostrils. Small lights were strung around the room, giving it an ambient glow. The room was filled with things she loved. A yoga mat. Candles. Books...so many books. Paranormal romance and histories of the empusae, witches, and fae.

Ophelia turned in place. "What is this?"

"I thought about your life in New York. How you managed to control your powers without knowing what you were."

"And?"

"And I think you have a strong mind, Ophelia. One of the strongest I've ever seen." Luka crossed the room to stand at one of the windows, looking out at the sea, one arm stretched out above him, his palm resting on the top of the window. "I think your yoga instructor probably understood your powers."

"You know Mira?"

He had the good sense to look embarrassed. "Not exactly. But sensed magic in her once. I think she may be a moira—a supernatural known for an ability to share visions of a person's destiny. I believe she helped you learn to calm your mind. It's your way of controlling the power. Whatever she taught you, you should practice it here. Maybe it'll help you remember who you are." He glanced at her, holding her eyes through those long lashes, waiting for her response.

In that moment, Ophelia's chest ached as she realized how much she missed her life in New York: her uncles, her best friend, her routine. She'd been gone weeks by now, and she was kicking herself for not checking in. Yes, she was happy to finally have answers, but these answers created new questions. And she had to admit to herself that she was more lost than ever, no closer to finding her mother or what happened to her. Much to her chagrin, she'd barely thought about her mom.

Without thinking, she crossed the room and threw her arms around Luka's waist. "Thank you," she whispered into his chest.

Luka stood still for a moment, tense. Finally, he wrapped his arms around her, bringing her even closer to him as he rested his chin on her head. "Of course." He cleared his throat. "You're welcome." They stood that way for a while, not speaking.

Finally, Ophelia leaned back and looked at Luka's face. She stood on her toes, in the same way she had when they first embraced in the bar in Trieste. She planted soft kisses on his lips.

"Ophelia, we shouldn't—" he tried to say, but she stopped him.

"Please, Luka." Her eyes met his, searching. "Don't say anything. Don't ruin this. I need you right now. We can worry about the rest later."

Those were the only words he needed. He bent to her, hungrily kissing and nibbling, exploring the contours of her mouth. She backed him into the wall and spread her hands over his chest, then dropped them to his waist, grabbing his shirt and pulling it over his head.

In one movement, he lowered her to the ground, his body over hers, sinking his hips between her legs. As he propped himself up on one forearm, he moved his other hand to her side, slowly running his hand up and down her body, enjoying every curve, as he kissed her mouth, more slowly this time.

"Fuck, Ophelia," he said reverently as he pulled away from her, sucking in his breath as she ground her hips into him at the same time that she pulled him in tighter, her legs wrapped around him. She felt him harden against her.

"That's the idea," she said, breathless.

"Gods, everything about you is intoxicating to me," he said, running his lips along her jaw, down her throat. "But," he said as he pulled away from her and rolled onto his back, careful not to touch her, "we can't."

The absence of his body instantly made her feel empty. "Why?" She was confused. Hurt. She knew he wanted her. She wanted him, despite the complications in their lives.

"For starters, we are distracting each other. I know you were struggling with magic today. Because of me."

"But..."

"No, we can't. I need you to know everything, Ophelia." He turned to look at her, propping himself up with his bent arm.

"I'm not a child that needs to be coddled," she said as she adjusted her clothes, pulling down her top that had ridden up. Humiliation crept into her cheeks as she felt herself flush.

"No, I don't think you are. I think you are a strong woman who is thriving despite what you have been through."

"But?"

"But there's a lot I need to tell you. I don't want to betray your trust again. I promised you that."

"So, tell me," Ophelia said. She could feel frustration deep in her body, wanting him and wanting answers all at once.

"Time is rushed for you. You grew up human," he said, tracing his fingers absentmindedly along her stomach. "But, as an empusae—"

"Wait," Ophelia cut him off. "Do you hear that?" She stood up quickly and dashed to the window facing the front of the castle. She spotted a figure she'd recognize anywhere at the front door of the estate, arguing with Brisa. Ophelia raced down the winding stairs, through the courtyard, through the kitchen and house, and to the front door. She felt Luka on her heels, but she didn't wait for him.

As she reached the front door, she heard the familiar voice. "You will let me in right now. I know she's here. Let me see her."

"Alex?"

FIFTEEN

"Ophelia!" Alex said, rushing forward and collecting her friend in a fierce hug. She squeezed her, not letting go until Ophelia peeled herself away, trying to put a little distance between them.

"Are you okay? What the hell is going on? Why haven't you been answering my texts?" Alex's questions were rapid-fire, one sentence after the other, not giving Ophelia time to answer. She looked from Brisa to Luka and back to Ophelia. "And who the hell are these people?"

Ophelia was stunned to see her best friend standing there, in Luka's doorway. "How did you find this place?" Ophelia asked, instantly regretting the words. Alex's face morphed from concerned to enraged.

"What do you think?" Alex's eyes were incredulous, rounder than Ophelia had ever seen them, anger burning her blue eyes into a deeper shade. "You've been MIA. No calls. No texts. I tracked your phone until the battery died. Or maybe you turned it off. I've been worried sick. Covering for you so that your uncles wouldn't panic. What the hell is going on with you?"

"Oh." Ophelia frowned. She didn't know what to say. She'd been so preoccupied. "I don't even know where my phone is," she admitted, trailing off. It wasn't an excuse. And it wasn't good enough. Why hadn't she reached out? She knew why. Because they never believed her. Always tried to fix her. And for once, she was learning who she really was.

"Why are you here?" Ophelia asked.

"What do you mean, why am *I* here? You disappeared from Trieste. Didn't tell me you were leaving. This bitch," Alex said, pointing at Brisa, "convinced me at first that you were on some love quest. I left with hot Marco, but then came to my senses after a few days..." Her words trailed off as Luka walked up behind Ophelia, resting his hand on the small of her back. Ophelia stepped forward slightly, unwilling to go along with the charade he and Brisa had concocted.

"What in the hell is going on?" Alex asked again.

Luka looked at Brisa. "It wore off?" he asked. "I thought that was long-lasting," he said, brows furrowed in concentration.

Ophelia was confused by his question until she remembered that Brisa had used a potion on Alex, to convince her to leave for New York.

"Apparently not. She shouldn't be questioning anything right now. She must have some magic in her bloodline. Wasn't researching that your job?" Brisa asked Luka, the accusation sharp in her tone. The air was stiff with tension.

"What?" Alex blinked, confused. Then she started tugging at Ophelia's arm with rising urgency, as if determined to get her out of there. "We're leaving."

Ophelia placed her hand over Alex's, stopping her. "Alex,

no. I need to talk to you. I need you to understand." Her words came out low as a tentative plea.

"We can talk at the hotel. Once we're away from this place." Alex's head tilted with that familiar, stubborn expression Ophelia had seen a hundred times. When Alex set her mind to something, almost nothing could stop her. But not this time.

"No. I'm not leaving." Ophelia said. The softness vanished from her tone, replaced with steel. Her lips pressed into a line.

Alex glared between her, Luka, and Brisa. Ophelia could almost feel her friend calculating, weighing the odds, and strategizing how to drag her out by force if she had to.

"Why don't you come with me?" Ophelia asked, not giving her the chance to object. "I want to show you something." Without another word, she turned and walked toward the courtyard. She could feel Alex's hesitation behind her, but she knew her well enough to trust she would follow.

Mo sat in his usual spot at the table, surrounded by open books in half a dozen languages. She gave him a brief nod, then gestured to Alex. "This is my uncle, Marcello."

"Your what?"

"He's my mother's brother. Half-brother."

Alex was clearly baffled, but she offered Mo a polite nod. Mo arched a brow as he scanned the room, taking in Brisa and Luka trailing after them.

"Luka, will you light a fire? Brisa, will you help me with a demonstration?"

"I don't think that's a good idea," Luka said, worry etched across his face as he glanced between the two women.

"We don't show humans—" Brisa began, her protest echoing his.

"I don't care what you think." The words came out taut, barely held together. "I don't care what you normally do. What your supernatural rules are. They don't apply to me. This is my best friend, and I won't lie to her." Ophelia turned to Luka, holding his gaze until he finally turned away.

Brisa held her cousin's gaze, refusing to look away as she said, "I don't do dog tricks. And this won't help. I can tell."

Ophelia knew Brisa was reading Alex's mind, studying her thoughts, but she still had to try. "Brisa, please," Ophelia pleaded. She needed her friend to see what she could do. To not dismiss her episodes, and to finally see her for what she was: a witch with real powers.

To Ophelia's surprise, the intractable, stubborn Brisa relented, sighing as she stepped forward, picking at nails that were now a deep purple. Luka lit the outdoor fire, his jaw set. So what if they didn't approve of what she was about to do? After years spent on the fringe, afraid of herself and her episodes, feeling misunderstood even by her closest friend and uncle, she needed this. Proof that she wasn't crazy or overstimulated or having psychiatric episodes due to her mother's disappearance. She hurried to the edge of the pool without being asked, ready to be doused or dunked if necessary.

As Brisa raised her hands to call the wind, Ophelia closed her eyes, centering herself as she thought about nothing but the fire. She raised her left hand and reached for it, calling it to her. At the same time, she focused on countering Brisa's air assault. She breathed the air and held her right hand out in front of her, as if she were holding Brisa's attack at bay with a flick of her wrist.

When she heard Alex gasp, Ophelia opened her eyes. A stream of fire surrounded Brisa, spinning in a raging typhoon of flames. Ophelia was also controlling the air spinning around her, never letting Brisa's magic hit her, countering Brisa's attack with her own magic. The magic was surging through her, stronger than she'd felt before.

Mo's eyes were wide, and Luka was staring at her with his brows knit together.

"Too much, Ophelia," Luka said. "You need to stop."

Mo stepped between his daughter and Ophelia, careful to avoid the fire. "Ophelia, the next lesson—the most important lesson—is control. It's important to know when to let go of the power," he said. "Let it drop from your mind. Allow the magic to dissipate. Not control you," he said. Mo's voice was soothing and calm, but there was an urgency, as if concerned about his daughter's safety.

Brisa was straining to keep the flames away from her. Sweat had started to drip down her brow, and her face was creased in concentration. Every instinct in Ophelia's body wanted her to keep fighting, to conquer and win. But she also didn't want to hurt her cousin. Exhaling deeply, Ophelia closed her eyes and thought about the fire moving back to the hearth, extinguishing itself. The air slowing to stillness.

When she finally opened her eyes, it was eerily quiet. Even the ocean waves seemed too far away, and the birds had stopped chirping. Ophelia found four sets of eyes trained on her, mouths gaping, their faces fixed with a combination of fear and admiration.

"That was..." Mo trailed off, unable to finish his sentence.

"That was terrible," Brisa said as she heaved, trying to catch her breath from the exertion. "You have work to do. We'll address the inadequacy in training."

Ophelia grinned at her cousin, knowing she had improved if Brisa was breathing that heavily. But her smile fell when she saw Alex's face.

Alex's lips were pressed into a thin line, her eyebrows were raised, and her body was rigid. She was trying to control her breathing, trying to control the angry look on her face. Ophelia had known her friend for over twenty years, and she recognized the expression and emotions radiating off of her. She had seen it so many times before. Alex simply didn't believe her.

"I can see that it didn't work, cousin," Brisa said, uncharacteristically quiet and free of sarcasm as she broke the news to Ophelia.

Ophelia knew what she meant. Brisa had read Alex's mind, and Alex didn't believe her own eyes. Alex turned abruptly and left the courtyard, walking briskly through the kitchen toward the front of the house.

"Alex," Ophelia called, trailing after her through the kitchen and to the front door. "Alex, stop, please," Ophelia yelled. She hated that her need was so strong, that despite finding this other family, she still needed Alex to believe her.

Alex whirled on her, spinning on her feet and almost colliding with Ophelia. "You are smarter than this. These people are con artists. Is this some kind of cult?" Alex's face was split into an anger Ophelia had never seen.

"What are you talking about? You saw the magic with your own eyes," Ophelia said, practically pleading.

Alex snorted and crossed her arms in front of her chest. "Smoke and mirrors, Ophelia. Tricks of the mind. These people know that you inherited some money after your mom died, and they are preying on your weaknesses," she said.

Ophelia laughed in response. "And what weaknesses are those, Alex?" she asked, holding her eyes. Feeling a wisp of wind swirl in response to her anger, she forced herself to let go of the magic. She'd fight this battle with words.

"You know what I mean," Alex said, averting her eyes towards the ground.

Ophelia stepped even closer to her. They were inches apart now. "I know exactly what you mean. You've never believed me. You've never believed in my 'episodes,'" Ophelia said, now disgusted with the term. "You thought I was just crazy. Sad about my mom disappearing. Causing a scene. That I just needed more therapy," she continued, her voice climbing an octave with each sentence.

"That's not—" Alex tried to deny it, but Ophelia wouldn't let her. Not this time.

"That's exactly what you meant, Alex." Ophelia was yelling now, the rage building as her fists clenched at her sides. "Guess what? I am different. But I'm happy that I'm different. For the first time, I know what has been missing in my life. I know why I had the episodes." Ophelia stopped herself. "No, not episodes. It's magic. It's power," she said.

Alex rolled her eyes and lifted her arms in the air, letting them fall to her sides with a slap. "Ophelia, some man who makes you feel good for the first time in your life is not magic," Alex said, lifting her hand to touch Ophelia's hair. "Look at you. Your clothes are wrinkled, and your hair is a mess. I see what is going on. Sleeping with him is not magic."

Ophelia jerked back. "Is that what you think this is about?" Ophelia barked a deep laugh. "Hardly. I've found people who understand me. Who can teach me about who I am. Who actually care about me."

It was Alex's turn to jerk back, like an invisible hand had slapped her across the face. She put her hand to her chest as if her heart physically ached. "And I haven't been there for you? All these years? Supporting every whim? Ignoring your idiosyncrasies? Ignoring the flakiness?" Alex asked.

"Idiosyncrasies? Flakiness? This is how you really feel about me?" Ophelia scoffed, her stomach dropping in knots.

Alex was unable to stop herself now that she'd started. "Supporting law school when you didn't even want to go? Going with you when you wanted to travel the world to find yourself? Lying to your uncles for you? Keeping your secrets?"

"That's not why I'm here," Ophelia said, almost a whisper,

so hurt that she was afraid to speak louder, afraid of her magic coming to the surface. "You know I want to find my mom."

"And that requires you to lie to all of us? To keep secrets? To lie to Sebastian and Elijah? Not even checking in?"

"I knew you wouldn't understand," Ophelia said, allowing a bit of shame to seep through.

"Our friendship is supposed to be based on trust," Alex said.

"No, our friendship is based on me hiding anything that might upset you. That might upset Elijah. That might upset Sebastian. As long as I keep my episodes—my magic—to myself. My thoughts to myself, my real intentions to myself, you all are happy. And what am I?" Ophelia asked.

"Ophelia, no one asked you to lie," Alex said, crossing her arms over her chest again.

"You didn't answer my question," Ophelia said, seething, her hands clenched at her sides as her nails dug crescent moon notches into her skin. She could feel the magic brimming, but she wouldn't allow it to come to the surface. "What am I, Alex? When you all get to hear what you want? Avoiding the real me?" Alex was silent, staring at the ground and refusing to look at Ophelia any longer. "I'll tell you. I'm a shell of my true self. A shell. Unhappy. Broken. Sad. Lonely in a room full of people who say they love me, but who won't even see the real me," Ophelia said, the words cracking.

Alex finally stared at Ophelia's face, searching as she said, "Ophelia, we have been best friends for twenty years."

"Yet you don't even know me. The real me. You refuse to believe what is in front of you. What kind of friend is that?" Ophelia asked.

"Wow. After all these years. This is how you really feel?" Alex asked, echoing the earlier question. A single tear fell down her cheek as her chin quivered. The sight of it made

Ophelia's eyes well with tears, but she refused to let them fall.

"And you've shown me how you really feel about me. Over and over." Ophelia said.

The tears finally flowed steadily down both of their faces. Alex took a deep, raspy breath. She turned without another word, opened the front door, and closed it gently behind her.

And it felt like a door had been closed on Ophelia's heart. She sobbed without a sound, her chest moving up and down as the tears flowed down her cheeks. She felt Luka behind her, and she didn't want him to see her cry. Gathering herself, and wiping away the tears, she still didn't face him as she asked, "Will you please make sure she is safe?"

"Of course. I'll make sure someone follows her home," he said softly.

Ophelia felt him reach his hand out to touch her arm, but she shook him off, moving so that his hand touched empty air. She had been alone her entire life, and she knew that she deserved that loneliness. Retreating to Luka's bedroom, she crawled into the bed and pulled the covers over her entire body, wanting to disappear into the darkness. Sleep did not find her for many hours.

CHAPTER

SIXTEEN

Ophelia was irritated, like she had an itch under her skin that she couldn't scratch. She'd tossed and turned all night, thinking of her fight with Alex. Wishing she could take back her angry words. But did she really regret what she'd said? Maybe the delivery, but not finally speaking her truth. When sleep finally took her in the early morning hours, she slept fitfully. And Luka had not come for training.

After dressing quickly in workout clothes, she jerked open the bedroom door to find Luka sitting in the hall, on the floor across from her. His green eyes searched her face, waiting for her to speak.

Narrowing her eyes at him and clenching her fists at her side, she asked, "Why didn't you come get me?"

"I thought you might need sleep. After what happened—" He rubbed at his jaw.

"No. I need training and answers. I don't need a break. Or to talk." She paused, hesitating for just a moment before asking about Alex. "Is she safe?"

"Of course," Luka said.

Without answering, she walked down the hall, ready to train.

Sighing, Luka followed her to the front door.

Ophelia trained hard that morning. Ran faster than she had the day before, even besting him at times, as the hurt carried her toward the sea. When she reached the water, she didn't hesitate, angrily launching herself into the water and then swimming to break the surface. Without confirming Luka was behind her, she started climbing up the jagged edges that jutted into the sea. She didn't speak, and Luka let her silence fill the space around them, suffocating them. When they were back at the estate, she practiced sparring with him. After a few rounds, when he suggested a break, "Again" was her only response.

In the afternoon, she trained with Brisa, clearing her mind of everything except her training, not wanting Brisa to read her thoughts. That evening, Ophelia went to the tower to be alone. Looking out to the sea, she tried to calm her mind in the way Mira had taught her over the years. But her thoughts often returned to Alex. She'd wanted to call her friend several times after finding her phone at the bottom of her suitcase, but her stubbornness held her back.

This pattern repeated for weeks, stretching through November as the air grew colder. At night, Ophelia would emerge from the tower, barely eat, and sink into bed from exhaustion. Alone. Luka and Mo pored over ancient texts, searching for clues about the Lunula Amulet and Ophelia's connection to it. Although Ophelia was withdrawn, she was making strides with her powers as she learned to control the magic, despite Brisa telling her repeatedly that a witchling had better control.

And Luka confused her. Although he trained with her, he was brusque—almost impatient—and they barely spoke outside of training. At night, he stayed up late with Mo, reading, never alone with Ophelia.

Finally, one morning, he came to her room earlier than usual. After knocking briefly, he spoke through the door. "Wear something warm. We're taking a break from training."

She was already awake, staring out at the courtyard. As she heard him walk away, the familiar vibrations began in the tips of her fingers. Something was off. It had been a while since she'd had any warnings—not since Trieste when she'd been attacked. Hesitating, she let curiosity win as she quickly dressed in a pair of jeans, a soft white sweater, and her boots.

Instinct led Ophelia to the estate's garage—in a separate building from the rest of the house—where she found Luka sitting astride a black motorcycle. Wordlessly, he held a helmet to her, motioning for her to put it on. Something felt very wrong, but she put it on anyway. "Where are we going?"

"I need to talk to you. Privately." His troubled eyes were a deeper green than usual. "Please."

Despite feeling a buzzing under the surface of her skin, she slid behind him and wrapped her arms around his waist, her legs flush against his. At first, he tensed at her touch, but he slowly relaxed into her, started the motorcycle, and drove down the gravel drive. They wound their way down the narrow road toward the sea, as the sun made its slow creep higher into the sky. Finally, Luka stopped the motorcycle on a strip of dirt between the road and a cliff overlooking the sea.

As Ophelia dismounted, Luka extended his hand, palm up, silently inviting her to take it. "Trust me," he said when she hesitated.

She slipped her hand into his without a word, and he

guided them down a barely visible dirt path. Overgrown grass brushed against her legs as they descended in silence. When they rounded a bend, a small beach came into view, concealed from above by the jagged cliff edge.

At the end of the trail, a three-foot drop led down to the sand. Luka jumped easily, landing with feline grace. Before Ophelia could follow, he reached for her waist, lifting her effortlessly and setting her down in front of him. Her breasts brushed his chest in the descent, but he kept a respectful distance otherwise. Without another word, he moved toward the shoreline, his gaze fixed on the horizon.

She followed him across the sand. When she stopped beside him, he offered a faint smile, lips pressed in a thin line. "I've been coming here for centuries," he murmured. "It's where I go when I need to think." His eyes swept the sea before he drew in a steadying breath. "I found something."

As fear crept along her spine, Ophelia waited. Based on Luka's face, she wasn't going to like what he had to say.

"Have you ever wondered why your mother kept your father's identity a secret? Or your birth a secret from the witches?"

"From what I know of my mother, she did things her own way," Ophelia said. Of course, she'd wondered. Many times. But she kept that locked away.

"She was...unique. Stubborn. A lot like you in that way," he said, smiling down at Ophelia. "She would bend rules—push hard to get her way."

"What did you find?" Ophelia asked, her voice quiet, wanting him to get to the point. It occurred to her that she hadn't asked about her mother much since she'd arrived, although that had been the plan. Fear had held her back. Fear of whatever Luka had to tell her.

Shoulder to shoulder, staring out at the sea, Luka found her fingers, interlacing his own with hers.

"Supernaturals usually stay away from each other. Avoid congregating unless necessary. And only then in neutral areas like Trieste," he said.

"But you and Mo and Brisa are friends. How did that happen?" she asked.

"Your mom. We met at a meeting for supernaturals in Trieste. We discovered our shared affinity for peace. She introduced me to Mo, and I met Brisa as a child," Luka said, smiling at the memory. "When Mo learned about the Lunula Amulet from an ancient text and the search for it, we decided to search in secret, working behind closed doors."

"But why the secrecy?" Ophelia asked.

"Our friendship is not necessarily forbidden, but it is unusual. And that's just the way things have been since supernaturals first roamed this world," Luka said.

"Why would anyone care who you're friends with?" Ophelia asked, interrupting him.

Luka shrugged. "Old prejudices that no longer make sense. The usual reasons people fear those who aren't like them." He paused, inhaling deeply. "But there are some rules that are foundational to supernaturals. That are forbidden and carry grave consequences. For starters, we aren't supposed to work together toward a common goal, like searching for the Lunula Amulet," Luka said.

"So, basically, supernaturals are living in the 1950s still, but worse?" Ophelia asked.

"As you can imagine, combining our powers and pooling resources presents a threat to the governing bodies for supernaturals. That's why my friendship with Mo, Brisa, and Celeste was always behind closed doors," Luka said.

Luka cleared his throat before speaking again. "Supernaturals can't be together," he said.

"But you just said friendship isn't forbidden," Ophelia said.

"I mean together as lovers. Mates. Partners," he said.

Ophelia felt a shudder run deep in her. Was this why he'd been avoiding her? Refusing to continue what they'd started in the tower? "But why?" she asked.

"Who knows? I haven't found the answer yet. The rule is centuries old. I suspect it is because any offspring could be too powerful. A threat to the governing heads and their hold on power."

"Can vampires even reproduce?"

"I didn't think so. But if I've learned anything, it's that there is always an exception where magic and supernaturals are involved."

Ophelia felt the water swirling around her feet. Squeezing Luka's hand, she was afraid of where this conversation was going.

"I've been searching for a witch like you. To understand why you have such strong powers. I've been reading with Mo, searching day and night," he said, hesitating again.

Ophelia hadn't seen him so unsure like this before. It made her nervous. "And?"

"I finally found something last night. I found a journal written in ancient Greek, my native language. Centuries ago, another witch had the ability to call all elemental powers. And he had a similar gift of foresight. Like you," Luka said.

"What happened to him?" Ophelia asked, her voice barely a whisper. She was squeezing Luka's hand, the whites of her knuckles showing.

"He was executed," he said, giving her hand a reassuring squeeze.

She felt her stomach drop. "Why?"

"Too powerful. Leaders of the supernaturals sanctioned his murder. And kept his existence—and death—a secret," Luka said. "The journal was written by his half sister and was hidden in San Marino. I may have snuck a few books out for Mo the last time I was there," Luka said, smirking before the humor quickly faded.

"But why would he be executed because of his powers?" Ophelia asked, feeling that she was missing a puzzle piece. After a long silence, she felt Luka's gaze on her face. "Why are you staring at me like that?" she asked, keeping her eyes fixed on the sea.

"His mother was a witch. And his father was an empusae. That's why he was killed. His powers threatened both witches and vampires—their way of life. Do you understand what I'm saying to you?" he asked.

"I...no," she said, though a cold certainty curled along her spine. She understood all too well—and she hated it.

"You can control all the elements," Luka said.

"No, I can't," Ophelia said, shaking her head and squeezing her eyes shut. "I can't even call fire, and I can barely control air."

"Yes, you can." He reached up and touched her cheek, guiding her chin with gentle pressure. "Don't be scared. Just— look down." His voice was soft, his thumb brushing her skin in slow, calming strokes.

Reluctantly, she lowered her gaze. Though the rest of the sea remained calm, the water at her feet swirled in turbulent circles, licking up her calves with surprising force. She stumbled back, breaking contact, and dropped to the sand. Pulling her knees to her chest, she rested her forehead against them, willing the ground beneath her to stay still and begging the world not to move with her.

"This doesn't mean that my father was a vampire," she

said. Why hadn't her mom given her this information? Why the secrecy?

"There's more," Luka said, walking toward her and sitting down next to her in one graceful movement, their legs touching.

"There is always more," Ophelia said.

"The empusae who attacked you in Trieste. He tasted your blood," Luka said.

Ophelia shuddered, remembering the attack. "So?" she asked.

"When empusae drink blood, we can see snippets of memories from our victims. And we can taste whether someone is a supernatural or human. Different blood has different compositions. Empusae can tell which is which," he said, looking at Ophelia. "The one who attacked you knew you were more than a witch. I saw his memories when I ripped into his throat and his blood entered me. That's why I killed him. I couldn't risk him telling others."

Ophelia jerked her head up from her knees, rage building inside her. "And you didn't tell me? Why would you keep this from me?" she asked.

"This world is so new to you. And I didn't understand why you had empusae blood either. There could have been several explanations," he said, sounding apologetic.

The sand under them started to sift as the sea stretched toward them. Shivering at her power—at the implication of what Luka had told her—Ophelia breathed deeply. As her body continued to shake, Luka wrapped his arms around her.

"Ophelia, I think this is why your mother kept you from the witches. Kept you from knowing your father. Kept you away from the supernatural world. She didn't even tell her brother. She was afraid for you," Luka said.

"What now?" Ophelia asked.

"I don't know," he admitted.

"Do you think this is why people are after me? And how is this connected to the amulet?" she asked.

"I don't know that either," he said. His voice was laced with regret, frustration just below the surface. "I think someone discovered your witch bloodline. That's probably why you were being followed in the park. But I don't think anyone knows about the blood. Or you would have been called to come before the Council."

Ophelia furrowed her brows, shifting toward Luka. "Why?" she asked, edging closer until their legs touched, drawn to the quiet steadiness of his presence.

"All empusae must answer to the Council. Witches must answer to the High Priestess. That's probably why your mother kept you a secret. From everyone," he said.

"But if this is true, I'm not really a witch or a vampire," she said.

"What do you mean if it's true?" he asked.

"What if I don't have vampire blood?"

"Ophelia, it has to be true. Magic and power radiate off of you. It's stronger than any witch I've ever seen. And more reckless. Harder to control," Luka said.

"But there's really only one way for you to know for sure, right?" Ophelia asked, building the courage to ask him. "I mean, you would need to tas—" Ophelia couldn't bring herself to finish the sentence.

Luka went rigid next to her. "You do not understand what you are asking," he said.

"Tell me, then," she said. Her voice was quiet as she watched his mouth, realizing they hadn't been this close since the tower. She reached her hand to his mouth, running her thumb along his full lower lip.

Grabbing her wrist, Luka stopped her. "Sharing blood with

an empusae the way you are asking is...intimate." His voice had lowered a few octaves as his eyes roamed her face.

"And if I want to share that with you?"

"It would bind you to me. You don't understand what that means," he said again.

Without asking another question, Ophelia closed the final distance between them, placing a soft kiss on Luka's mouth. As his lips parted in surprise, she explored the shape of his mouth, darting her tongue in to meet his. She wanted to forget about this conversation. Needed the distraction.

Restrained at first, Luka let her lead until finally giving in and pulling her onto his lap to straddle him, running his hands up and down her back. She wrapped her arms around him, running her hands through his hair. With one hand on her bottom, Luka allowed the other hand to roam up her shirt, underneath the hem, where his fingers traced her stomach to the curve of her breasts.

Just then, Luka's phone rang out with a shrillness that interrupted their peace. They ignored it, kissing as Ophelia ground her hips, wanting to feel him.

The phone rang again. He groaned and leaned back from her. "Sorry, love. Only a few people have this number," he said, answering his phone with audible annoyance. As he listened, she leaned back toward him, planting kisses down his neck. But she stopped when she felt his mood change, his body tensing. "We'll be right there."

Hanging up the phone, he gently pulled Ophelia off of his lap, placing her next to him. "We'll have to continue this later." He kissed her hard on the mouth and then pulled away again. "Mo found something. We need to go."

She scooted away from him, groaning with frustration as she ached between her thighs. Smoothing her sweater, she accepted his offered hand to help her stand. Luka patted sand off her clothes before placing his hands on her shoulders, turning her to see his face. "I will do whatever is required to keep your secret. To keep you safe. We keep this to ourselves for now," he said.

"Even from Mo and Brisa?"

"Yes. If they know the truth, they may be required to tell the High Priestess. I'm beginning to understand why your mom kept you a secret."

CHAPTER
SEVENTEEN

Side by side, Ophelia and Luka bent at the waist, staring at the brittle, ancient pages, yellowed and partly fading from the passage of time. They were in Luka's home, in an opulently decorated parlor.

"Latin?" Ophelia asked, eyes scanning the dense script.

Mo seemed impatient, his excitement palpable. "Yes, but you don't need to read the text. Focus on the images."

Luka spotted it first. "Well done, friend," he said, clapping Mo on the back.

Still confused, Ophelia glanced between them and then back to the book. The pages depicted several images of the same open-air, square marble altar—large enough to be its own room. It was carved with ornate figures, including statues of people and animals. "What am I missing?" she finally asked.

Mo pointed to one drawing, careful not to touch the delicate parchment. "It's the Ara Pacis, an altar to Pax, the Goddess of Peace." He indicated a section on one side. "See? That's a carving of Pax. An ode to her greatness," he explained.

"But how is this helping us?" Ophelia asked, still puzzled.

"According to the text, the altar was built in 13 BC in the flood plain of the Tiber River, where it lay buried beneath thirteen feet of silt and sediment. Long after the Alliance between supernaturals was formed." He gestured to a carved image of a child on the interior of the altar. She wore a necklace: a carved upside-down crescent moon with three jewels embedded in its belly.

"She's wearing the Lunula Amulet, Ophelia. It's a clue," Luka said. "The best one we've had since we started searching."

Mo began pacing, his attention no longer on the book. "For centuries, rumors swirled about Alaric's treasure—mainly that he died fleeing the vampires and was buried in the bed of the Busento River in western Italy. But what if he died close to Rome? In the flood plain of the Tiber?" He finally exhaled. "That's what I think the Ara Pacis reveals."

Luka picked up the thought, rubbing his hand across his jaw. "Perhaps," he said. "Perhaps the Busento has been a ruse all along. That would explain why no one has found the treasure in all these years."

"Do you think the amulet is with the Ara Pacis?" Ophelia asked.

"No," Mo answered, "the Ara Pacis was excavated a long time ago. The amulet would have been discovered at that time."

"Where is the flood plain?" Ophelia asked.

"That's a good question," Luka said. "It has changed in modern times. Back then, when the Ara Pacis was buried, it was on the outskirts of Rome. North of where Alaric attacked. In the opposite direction from the Busento, where treasure hunters have searched for centuries for Alaric's treasure and the Lunula Amulet."

They were all quiet for a moment until Luka spoke again.

"You know, I remember when the excavation of the Ara Pacis began. In the early 1900s."

Brisa finally spoke from her seat in the corner. "Damn, vamp, I knew you were old as dirt."

Luka ignored her. "It's now in a museum in Rome, not far from the Trevi Fountain," he said.

"I think you and Ophelia need to see the Ara Pacis in person," Mo said.

"How would that help?" Ophelia asked.

"I've been trying to learn about your foresight. I don't think it's just danger that you can sense. I think you might have the ability to perceive what others can't. If I'm right, visiting the Ara Pacis in person—perhaps touching it—may allow you to find a clue about the amulet's location," Mo said.

"I agree," Luka said, surprising her. She'd thought he would object.

"But, what about finding my mother?" Ophelia asked, pausing because she didn't want to disappoint this newfound family, but she'd already been sidetracked enough. "I'm truly grateful for your help, but I came here for a reason. I've been delayed for weeks, and I'm really no closer to learning more about her."

"We know, Ophelia. We promise we've searched for clues about her disappearance, and we will help you," Mo said, his expression softening and reminding her so much of Elijah. A pang of homesickness swept over her as she thought of her uncles. And Alex. "But for now, we very much need your help finding the Lunula Amulet. If we don't make it our top priority, it could fall into the wrong hands. And we have no idea who might be after it."

Brisa chimed in, blunt as ever. "Cousin, all we know is that, at first, the amulet was used for good, to eradicate evil. Eventually, it became a weapon, but at least it was hidden away in a vault. Until Alaric stole it. Now, anyone could use it to control minds, supernatural or otherwise. We can't let that happen. We want to destroy it. And we think we need you to do that. So, your choice: search for your mother—who, frankly, no one's been able to find—or help us save the world. Entirely up to you, of course."

Ophelia dropped her gaze to the floor, her feet shifting as guilt pricked at her. She hated that she didn't answer right away. The truth was, there wasn't much of a decision to make. Not really. She'd waited twenty years for answers about her mom. She could wait a little longer.

She exhaled and lifted her head. "All right. I'll help you," she said, meeting each of their eyes in turn, making her promise. Willing to set aside the mystery that had haunted her life, at least for now.

"Thank you," Mo said, placing a hand on her shoulder and giving it a grateful squeeze. "And...there's something else." He wrinkled his nose as he said it.

"There's always something else," Luka said dryly.

"You two will have to go alone. Brisa and I have been called to a meeting at Mt. Slivnica."

Luka sighed deeply and pinched the bridge of his nose. "Really?"

"Mt. Slivnica?" Ophelia asked at the same time, her eyebrows lifted.

Mo answered, "Slovenia. Where the witches and High Priestess meet in communion. We've all been commanded to convene." Mo hesitated. "The reason for the meeting has been kept a secret. I understand now why your mother kept your powers from me. If they ask about you...I don't want to put Brisa at risk. If I keep information about you a secret, then Brisa could be harmed," he said. His voice was apologetic.

Luka's face went rigid, his jaw set. He stood tall, leaning

toward his friend. "You wouldn't dare put Ophelia at risk by revealing what you know."

Ignoring Luka, Mo looked at his niece. "If the High Priestess demands information about you, I would be required to tell her. I'll have no choice. If I refuse, my family will face severe punishment," he said.

Understanding knocked into her. Luka had already explained that Mo and Brisa may be required to reveal her secrets if requested by their High Priestess. Mo was confirming it. That's why the two of them were keeping her lineage a secret, for now.

She stepped closer to Luka, placing her hand on his arm, blocking his anger. Turning back to Mo, her face serious, she said, "I trust you. And Brisa. I want you two to protect your-selves, even if it means that you reveal my identity." Sensing Luka had calmed down, she stepped away from him and toward Mo. "I just found my family. I don't want to lose you."

Mo bent to hug her, his tense face softening with relief. "Thank you for understanding. I will do what I can, within the confines of the Covenant."

"Covenant?" she asked.

"The Witch's Covenant contains all the ground rules we must follow," Mo answered, turning to search the room. "Ah, here," he said, selecting a book from his stack and handing it to Ophelia. "This book may help you understand your lineage and our history."

After taking the book and thanking him, Ophelia excused herself early that night. When she spoke briefly with Brisa, she sang "Happy Birthday" to herself in her mind, over and over, so that Brisa couldn't read her thoughts and learn her secret. When she saw Brisa glaring at her through narrowed eyes, she knew it was working.

It was a relief to let her guard down when she finally closed the bedroom door. Eyeing the fireplace, she decided to play with her magic. Relaxing, thinking about nothing but the logs in the fire and her desire to be warm, she yelped in surprise when fire sprang from her fingertips. She squealed when the flames roared to life in the fireplace.

Immediately, there was a knock at the door, and Luka poked his head in the room. "I heard you yell. Is everything okay?" Hunting for danger, his tense eyes roamed the room. When those emerald orbs landed on her beaming face, he visibly relaxed, his tense jaw softening.

"I just brought *fire* to my fingertips," she said, marveling at how everything had finally clicked into place. Luka's lips curved in response, but the warmth in her expression faded, shadowed by the memory of their conversation on the beach. "Come in?"

Luka hesitated, but he slipped into the room and leaned against the door after closing it. Wanting him near her, Ophelia held her hand out to him. Wordlessly, he took it, intertwining their fingers together as they both stared into the fire.

"Will you stay with me tonight?" she asked.

Luka didn't respond immediately, hesitating a moment too long, leaving Ophelia feeling embarrassed. "Forget it," she said, dropping his hand and walking away from him.

He grabbed her by the waist, slamming her back to his chest. "It's not what you think," he said, whispering in her ear. "I want you. I'm afraid to tell you how much I want you because I don't want to scare you. I want every moment I have left to be with you," he said, inhaling her scent as his breath sent shivers down her neck. "I've lived hundreds of years, Ophelia, and I haven't been scared in a very long time. But I don't know how to keep you safe. I don't know what the Council or the High Priestess will try to do with you when they inevitably discover you. And I can't protect you from it. I'm trying, but I know I can't." He released her waist, turning her to face him and running a hand through his hair. "And there is more I need to tell—"

Ophelia placed a finger on his lips. "Let's save the rest of the confessions for later. Please?"

Relenting, he pulled her to him, moving his hands up to her face, pulling her closer. he kissed down her neck to the soft spot between her collarbones. Hurriedly, she grabbed at his shirt, barely able to reach, yanking it over his head. His hands roamed her body as he moved to the hem of her shirt, pulling it over her head. He unhooked her bra to free her breasts, heavy and aching to be touched. Not taking their eyes off each other, they parted briefly to slip out of the rest of their clothes.

As soon as they were bare, their bodies met again. Luka ran his hands down the sides of Ophelia's body, feeling every curve. He stepped back to stare at her. When she tried to move toward him, he stopped her.

"No. I want to learn every inch of your body."

Getting down on his knees in front of her naked body, he ran his hands up the back of her legs, cupping her ass as she shivered, waiting. "Do you know how hard it is for me to focus on training you when your long, gorgeous legs are taunting me?" he asked, kissing the tops of her thighs. "When all I want to do is taste you?" he asked, running a tongue up her inner thigh. "To bury myself in you? To bend you over and fuck you in the woods?"

Kissing her hip bones, his lips made their way up to her pebbled nipples. "These are also very distracting during training." He bent down and flicked his tongue over her right nipple before moving to her left, sucking and nibbling.

"Luka," she moaned as she grabbed his hair, squeezing.

"Gods, I love hearing my name from your beautiful mouth." To her great disappointment, he left her breasts. "Your fingers are also beautiful." He started kissing down each one. "I love watching your hands. Watching the magic that ripples from them." He kissed her fingertips, one at a time. "But what I really love," he said, with a grin on his lips, "is remembering the taste of your mouth on mine. And now I want to taste you again."

Luka cupped her around the ass and lifted her easily, in much the same way he had that first night together. But this time, nothing separated them as her heat pressed into him. He held her with one hand, the other snaking around to part her lips with his thumb. He moved his finger up until he was stroking her center, stopping before she could climax and forcing a frustrated groan.

"Gods, love, you are so wet. But I don't want you to come just yet. Not unless it's on my tongue." He dropped her on the bed and pinned her waist with his hands, lowering his head between her thighs. He didn't bother with teasing her, instead parting her with his tongue briefly before licking and sucking her clit.

Ophelia didn't hold back. "Luka, fuck." She gasped and moaned until her body finally rocked with an orgasm. He didn't stop until the last shudder had passed.

"I want you inside of me now," Ophelia said, her voice hoarse and breathless. She tried to sit up, reaching for him, but he stood out of reach, slipping those sweatpants over his hips and legs to reveal his large cock, swollen with need.

"God," Ophelia said.

"None here," Luka said, winking at her. "But, since we know about your lineage..." he stopped. "I don't have any condoms."

"I'm on birth control," Ophelia said quickly, understanding his concern and happy that was the one thing she managed to never forget. "What about..."

"The empusae can't carry infections or diseases," Luka said, assuaging any concerns about sexual health.

Ophelia thought this sounded like the absolute best part about being with a supernatural. And now she needed him buried inside of her. She stood in front of him, guiding her hand down his stomach to his throbbing erection, grasping his thickness. As she stroked back and forth, she turned his body, released his cock, and then pushed him to sit on the edge of the bed.

Putting her hands on his shoulders, she planted her knees on the bed on either side of him, straddling him. They stared at each other for a moment before she lowered her head to kiss his mouth. As they kissed deeply, she slid herself over the length of him, slowly working her way down until he filled her, stretching her.

For a moment, they were both still, and then Ophelia began rocking her hips in a rhythm. Luka placed one hand around her and grabbed her ass, encouraging her to keep riding him. Drawing one of her nipples into his mouth, he sucked and nibbled as he used his thumb and forefinger to tease the other nipple. Feeling herself tense with every stroke as she slid up and down, she started to moan as her sensitive clit rubbed against his base.

Finally, she felt the heat build in her core as she climaxed around his cock, moaning his name. As she came, Luka followed, grabbing her hair and pulling her mouth to his, kissing her until their bodies stilled.

They stopped kissing and sat that way for a while, Luka still inside of her, with her head on his shoulder as he rested his hands on her hips. Finally, Luka moved them up the bed, supporting her in his arms. He separated their bodies briefly, easily lifting Ophelia off of him, and covered them with a blanket before pulling her in closer to his chest.

They stayed that way for several moments until Ophelia let out a short, nervous giggle. "Shit, my uncle and cousin definitely heard us," she said.

Luka propped himself up on an elbow, tracing her breast with his finger. "Not to worry. This place is made of old stone. Built for an age of fellowship and banquets and soldiers fucking in dark corners." He traced her nipple in lazy circles, a smirk on his lips. "And why do you think I put you here? On the opposite side of the house."

She laughed again and playfully swatted at him. "You are very naughty."

"Mmmmmm... I don't think you really mind." He lowered his face to nuzzle her neck, inhaling the scent of her body and hair.

"And how did you come to own this home?" she asked, curious about his history.

He leaned back as she draped her body around him, running her hands along his chest and over his arms.

Luka glanced around the room before answering her question. "My maker built this castle for me. Because the empusae are mostly immortal, we have learned how to harness the world's wealth. Some of us have used it for our selfish desires. And some of us, I would like to think including me, have used that wealth to make the world a better place. My maker hoped that I would fill this home with empusae loyal to her. But that never happened. Instead, I have filled it with all manner of supernaturals over the centuries, with the hope of promoting peace," he said before kissing her on the side of the lips. "But enough about my history," he said, planting kisses along her jaw before grabbing her hips and pulling her back on top of him. "I think we should make the most of our time in this bed."

Ophelia sucked in a breath, almost forgetting the question she wanted to ask. "Luka, stop. Wait."

He stopped immediately. "What's wrong? Am I hurting you?"

"It's just..." Ophelia suddenly felt shy, looking away from him. "It's just that I want you to—to taste me." She felt ridiculous asking, feeling her cheeks redden with embarrassment.

Luka understood immediately, taking her chin and gently turning her to face him. "Love, I don't think you know what you are asking. I've tried to explain, but I don't think someone raised human would understand the empusae. And what you willingly giving me blood means to our kind."

"But I need to know. Need to know if it's true. What you think you discovered about my lineage," she said. "I trust you, no matter what it means to your people."

"Are you sure?" he asked, eyes searching her face.

"I am," she said, nodding her head in agreement.

In one quick motion, he flipped her over onto her back, now on top of her with his hips flush with her. She felt him harden and spread wider for him as the tip of his cock pressed against her entrance. "This may sting at first," he said, "but then I will make it feel good."

Leaning back so she could see his face, he extended his canine teeth. Curious, she reached her hand to his mouth, touching the extended fangs. Shuddering, he bent to her, scraping his teeth down her throat to her left breast, where he allowed the fangs to brush her nipple. At the same time, he pressed ever so slowly into her, letting just the head of his cock enter her.

Moving his attention to a spot above her heart, he pricked her skin, causing her to shudder with anticipation. Ophelia gasped as he bit down at the same time he thrust into her to the hilt. The skin burned under his touch as the blood rushed to his teeth. But then the sensation became something entirely different, something pleasurable.

The combination of sensations—Luka sucking on her while fucking her—made Ophelia's entire body sing with pleasure. He pumped in and out, building another orgasm. As she held his head in place, she started to convulse under him, coming around him as he emptied himself into her again. When they were both done, Luka pulled his head back and retracted his teeth. Two fang marks were left on her chest, and he bent to flick his tongue over them, cleaning the remaining blood.

Ophelia's legs were shaking, her body spent. Luka gently lifted her to a comfortable position on the bed, her back pressed to his chest, his arms tight around her.

"Are you okay?" he asked, stroking her arm up and down.

"I didn't expect it to feel—" Ophelia didn't have the words.

"Feel what? Did it hurt?" His voice held an edge of concern.

"No. I mean, yes, at first. But it heightened the, uh, sex."

Luka chuckled before responding. "The empusae have the ability to make their prey feel no pain. Otherwise, a bite can be very painful. I wanted you to feel absolute pleasure in that moment, of course." He lazily ran one of his hands along her arm, to her hips, and back up again.

"And, what about—" Ophelia couldn't bring herself to finish the sentence, but he understood.

"You taste uniquely you. Like magic. Witch mixed with empusae. There's no doubt. I've never had blood like it in all my years."

Ophelia sighed. "That is not what I wanted to hear." But she knew he was telling the truth. "I just don't understand. Why am I not like you? Why don't I need blood to survive?" she asked, turning her body to face him.

"There is a lot we don't understand because your bloodline is rare. And we don't know anything about your paternal line.

My guess is that the witch magic is stronger and prevents you from needing blood to survive."

"I wish I knew more. Why wouldn't my mother have given me this information?"

"There are other subtle signs that you have empusae blood. I wouldn't have caught it if we hadn't spent this time together," he said.

"Like what?" Ophelia was intrigued.

"You are fast—really fast. Not as fast as an empusae, but you can run faster than any human I've ever seen. Or witch, actually. You are also strong. And you seem to heal quickly. When you were hurt in Trieste, you needed relatively little time to recover from grave wounds. Even the fang marks are almost gone."

Ophelia sighed but didn't respond. She needed answers. Wanted her mom more than ever. Not for the first time, she wanted to know the identity of her father, too. Wanted information about him—any information. But that would all have to wait for now. "Thank you," she said finally.

He was still watching her, and his eyes widened in surprise. "For what?"

"For helping me. For keeping my secret. For not telling Mo and Brisa. For giving me a chance to figure this out on my own first."

He draped his arm across her stomach, holding her tightly as he responded. "Don't you understand, Ophelia? I would do anything for you. Anything to keep you safe. No matter what happens next."

CHAPTER

EIGHTEEN

Ophelia and Luka landed in Rome the next morning, having flown on Luka's private jet. One of the perks of being an ancient, rich vampire, she assumed. For the first time in weeks, they were dressed in something other than workout clothes. The early December air was chilly, so Ophelia had opted for a form-fitting black long-sleeved sweater dress with a v-neckline. The dress hit mid-thigh, and she paired it with soft, opaque black tights and her weathered black combat boots. Luka was dressed in black slacks and an emerald-green shirt that showcased his eyes.

Marco collected them on the tarmac of a private airport terminal. When Ophelia saw him, she glared, remembering his deception with Alex.

Marco held up his hands. "I didn't touch her. I promise."

But then Ophelia was worried again. "But who is keeping Alex safe?" she asked, directing her question to Luka.

"I have a team watching her around the clock," he said.

Marco drove them directly to the old flood basin of the Tiber River, where Mo had directed them to start the search.

Ophelia had expected ancient ruins and a quiet place to roam, to allow her magic to explore. Instead, she found ancient buildings converted into modern clothing stores and souvenir shops. The streets were flooded with tourists gawking and taking selfies, heads bent over phones to post them on social media.

As the car came to a stop at a curb, Luka opened the door and stepped out, offering his hand to Ophelia. As she slid across the seat, taking his hand and stepping onto the streets of Rome, her senses were overwhelmed. After weeks spent on Luka's estate, the sounds and scents of the city washed over her. Although they were standing near ancient ruins and former temples, she heard the modern sounds of cars honking and storefront doors dinging open and closed. Her nostrils were assaulted by the smells of dust before rain, food wafting out of restaurants, and millions of people living in a small space. But being back around the sights and sounds of a city made her homesick. She missed New York. She missed her uncles. And she really missed Alex. But she had work to do now.

"We need to move quickly," Luka said to her as they walked down the narrow sidewalk, joining the throngs of bodies. His voice was low so that only she could hear as he interlaced his fingers in hers, gripping her firmly. "We don't know who is in the city. We gather information. Then we leave."

"To the Ara Pacis museum first?" Ophelia asked as they walked briskly away from the tourist attractions and toward the faint tang of river water.

Luka squeezed her hand and gazed down at her. "Yes, it's in this direction. But you've been leading from the moment we stepped out of the car. Do you feel a pull? Toward something?"

Taking a deep breath, Ophelia closed her eyes. A familiar hum coursed through her. But it wasn't fear or danger. Rather, it was her body guiding her. Urging her forward. When she opened them again, she pointed west. "What's in that direction?"

Luka's eyes followed Ophelia's hand, pursing his lips. "The Tiber. And the Ara Pacis," he said.

Without responding, Ophelia started walking briskly in that direction. Luka shadowed her, matching her pace but not interfering. When they reached the bank of the river, Ophelia paced up and down the sidewalk, feeling a magic calling to her, but too inexperienced to follow it.

In frustration, she leaned over the guardrail and stared at the Tiber. A wind stirred around her, and she pivoted to track its path north, until her eyes landed on a modern building of glass and aluminum, jarring against the backdrop of crumbling ruins.

"What's in there?" Ophelia asked, her gaze lifting to the structure as a powerful pull surged inside her. The warning vibration thrummed louder beneath her skin.

Luka's eyes flicked toward the building, then down to meet hers. "The Ara Pacis, Ophelia."

She took a step back, her heart thudding. Her attention shifted from Luka to the sleek museum ahead. Somehow, her magic had brought her straight to the altar—the very thing they had come to find. And now, she had to get inside.

They walked up the long, deep stairway to the entrance, joining the line of tourists. Luka wrapped his arm around her waist, scanning their surroundings. "Stay close," he said in her ear. "I don't like how crowded this is. Something feels off."

Ophelia shifted on her feet, barely hearing him, impatient to be at the altar. A thrumming sensation spread through her as they entered an asymmetrical lobby with subdued lighting. The walls, covered in travertine, traced the path of the Tiber River, and they wound their way through the corridor until they found the large room that housed the Ara Pacis. The altar was framed by glass windows that cascaded like curtains, lit by skylights. The December sun shone throughout the room, casting shadows that bounced on the altar.

Moving deeper into the room, Ophelia felt a pull up the stairs to the interior of the altar, where she found the statue of the child wearing the Lunula Amulet. But it was in an area that was roped off and inaccessible to visitors. She needed to be closer to touch it, to see if it revealed anything to her as Mo suspected it would.

She glanced back at Luka and spoke in a low voice. "Think you can keep the guards busy? I need a better look." Luka frowned, head tilted in disapproval, but she didn't wait for a response. He cursed as she ducked under the rope and stepped within inches of the wall, leaving him no choice but to help her.

With her hand trembling, she extended her fingertips toward the sculpture of the stone child. The moment her skin brushed the marble, visions flickered behind her eyes. She recoiled instinctively, heart pounding, scanning the altar with wide eyes. No one had noticed. Forcing herself to steady her breath, she closed her eyes and pressed her hand once more to the amulet.

The moment she made contact, images surged through her —vivid and dreamlike. A woman emerged from the haze, a witch standing in the basin of a river. Her skin was golden, kissed by the sun, and her long black hair flowed to her waist. She wore a white gown, fitted through the bodice and loose through the skirt, the fabric billowing in a wind that didn't touch the water.

Water parted around her, splashing to both sides of a river basin, forming a levee. Her dress remained dry as she walked the path she'd opened to reach the Ara Pacis when it was still buried in the Tiber River. Once the witch reached the altar, she brought fire to her fingertips and used it to carve the Lunula Amulet onto the child. After the witch was done, she climbed out of the riverbed, lifted her arms, and allowed the water to settle back over the altar, refilling the Tiber. Water poured over until it settled again, smoothing to stillness.

As she stood on the bank of the river, the witch lifted her gaze to Ophelia. Deep green eyes, speckled with yellow, pierced Ophelia's own. "Follow the fog above the disappearing lake and your questions will be answered beneath the peak."

Ophelia snatched her hand back, startled that the witch had spoken. The atmosphere inside the museum shifted, currents stirring around her in response. She inhaled deeply, forcing her magic—and her nerves—back into stillness. For a brief moment, pride flared. She'd done it. She'd controlled the surge.

But then a deeper vibration pulsed through her body, strong and insistent. A warning.

She circled the exhibit space, but Luka was nowhere in sight. The pressure in her chest intensified, thrumming like a warning bell. Something was wrong—terribly wrong. But instead of retreating, she advanced, letting instinct sharpen her focus. Her magic tugged her forward, past displays and distracted tourists, toward a staircase tucked near the back of the museum.

She hesitated at the top for only a heartbeat before descending two steps at a time. The air grew cooler, the light dimmer. As her eyes adjusted to the dark, a prickling awareness crawled up her spine. Someone was watching. From the corner, a shape stirred, detaching from the darkness with lethal grace. Not a man. A vampire. He moved with quiet menace, dark eyes fixed on her, his warm-toned skin in sharp contrast to the chill he brought with him.

"I've wanted to meet you for quite some time," he said, his voice soft and pleasantly husky. It was an unsettling mismatch for the sharp angles of his face and the predator's stillness in his posture.

"Who are you?" Ophelia asked, her fingers brushing the wall behind her as she edged back.

"Gabriel Lombardi, at your service," he replied, inclining his head with courtly precision, though his gaze never wavered from her. As he shifted, she caught sight of tattoos crawling out from beneath his collar and cuffs, curling like smoke along his hands and neck.

"What do you want?" Ophelia resisted the urge to glance back up the stairs, even as she pressed her palm against the wall behind her. Despite her blood, she couldn't outrun this vampire. She could feel it. He was ancient. And terrifyingly powerful.

"I'm afraid you aren't ready for that answer," Gabriel said, his voice low and measured as his gaze swept over her face. "But I can tell you what the Concilium wants."

Blood surged in Ophelia's ears, a high-pitched ringing rising with her dread. Something was deeply, unmistakably wrong. The vibrations in her body sharpened into alarm. "And what is that?" she asked, her voice steadying as she fought to stay calm. She needed to keep him talking, stall him— anything to buy time while she scanned for an escape. Where was Luka? And why the hell hadn't they brought weapons?

"It's a simple request. Help us find the Lunula Amulet." His voice was firm, a man accustomed to getting his way.

Inching away from him, Ophelia stepped sideways, trying to put distance between them. "I didn't hear a question, but the answer is no."

Without taking his eyes off her face, Gabriel moved toward her with preternatural speed, stopping inches in front of her and blocking her exit as she was forced back against the wall. Planting his hands on either side of her head, he caged her. This close, she could see that his hair was velvet black, almost blue.

No longer trying to hide what she was doing, Ophelia turned her face away, scanning the room for another exit. But he caught her by the chin—firm, but not rough—and angled her head back toward him. His grip was steady, and she had to tilt her neck to meet his gaze; he towered over her. Despite her efforts to stay calm, her body betrayed her, trembling with adrenaline.

"You're not what I was expecting," he said, eyes sweeping her features with unnerving curiosity. "But I wouldn't be so quick to refuse. The Concilium doesn't take kindly to defiance."

He let go of her chin, his fingers trailing down to her arm. Without waiting for permission, he half-guided, half-dragged her toward a door farther down the corridor. Just before opening it, he paused, studying her like a painting he meant to commit to memory. Then he pushed the door wide, stepping aside to reveal what lay beyond the threshold.

Two vampires were holding Luka, a small knife pressed to his heart. Droplets of blood were starting to stain his green shirt, the blade already piercing his skin, but not deep enough yet to find his heart.

At the sight of Luka being harmed, a storm started to build in Ophelia, the air around them stirring. They hadn't brought any weapons, but she didn't need one. She was a weapon herself. One Luka and Brisa had trained, and these vampires were grossly underestimating her. Gabriel still held one of her arms. Instead of pulling away from him, she stepped toward him, angling her body toward him, placing a hand on his chest. He met her eyes, and she let him see the rage that was building in her. "Let him go, Gabriel." She enunciated each word as she spoke.

Surprise flittered across his face as he flinched, glancing at the other vampires and back at Ophelia. "I can't do that." Something like regret tinged his words, replaced immediately by the cold voice that had been there earlier. "There are rules against harming you, witch, but not against harming him. You may come freely to hear the Concilium's proposal. Or not. Your choice entirely, of course." He nodded his head toward Luka, emphasizing what little choice she really had.

"Okay," she said, hoping Luka would understand. "And this is your choice, as well, Gabriel."

His eyebrows were drawn in confusion until she sent a powerful gust of air toward Luka, knocking the knife away from his heart. With a hand still on Gabriel, she stepped even closer, summoning a surge of heat that burst across his chest. At first, he refused to move, seeming to relish the burn and her nearness. But as the blaze spread, climbing her arm and radiating with furious energy, he jerked away with a growl.

"Next time, you'll think twice before you try to force me to do anything," Ophelia said. Gabriel's eyes never left hers as she stepped back and conjured a blazing ring around him. Smoke thickened in the corridor, and she manipulated the air to whip the heat toward Gabriel.

Without the threat of the knife, Luka morphed, his face shifting into a jaguar's. He mauled one of the vampires and ripped his head off in one swift movement. The other vampire lunged for Ophelia, but she drove him backward with a concentrated gust, straight into Luka's waiting grip. The vampire collapsed as Luka drove the knife into his heart. Smoke now coated the narrow space as the fire alarms screamed to life. Sprinklers burst overhead, dousing them with freezing water.

"Shit," Ophelia muttered as steam hissed off her skin. The downpour was extinguishing her magic, and Gabriel would soon be free. She'd already played her only advantage—the element of surprise—and next time, he'd be ready. "Luka!"

He was at her side instantly, his features human again. "We have to go before others come," he said, casting a final glance at Gabriel before lifting Ophelia and racing up the stairs with supernatural speed. They emerged into chaos on the main museum floor, slipping into the flood of tourists fleeing through emergency exits.

Luka led Ophelia through an emergency exit and to the street, where the sun had disappeared behind muted clouds. Marco pulled the car to the curb, and Luka ushered her inside before sliding in next to her. As they sped away from the museum, Ophelia glanced back once more. She saw Gabriel standing on the steps they'd just left. He held her eyes as he tilted his head to the side, mouthing something she could barely make out: *Next time.*

She shivered at the words and turned away just as she saw Gabriel start to laugh.

"Are you okay?" Luka asked, placing his arm around her. They were both soaking wet from the sprinklers, but her hands were still warm from the fire she'd conjured.

Ignoring his question, she shifted in the seat to face him, her knees knocking against his. Instead of answering his question, she repeated the vision and riddle, watching as his eyes narrowed while she spoke.

"What is it?" she asked.

"Mount Slivnica."

CHAPTER

NINETEEN

An hour later, Ophelia and Luka were en route to Slovenia aboard his private jet. She scanned the cabin—plush leather seats, polished woodgrain, everything quiet and absurdly expensive. Just how rich was he, exactly? Chartering two last-minute jets suggested the kind of wealth that came with centuries of life. Now didn't seem like the time to ask about his investment portfolio.

From the corner of her eye, she studied him. He hadn't spoken since takeoff, focused on an open book he clearly wasn't reading. His jaw was tight, the veins in his hands raised like cords, and he hadn't turned a page in half an hour. He was angry—furious, probably—that she'd revealed her magic to Gabriel. Not just one element, but two. And Gabriel was loyal to the Council. There'd be no hiding her power now. Which meant they'd want her more than ever.

Ophelia blew an unnecessarily loud breath out of her mouth. Squirming in her seat, she shifted her body to face him. "Luka, I know you're angry—"

"No," he said, cutting off her words, but not raising his eyes to meet hers. "I'm not angry." His grip tightened on the book.

He sure seemed angry. She sighed again, louder this time, and then smacked her lips. Her annoyance grew at this old-ass vampire behaving like a child. She finally gave up on trying to talk to him. Instead, she began reading a book Mo had given her, *Histories and Lessons of the Empusae, Laws that Bind, Vol. 10.* It was one of the many she'd now read about the world of supernaturals and vampire law. Admittedly, these were far more fascinating than the torts and contracts books she'd read in law school. But right now, she retained only a fraction of the words in front of her as she replayed the events from the Ara Pacis. Why was he so angry? What was she supposed to do? Let him die? Go with Gabriel, a man so obviously cruel and evil?

Mo collected them from a private airstrip outside Ljubljana. It didn't escape her that she was in the last place her mother had been seen alive. As she stepped off the last step of the plane, a bone-chilling burst of air slammed into her body. The late-afternoon sky smothered the day with dark clouds and wind. She hugged herself against the cold as Mo ushered her into a car—a tiny red Renault Clio. Luka slid into the back with only a nod to Mo. Ophelia withheld a snicker at how comical he appeared, his long legs and large body barely crammed in a seat meant for a child. His mouth was still fixed in a pout.

"We've got about an hour," Mo said as he buckled his seat belt. He glanced from Luka to Ophelia, eyebrows raised in silent question. She rolled her eyes and gave a small shake of her head. With a shrug, Mo started the engine and headed south, away from the city.

Soon, they were swallowed by a forest of beech trees. Snow blanketed the ground, broken only by dead leaves and the occasional stubborn brown one still clinging to the branches with the last breath of fall.

"Where exactly are we going?" Ophelia asked, watching the blurred landscape rush past her window.

Mo's gaze flicked to the rearview mirror, his brows knitting together. "Mount Slivnica. It's the ancestral home of the witches."

"And what does my vision have to do with this mountain?" Ophelia turned in her seat to face him.

"A vision from an ancestral witch is a rare gift, and this witch apparently walked the earth centuries ago if she spoke to you from a time when the Ara Pacis was still buried. She told you exactly where to go. *Follow the fog above the disappearing lake and your questions will be answered beneath the peak.*"

"So?" The word was drawn out as Ophelia's impatience grew. "What does that have to do with Slovenia?"

Mo chuckled at his niece, offering her a brief smile before refocusing on the road. "The witches' ancestral home rests above Lake Cerknica. It's a disappearing lake. When the witches gather, their collective power fills it. When they leave, the water vanishes. Beneath the peak of Mount Slivnica lies Coprniška Jama, a cave where witches have convened for millennia."

They were now passing through a small town lined with green pines and skeletal trees. Snow and ice draped the landscape in silence. "Where are we now?" she asked.

"The town of Cerknica," Mo said, answering the second question.

It was early evening now, but the small town was deserted. No one walked down the streets. Shops were closed, and there were no other cars. It was eerily quiet except for the sound of Mo's small car speeding along the snow-caked street. "Where is everyone?"

"The locals and witches have an understanding. When the lake fills, the locals know the witches are meeting. A dark cloud full of thunder and lightning spreads across the area around Mount Slivnica. The cave is difficult to find—unless you're a witch, or brought there by one—because it produces a fog that masks the entrance. All of this is magic, wards. They protect the witches when they meet," Mo said, pausing for a moment.

"Listen, Ophelia, I don't know all of your mother's reasons for keeping you from the witches. But High Priestess Sofija is angry that she wasn't told about you. And they know you've been training with Luka."

"And how would they know—?" Ophelia started to ask, then shifted her gaze to her uncle. "Oh. You had to tell her," Ophelia guessed.

Mo winced. "Brisa," he said as an explanation.

Ophelia sucked in a breath. She understood. Of course, she did. "But how is any of that my fault? I can promise you that I want to know, as well," she said.

"I know. I know," Mo said, shifting his eyes to Ophelia and reaching over to pat her hand, before looking back at the road as he slowed the car. "But you should tread lightly, especially with information about your powers. Sofija has ruled for two hundred years, and she won't like that your powers may be greater than her own. She'll view you as a threat. And she won't like that you've been, uh...fraternizing, with a vampire." Mo coughed and shifted in his seat, cutting a look at Luka in the rearview mirror.

"Witches can live that long?" Ophelia asked, brows lifting in disbelief.

Mo gave a noncommittal nod. "They can, if they are powerful enough to draw on the Earth and sustain their lives," he said, not offering more of an explanation but instead continuing his warning. "Sofija is required to allow you to enter the cave. You were summoned there by an ancestral witch. It's part of our Covenants. If Sofija ignores the call from the ancestral witch, she could be punished. Her magic could be weakened. She won't risk that. And she must allow you safe passage off the mountain. But she will force you to speak with her before entering the cave," he said.

Mo steered them off the main road and onto a gravel path, finally pulling to a stop at the base of a winding trail. Mist clung low to the ground, curling around their feet as they stepped out. Overhead, the deep gray sky dimmed toward dusk, and crushed stone crackled under Ophelia's boots as she circled to the back of the vehicle. Her phone buzzed in her pocket—Sebastian. Wincing, guilt bloomed. She hadn't called her uncles in weeks. She'd call them once she was off the mountain.

Luka leaned against the rear fender, arms crossed in brooding silence. Mo retrieved a heavy coat, scarf, and gloves from the trunk. "Your boots will do fine in the snow," he said, glancing down. "But you'll need more warmth for the climb."

Ophelia looked up at the path ahead, then higher to where the thick fog curled like smoke around the mountain peak. A shiver passed through her, an itch under her skin urging her upward. Something ancient stirred in her blood.

Mo placed a hand on her shoulder, guiding her to face him. "As a witch, your blood sings here. That's what you're feeling. But don't be alarmed. No witch can use magic on this trail. Wards neutralize it. You've grown used to wielding it, so the absence may feel...unsettling."

He shot a glance at Luka before shifting his gaze back to her. "Those same wards keep other supernaturals out. No vampire has set foot on Mount Slivnica in centuries. I'll go with you as far as I'm allowed, until Sofija draws the line." His hand dropped, and he headed to the driver's seat to lace up a pair of worn hiking boots.

Ophelia found Luka still slouched against the car, his expression locked in a sullen pout. She didn't indulge it. Closing the distance between them, she let the warmth of his body brush hers. "Will you be here when I get back?" she asked, tilting her head with a crooked grin. "And over your tantrum by then?"

His brows arched in surprise as he uncrossed his arms and grabbed her hands. "You can't get rid of me that easily." He leaned down and gave her a chaste kiss, barely brushing his lips against hers. "I'm not angry at you. I'm angry at the situation. At myself. I want to keep you safe. To protect you. And I'm not sure how to do that," he said as he zipped the winter coat she was wearing. Tugging at the ends of her scarf, he wrapped it around her, tucking it into the top of the coat. After inspecting his work, he pulled her into an embrace. "Be safe," he said in her ear, kissing her temple before he stepped back. Leaning against the car again in a false pose of nonchalance, he watched as she began her ascent up the rocky path.

As soon as Ophelia stepped into the fog, she felt as if the air had been knocked out of her. The magic thrumming through her was dimming, but it didn't completely disappear. Trying to ignore the sensation, she focused on the muffled press of their steps in the snow as they climbed. She and Mo didn't speak. They didn't know who could hear.

About an hour into the hike, a dilapidated cabin appeared at an opening on the trail. It was made of rotting interlocking wood logs, with no windows and a single plywood door at the center. Fog shrouded the cabin, touching every surface. As they approached, the force of the magic surrounding the cabin pressed into Ophelia.

"I thought magic didn't work here," she said in a hushed voice.

Mo looked at her sharply, his eyebrows drawn together. "Our elemental magic doesn't work here. But there are wards in place to protect this mountain. And some spells work in the cave." He lifted his hands in a helpless gesture. "If a witch has a special power, like Brisa's ability to read minds or my ability to know languages, those usually still work here. But that's it," he said.

The door to the cabin swung wide, banging against the logs.

"Sofija is inside," Mo said quietly. "I am being prevented from entering. You have to go alone."

Ophelia squeezed her uncle's arm and then walked forward with heavy steps. As she trudged up the steps and into the cabin, the door slammed behind her, sealing her in. The room was dark. The only light came from a plain wooden chandelier with three white candles that threw shadows on the wall. Wax dripped over the edge of the candles, somehow never touching the floor.

A short, hunched woman stood in the center of the one-room cabin. Sparse white eyebrows and deep grooves carved across Sofija's face marked every one of her years. But her piercing aqua-blue eyes remained unblinking as they fixed on Ophelia. Gesturing, the woman said, "Come in, girl. Let me get a look at you."

"Sofija, I presume?" Ophelia asked, taking cautious steps forward until only a few feet separated them. Power radiated from the old woman, thick and undeniable. Magic might have been stifled in this place—but not hers.

"That's *High Priestess*, you fool," the woman said with a toothless smirk, lips curled inward from age. Patches of her scalp were bare, with a veil of thin, silvery hair cascading to her waist. But her frailty was a lie. Power coiled beneath her skin.

"I wonder," Sofija said with mock confusion, "why do you think we are only meeting now?"

"No idea," Ophelia said, the lie hanging in the air as she scanned the room.

"You can do better than that," Sofija said, rapping her cane and striking it against the wood plank floor, the sharp sound demanding Ophelia's attention. "I see your uncle fulfilled his duty and didn't tell you about my particular power. That was smart of him. For his family."

The threat lingered, but Ophelia didn't take the bait.

Sofija stared at her for a long time. "Let's try this again. But lie to me again, and I'll know. It is a power that has come in useful over the last couple hundred years or so," she said, rapping the cane again.

Ophelia waited, shoulders tense, hands curling into fists at her side. Sofija's ability to detect a lie was news to her. It would have been helpful information to have.

"Why is this the first time we are meeting?" Sofija asked again, her voice almost a whisper, trying to coax the answer from Ophelia.

Considering her words, Ophelia waited several long moments before answering. She owed nothing to this woman. But if she had the power to sense a lie, Ophelia would at least try to make her own life easier. She shifted on her feet. "Because my mother didn't want me to be used to find the Lunula Amulet." It wasn't the entire truth, but it was a truth. She stared at Sofija, unblinking, and forced herself to breathe normally.

When Ophelia didn't offer more, Sofija changed topics suddenly. "Why are you here?"

Seeing no reason to lie, Ophelia answered truthfully. "I had a vision from a witch when I was at the Ara Pacis," she said.

Sofija's eyes widened slightly, revealing yellowed sclera around irises of endless blue. "What was this vision?" she asked, almost panting with eagerness.

Ophelia explained the vision, in full. Sofija had to let her pass. Mo had at least prepped her about that.

Sofija's mouth twisted as she took a step back. After a few moments, she collected herself. "I will allow you to pass. To answer your vision in Coprniška Jama. But, as High Priestess, I command you to help your fellow witches find the Lunula Amulet. For the good of our people."

Ophelia snorted as she widened her stance and crossed her arms across her chest. "And if I don't? You are not *my* High Priestess." She would not allow herself to be used by this woman, the very thing her mother had tried to prevent. She inhaled deeply, nostrils flaring.

Sofija shifted, her brittle frame creaking like old wood. "You will be placing your newfound family in a precarious situation. The choice is yours."

Anger sliced through Ophelia as she felt her face flush, heat rising up her neck as it turned molten red. There was that threat again. Everyone kept telling her the choice was hers, but it never was. She uncrossed her arms and clenched her hands into fists at her side. "I know you are required to allow me to pass and what you are required to do under the Covenants," she said, her voice a whispered rage. Without waiting for a response, Ophelia walked around the High Priestess, toward the back door of the cabin.

Sofija made no move to stop her, but she finally spoke as Ophelia twisted the handle and wrenched the door open. "You will yield to me. One way or the other."

Ophelia didn't answer as the door slammed behind her.

CHAPTER

TWENTY

The climb was arduous. The trail was cloaked in deep night, lit only by a smattering of muted stars and the pale arc of a waxing moon. Ophelia reached out to steady herself as she stumbled over the rocky, ice-slick path. The air thinned with each step higher, and the cold fog sank into her lungs. Her breath came in visible bursts, quickened by anticipation and effort. Still, the cave beckoned. Its pull threaded through her veins, the hum in her blood growing stronger with each step. The night remained quiet, disturbed only by the crunch of her boots on stone.

As that familiar vibration settled into her bones like an old friend, she knew she was close. Was it danger? The mountain's magic? It was hard to tell. Her magic had changed—evolved. It no longer warned her only of threats. Now it stirred when she needed to be alert, when focus was vital.

She hugged the side of the mountain at a narrow bend in the trail, one hand braced against the rock as she peeked over the edge, only to find a void of bottomless black. Carefully, she stepped onto a wider stretch, squeezing through a copse of beech and pine. Suddenly, she stopped short, shivering and nearly slipping on the ice beneath her boots. Here, the stars and moon seemed brighter, casting silver light over a glacier-carved field of lush green grass dotted with wildflowers in shades of yellow, purple, and red. Magic. Only magic could allow a meadow like this to bloom in an alpine tundra.

Her body moved on instinct, carrying her across the field until she stood at the mouth of the cave. She barely remembered the crossing. The entrance, carved directly into the mountainside, was limestone and framed in ivy that cascaded like a curtain. It rose just an inch above her head and was so narrow that only one person at a time could slip through.

Stepping back, Ophelia looked up toward the peak still rising another half mile above. It loomed sharp and proud, all jagged ridges slicing into the sky. Extending a trembling hand, she parted the ivy and ducked beneath the low entrance. The tunnel was narrow enough to brush both shoulders as she passed through. After shimmying sideways into a tighter gap, she stumbled to a halt.

A vast chamber opened before her, all soaring ceilings and sloping floors. Stalactites dripped from above while stalagmites rose to meet them, casting a soft glow as if lit from within. The air, though damp, smelled clean—crisp, untouched. No dust clung to the walls, only polished veins of limestone gleaming in the quiet.

Wide-eyed, Ophelia moved in slow circles, carefully stepping over fragile rock formations. The sound of trickling water drew her toward a spring bubbling from the base of a limestone wall, pooling into a basin of startling clarity. With a weary sigh, she sank to the ground. When her fingers brushed the water, she jerked them back in surprise. It was warm, in stark contrast to the chilled air around her. Crossing her legs, she leaned her elbow on one knee, chin in hand, gaze fixed on the surface.

Her breath deepened. Her pulse slowed. Her eyelids began to droop as a heavy stillness pressed down on her, until a sudden vibration jolted through her, crackling through her bones like a struck chord. She wasn't alone.

Scrambling to her feet, Ophelia turned—and froze. A witch stood just a few feet away, her yellow-green speckled eyes unmistakable. She wore the same flowing white dress from the vision. This was the one who had summoned her.

Ophelia instinctively stepped back, breath catching in her throat. "Who are you?"

The witch's mouth curved at one corner. "Galla Placidia," she said, her voice laced with a heavy accent. "But is that really what you want to know?"

Ophelia hesitated. "Did you—was it you who called me here?" Her voice wavered, the question clumsy in her mouth. She still didn't know the right language for this world.

Galla ignored the question. "What is most important to you in life, Ophelia?"

She didn't hesitate. "To find my mother. Or to learn what really happened to her."

"Really?" Galla's head tilted, eyes narrowing with disbelief. "After everything you've uncovered? That is still the most important thing? The one desire that eclipses all others?"

Ophelia held her gaze, spine straight, jaw clenched. "It is," she said, her tone flat.

Galla gave a slow shake of her head, one brow arching as she leaned in. "I must have misheard you. You've learned so much about who you are. About your gifts. Your power. You've met your twin flame. You could change the fate of the world. And yet, your heart still clings to a mother who vanished when you were a child?" She drifted closer, gliding across the cave floor as if untouched by gravity.

Heat surged in Ophelia's throat, and a fine sheen of sweat formed at the base of her neck. Her arms folded across her chest like armor. "She didn't leave—" The words caught. Her jaw locked tight as her eyes slammed shut. When she opened them again, they burned. "Wait. What? Twin flame? And how do you know all this? About me? My family? My name?" Her questions flew out in a rush as she took a half-step back, only to find the spring lapping dangerously at her heels.

"How does one know anything?" Galla asked.

Ophelia huffed, feeling herself grow annoyed. "Why can't you just say what you mean?"

"Because you must earn your knowledge," Galla said, ignoring Ophelia's other questions. "You have great power. You stand between two worlds, and you will have the ability to bring peace. But you will be tested in ways you can't even fathom. Your mother was wrong to keep this from you. She thought she was protecting you, but even she couldn't keep you from this destiny. Are you ready?"

"Ready for what? What do you want from me, other than to annoy me with your riddles and questions?" Ophelia crossed her arms over her chest.

"You know who I am, *nipotina*. The story is in your blood if you would only listen," Galla said. Her eyes softened as she tilted her head to the side again. She stretched forward to graze Ophelia's skin, and at the faint contact, something ancient surged into her: images, emotions, and a flood of knowledge not her own. Visions flashed too quickly for her to grasp them all. She tried to hold on, to make sense of them, but the torrent overwhelmed her.

"Wait. Wait. You were—you were with Alaric. He took you from Rome?" Ophelia asked, trying to piece it together.

"Good, good," Galla said, the corners of her mouth turning up again as she gripped Ophelia's wrist. "What else?"

"You—you know about the treasure." Ophelia's brows furrowed in concentration as she stared ahead, no longer seeing the cave around them. "And you buried Alaric with it. And the Lunula Amulet."

"And?" Galla's eyes sharpened as her grip tightened, fingers digging into Ophelia's skin.

"And you burned everyone around you," Ophelia said, gasping as her eyes flew wide. Galla's memories raged through her. She staggered under their weight. "To keep others from discovering the amulet, you destroyed them all. But you were in love." She tried to wrench her arm away, desperate to shut out the rush of sensation and truth. But Galla's grip held fast, unyielding.

Galla's lips curled into a full smile, though her unfocused gaze drifted in Ophelia's direction without truly landing on her. "It's true. Everyone thinks he kidnapped me from my father when he conquered Rome. At that time, supernaturals lived in harmony, and my family was one of the few witch families in the city." Her voice rose into a loud whisper, nearly a shout. "But he didn't steal me. He loved me. I wanted to go with him. He wasn't after gold or gems or coins or any treasure. He was searching for me. And I was happy to be found. I wanted a life with him. To be with him forever. He was my twin flame. I would have done anything for him...almost anything."

Galla's voice softened as she finally dropped Ophelia's wrist. "But then I realized he had the amulet. He became obsessed with it. Obsessed with what he could do with it. With control over the world. And other supernaturals were after the amulet—and us. And...and I knew what I had to do. I had to protect everyone. Even if it cost me," she said. Galla's voice was strained with memories, a soft whisper now. "I killed everyone. Even him. To hide the amulet. To keep it safe. To keep the world safe. It was my duty."

Ophelia brought her hand to her mouth, Galla's raw emotions touching her core, burning her senses. "I'm so sorry. That must have been an impossible decision."

Galla finally focused on Ophelia, taking several long moments before speaking as she searched Ophelia's face. "Not hard enough, I'm afraid. I was weak. So weak." Galla closed her eyes and then reopened them, her gaze clearer now. "I couldn't allow myself to die. I should have. I was the only one left who knew where to find the amulet. But you see, if I killed myself to protect the world, I would kill our child. And that, that I would not do. Could not do. So, I retreated. I hid. I delivered that babe with my own hands. And then I sent her away. To live in hiding."

A growing unease settled into Ophelia's bones. She moved a foot, trying to step back, as she kicked a loose rock into the water.

"And that, *nipotina*, is how you are here. I allowed the fire witch line to continue. Even though I should not have." Galla sighed deeply before speaking again. "It was the one thing I could not do. My daughter was a piece of him, and she was my blood. And so, the answers have continued on in my blood through generations. Through your mother. And you," she said, gesturing to Ophelia.

A roar built in Ophelia's ears, a pressure mounting beneath her skull. She rubbed the base of her neck, fingers digging into tense muscle. "I don't understand any of this," she said, her voice low, ragged with disbelief. "A few months ago, I was just someone searching for her mother. And now I'm supposed to navigate vampires? Witches? Fae?" Her words came faster, each one sharper than the last. "What do they all want from me? Why now? Why you?"

She shut her eyes for a moment, pressing her fingertips to her temples as if she could hold her mind together through sheer force.

Galla glanced toward the entrance of the cave and then back at Ophelia. "We don't have much time. I wish I could help you understand everything. But you must go soon. So I will simply say that my role in hiding the amulet has evaded discovery for centuries. But your blood tells the story of what happened. And somehow, the supernaturals know they can use you. I need you to do what I could not."

"But why me?" Ophelia shrugged her shoulders, releasing them with a heavy sigh. "How can I help?"

"I have been waiting for you. Someone like you. To destroy the amulet."

"We're back to riddles," Ophelia said, a stiffness forming in her neck as a headache started to form.

"You know what must be done."

"I don't," Ophelia said, shaking her head.

"You have to make the choice to destroy the amulet. To protect the balance of life. At all costs. No matter what. Or the world will be in danger of changing forever. No one group of people should have the kind of control the amulet affords. You are the first who can destroy the amulet. And you must follow your destiny."

"I don't know how," Ophelia gritted out, her words drawn out sharply, eyes narrowed at Galla. She did not have time for the riddles. She needed answers. And fast.

But Galla gave her a smile that didn't reach her eyes before she said, "Consider this riddle:

The power of three created thee,

So too shall three destroy.
In the depths below you shall summon thee,
But one of three will cease and be no more.

And then she disappeared, just as suddenly as she had appeared. Startled, Ophelia leaned forward, reaching out her hands to feel the air in front of her. Her skin prickled, and she shuddered. Galla was gone.

With a loud huff, Ophelia plopped back down on the floor, allowing Galla's words to slosh around in her mind over and over. Her muscles stiff from disuse, Ophelia finally stretched upwards, lifting her body from the earth. Making her way out of the cave, she stumbled into the meadow, which was now highlighted by a pre-dawn light. Dew formed a mist over the flowers and grass. She shivered at the unnatural beauty, not lingering as she rushed through the field and back through the thicket of trees.

Looking back, she saw the early morning light creeping to a slow rise above the peak of the mountain. The sun hit her face and began warming her as she walked, sure-footed, down the mountain. She shuddered when she saw how close she'd been to the edge the night before, unsure how she'd managed not to fall.

As she passed the dilapidated cabin, it appeared newer in the light of day. Perhaps her mind had deceived her the night before. She instinctively knew that Sofija was gone, as Mo had promised. Ophelia would escape the witch's wrath. For now.

As she emerged from the woods, she found Luka still leaning against the car. Although he had an air of nonchalance about him, she knew he was alert. Mo was sleeping in the car, the seat laid back.

When she stepped on some leaves, Luka turned to her and then moved swiftly to the edge of the wards. As she left the forest, the rest of her magic flooded back to her. Bending at the waist, her stomach emptied itself as she retched what little food she had inside her.

Luka wrapped one hand around her waist as he used the other hand to pull her hair back from her face. "Are you okay?"

Mo yawned from the car. "It's normal the first time you come off the mountain. The returning magic floods your system and causes nausea. It should pass," he said.

When she was finally done, she wiped her mouth with the back of her hand, her tongue coated with grit and bile. She felt filthy; her skin was clammy, her body heavy with sweat and magic. All she wanted was to get far away from this place.

Luka kept his arm around her as he stroked her hair. But her power surged suddenly, warning her that something was very, very wrong. "What is it?" she asked.

"Alex and Sebastian. The Council took them."

CHAPTER

TWENTY-ONE

"We can't just barge in. We need a plan," Luka said, standing in his bedroom, wearing a pair of sweatpants that hung low on his hips. And nothing else. They'd immediately made the thirty-minute flight back to Trieste, arguing the entire time about what to do next. Ophelia paced back and forth in front of him, wringing her hands. "And you need to rest," he said.

She stopped, turning to him with her hands on her own hips now. The sudden movement caused her hair to slide over her shoulders, down her chest. She wore a T-shirt and a pair of his shorts. "I don't need rest," she said, her voice edged with ice, tired of the argument. "I need to get my uncle and my best friend away from those monsters. Once I show up, the Council will let them go."

"That's not how it will work, Ophelia," Luka said, stepping closer to her and placing his hands on her shoulders, his voice soft. "And even if it did, then what? They want to use you to get to the amulet. To get what they want, they will use those you love. There's no middle ground here. We have to be smart about this."

"That's why I want to go alone," she said.

"Absolutely not," he said, squeezing her shoulders. "I agree that Brisa and Mo shouldn't go. They would be violating the Alliance by entering San Marino without an invitation. But I'm not letting you walk in there alone. You may never come back to me."

Ophelia brought her hands up to cover his. "Please. I can't," she said, her voice breaking. "I can't allow someone to be hurt because of me. What if that's what happened to my mom?" She lowered her eyes, not letting the tears spill over.

Luka pulled her in close, their bodies touching as she rested her head on his chest. "I won't let you face this alone," he said.

She took several deep breaths, cleansing the ache in her chest. "And if you go? They'll know there is something between us and will try to use you against me, as well. I can't lose all three of you. I can't," she said, her voice cracking again. "I've— I've already lost my mother. And I'm just starting to find my way and learn what has been missing my entire life," she said.

He held her tighter. "We face this together," he said more firmly this time.

Ophelia lifted her head and leaned back to look at him. "Fine," she said. "We'll go together. Tomorrow." She lowered her head back to his chest. "And you're right. I've been up for twenty-four hours. I'll feel calmer, ready to face all of this, after I get some sleep."

She felt him tense in surprise and then relax beneath her. "Good." He kissed her forehead. "Good," he said again before chuckling. "I never thought I'd see the day when Ophelia Wildes agreed with me."

Ophelia's laugh echoed his, but it rang false. It was too high and brittle. Before Luka could question it, she changed the subject. "Do you know what a twin flame is?" She'd told him what Galla had said, but they hadn't discussed the meaning.

Luka released her, rubbing his jaw with both hands and avoiding her gaze. "For supernaturals, it's the rarest kind of love. Different lineages call it different things—life mates, soul mirrors, divine counterparts. Witches call it the twin flame." He began pacing in a slow circle, hands braced on his hips as he stared at the floor. "It's when two souls reflect each other. A bond so intense, it rewrites your path. They say meeting your match transforms everything because you're constantly being pushed to grow. It's powerful...and incredibly hard to hold."

Ophelia shifted from one foot to the other, unsettled by his discomfort. "Galla said I've already found my twin flame."

"Is that so?" Luka asked, still not meeting her eyes as he stepped closer to her, bringing their bodies to touch. He lifted her chin and kissed her mouth, tracing his hands down her arms. Wrapping his hands around her waist, he lifted her and tossed her onto the bed.

She gasped and grabbed Luka by his pants, pulling him over her as he smothered her body with his warmth. Their kiss was hard, all tongues and lips as they tasted each other. Her moan undid him, snapping whatever restraint he had left. There was nothing slow about what came next as they sought release from one another, frenzied and needy. When Ophelia slipped his pants down, the hard length of him sprang free. Luka ripped Ophelia's shorts down the middle, causing a giggle to escape her. The giggle dissolved into a moan as he dipped his fingers to her center, pressing on the bundle of nerves.

"Fuck, you're already ready for me." He flipped her over onto her stomach and lifted her hips so that she was on her knees, her chest lowered so that the T-shirt bunched around her breasts. Plunging into her, he stretched her until their bodies were flush. Over and over, in and out, he pumped with long, hard strokes. The sound of his thighs hitting her ass built into a crescendo.

"Luka," Ophelia gasped, moaning and then screaming as she came around him. He hilted deep inside her, shouting his own release.

He leaned over her, staying that way as they took deep, long breaths to recover. Finally, he eased out of her. She rolled to her side as he moved up the bed behind her, their bodies intertwined.

After several long moments, Luka broke the silence as he stroked her arm, running his fingers from her shoulder to her wrist and back again. "Ophelia, I know you are just learning this world. But I want you to know how sorry I am. About everything. About following you. Lying to you."

Ophelia stilled under him as he spoke.

Luka paused, swallowing hard. "I know the supernatural world has already taken so much from you. And I want you to have a life of joy. Of adventure. Of love. And with the time we have together—however long that may be—I want you to know how loved you are. Because I do—I do love you. With my whole being. You don't need to say anything, but I need you to know how I feel about you," he said.

Ophelia bit her lip, glad Luka couldn't see her face. The tears threatened to fall again as she felt her face flush. So she didn't speak, afraid of what she would say or what her voice would convey. Instead, she squeezed the arm he wrapped around her, his body cocooning hers.

As Luka's breathing slowed and deepened, his chest rising and falling in the soothing rhythm of sleep, Ophelia slipped out of the bed. Quickly and quietly, she put on dark jeans, a dark T-shirt, and her black leather jacket. She donned her trusty leather boots and slipped a knife down the ankle of each boot.

Looking back just once, she whispered, "I love you, too, Luka."

As she strolled out of the flat, closing the door softly, her steps were light and stealthy like Luka had taught her. Allowing one tear to slip down her cheek, she wound her way through the cobblestone streets. At the edge of the Old City, the vibrations in her blood stirred. She was close.

Ophelia spotted those dark eyes—molten brown, brimming with chaos and danger. He leaned against a sleek black sedan, dressed in charcoal slacks and a fitted black sweater, arms crossed in practiced indifference. The moment his gaze locked onto hers, her chest seized. For a second, she nearly turned to run. But no, she wouldn't leave. Not without Sebastian and Alex.

As she neared him, footsteps scraping against the street, he pushed off the car and reached for her.

"Don't you fucking touch me." She snapped back, glare sharp as glass.

He sighed, loud and theatrical, before his lips curled. "That beautiful mouth of yours has quite the tongue."

Ophelia lifted her chin, nostrils flaring. "I came here willingly. That doesn't mean you get to lay a hand on me."

Gabriel clicked his tongue. "It would be my pleasure, Ophelia." Her name slid from his lips like a caress, sending a shiver up her spine. "But I'll only touch you when you beg me to."

He paused, winked, then sobered. "For now, I need to search you for weapons. Unless you'd prefer one of them to do it," he said, gesturing behind her.

Spinning, Ophelia's breath hitched as she caught sight of three large men—vampires—closing in. Shit. She should've sensed them. She'd let herself get distracted. But she didn't need weapons to defend herself. Not anymore. Still, delay wasn't an option. Luka could wake up at any moment, and if he found her gone, he'd do something reckless.

She stepped backward instinctively and slammed into Gabriel's chest.

His hands caught her arms, firm but not aggressive. "Well," he murmured, clearing his throat, "we don't need to be this close for the search."

He guided her forward a few inches, then lifted her arms into a T. With an exaggerated sigh, Ophelia left them there. His hands swept from her wrists to her shoulders, then traced the sides of her body, pausing at the small of her back. Despite herself, she shivered. He lowered her arms and appeared before her in a blink, crouching to one knee, both hands curling around her ankles. Tilting his head, he raised a brow. "Really?" he drawled.

Suppressing a grin, Ophelia rolled her eyes and gave a one-shoulder shrug. "I had to try," she said.

He lifted the hem of her jeans, retrieved the knives from her boots, and tossed them down the alley. Then he smoothed the fabric with surprising care before letting his hands travel up her thighs, giving them a squeeze. She sucked in a sharp breath, staring ahead, refusing to meet his gaze. His palms skimmed around her hips, up her torso, stopping just below her breasts. The heat of his touch left a blazing trail on her skin, like he'd burned a map into her nerves.

He rose to stand a breath away. For a long moment, he said

nothing and just waited until she finally looked at him. When she did, he inhaled deeply and leaned in, his voice low and close enough to stir the hair at her ear.

"I'm sorry for what comes next."

"What do you—?"

Darkness swallowed her before she could finish.

CHAPTER

TWENTY-TWO

Ophelia jolted awake, sprawled on cold stone, panic crashing into her like a wave. Disoriented, she winced as a dull pulse throbbed in her head.

"She's awake," said a man with a deep, gravelly voice. "Bring her here."

She scrambled to a sitting position, shaking as she scanned her surroundings. Her body was screaming at her that this place was dangerous. Very dangerous. She was in a large, ornate chamber, surrounded by gray stone walls and floors. Stained-glass windows in shades of red and yellow allowed some evening light to seep through, casting the room in shadows. Black sconces with lit candles were spread around the walls.

Three chairs—more like thrones—crafted from interwoven gold vines, thorns, and roses stood at the front of the room, evenly spaced and occupied by three men. Vampires. A semicircle of others surrounded her, their faces blurring in her vision.

Gabriel grasped her by both elbows, hauling her upright

until she stood face-to-face with him. She tried to pull away. "I can stand on my own," she snapped, low and furious. "Let me go." Each word landed sharp, bitten off with rage.

He stared at her, as if trying to convey something unspoken. Then he let go abruptly. She stumbled back, nearly falling into the crowd before instinctively moving closer to him, choosing the devil she knew over the ones watching. Still glaring, she reached up and touched the side of her head.

The vampire seated in the center motioned for them to approach, his long, slender fingers curling in command. Jet-black pupils fixed on her, unblinking, as shoulder-length dark hair slipped forward, framing his face. Though he sat hunched like a withered elder, his face was smooth, untouched by time.

Gabriel gripped her arm, sending a jolt through her as he began to drag her toward the thrones. When his fingers brushed along the inside of her arm, she yanked herself free with a snarl. "I can walk, as well," she said, feeling the urge to punch him as hard as she could.

Straightening her shirt and smoothing her hands along the sides of her jeans, she walked slowly toward the three imposing figures. With the fogginess finally clearing, it dawned on her that they were in one of the towers of San Marino, and these three were the leaders of the Council. She'd read about them in one of the books Luka had given her, and she racked her brain to remember the laws of the empusae, seeking some kind of edge. Luka had been right. She should have had a plan.

"You can stop right there," said the vampire seated on the far-right throne. His salt-and-pepper hair and the deep creases at the corners of his face marked an older turning. She wondered when he'd been changed—it was clearly late in life.

Ophelia halted as instructed, watching and waiting.

"What an enigma you are, Ms. Wildes," said the one in the

center—Leander. She recognized the name. The oldest known vampire. "Your mother hid you all these years. Why do you think that is?" he asked, deliberate, as if each word was chosen with care.

She ignored the question. "I know you have Sebastian and Alex. Let them go, and I'll cooperate."

"So impatient," the man on the right said. "Your thoughts are darting everywhere." Zeon. She remembered now. He was one of the rare vampires who could read memories without drinking blood.

Ophelia centered herself, forcing calm. She'd taught herself how to shield her thoughts, poring over ancient texts while Luka and Mo searched for the amulet.

Zeon gave a low chuckle, the corners of his mouth curling. "I see you've been studying our ways." His fangs slid into view, sharp and eager. "Perhaps we'll just have to uncover your secrets the old-fashioned way."

As her temper flared, Ophelia forced herself to take a deep breath. "You know they're the only reason I'm here. Let them go, and I will help you," she said.

"Why don't we bring them out so that you can decide for yourself whether you really came for them," said the final member of the Council, Durante. He was a cruel abomination who had been turned as a teenager and still appeared child-like, his cherubic face masking his brutal and violent nature. Waving his hand in a dramatic fashion, his face contorted in a smile as two separate wooden doors on either side of the Council were opened.

Sebastian was dragged through the left door, his sneakers skidding across the stone floor as two vampires hauled him forward. His hands were bound behind him, dried blood streaked his running shirt and shorts, and a raw wound pulsed above his brow.

The moment he saw Ophelia, he stopped struggling. His shoulders sagged, and defeat washed over him. Tears blurred her vision as their eyes met. "Are you okay?" she mouthed. He held her gaze for a beat, sorrow etched deep in his features, then gave a small nod and lowered his head.

Before she could process his reaction, a soft whimper from the right snapped her attention around. Alex stood there, trembling, eyes wide and brimming with tears. When she spotted Ophelia, a guttural sob broke from her throat.

Ophelia surged forward instinctively, but Gabriel caught her. His arms wrapped around her waist, lifting her slightly, her spine flush against his chest.

"No," he said, low against her ear.

"Let them go," she demanded. The air stirred, and the candles lining the chamber flickered in warning.

Leander regarded her, fingers steepled in front of his face, his forest-green gaze unreadable. "I believe the rumors may be true," he said slowly.

Ophelia tamped the magic down, though it burned in her blood, screaming to be unleashed.

"We did promise we would let them go," Leander continued, "if you came to us willingly."

"But," said Durante, practically giddy, "you should have all the pertinent information first. Especially about your dear uncle Sebastian. The man who magically came into your life when you were—what was it—eleven?" Durante stood abruptly, walking to Sebastian as he glanced between Ophelia and the man who had raised her. Durante's expression was smug.

Ophelia went still, the ache in her body intensifying as magic thrummed beneath her skin. Gabriel had set her back on her feet, but his arm remained tight around her. She didn't resist as she stared at Durante, every nerve pulled taut.

Zeon shifted to regard Sebastian. "Your mind is wide open, Sebastian. With all your deception, did you not learn to guard your thoughts?"

Ophelia felt a flush creep over her body. "What are you talking about?"

"Ophelia, listen—" Sebastian began to speak, but Durante put a warning finger over Sebastian's mouth.

"No, no, no," Durante said, "no more lies to your beloved niece. Tell her who you are. Isn't your relationship built on trust?" His voice was gleeful, reveling in every second of it.

"Ophelia, I love you. You are my daugh—" Sebastian tried to speak again, but Durante lost patience and slapped Sebastian across the face, once on each cheek. A red line appeared where Durante's nails had gouged a deep groove in his face. Durante leaned over and licked the droplets of blood that formed. As Ophelia shuddered in disgust, Gabriel tightened his hold on her.

"Sebastian doesn't want you to know the truth," Durante said, turning back to Ophelia with a faux frown on his lips.

Closing her eyes, Ophelia tried to force her magic down, trying to tame it before she lost control of a situation she had badly underestimated. "I don't know or care what you are talking about. Let my family go. That was our deal."

"Haven't you learned that hiding from who you are—who others are—is never a good idea? Don't you want to know who Sebastian really is?" Durante asked.

"No," she said in a whisper. Of course she did, but she didn't want to hear it from this lunatic.

"You forget, girl, that I can read your mind," Zeon said, his words a slow drawl.

Shit. She had left her mind open, forgetting to shield herself as her emotions spiraled.

"So you do want to know," Durante said, that revolting grin

twisting his lips. He paused, savoring the moment. "Your dear, sweet Sebastian has been lying to you since the day he joined your household. A low-level witch. A plant. Sent to watch you." He clapped his hands in delight, practically euphoric.

"No, that's not true. That's absurd," Ophelia snapped, her brows knitting as she turned to Sebastian, silently begging for his denial.

But he said nothing. His gaze stayed fixed on the floor, shoulders slumped in shame.

"That's not possible," she whispered, the conviction draining from her.

"You know it's true, Ophelia," Leander said, his tone devoid of emotion. She wondered if anything could move a creature like him.

"Tell them, Uncle Sebastian," she pleaded, her words cracking. "Tell them it's not true."

Tears welled as Sebastian finally looked up, straightening his posture. He met her eyes. "You and Elijah mean everything to me," he said, voice hoarse. "Everything." His expression shattered her. "But yes," he continued, "I was sent to monitor you. That's how it started. I was placed at your school to observe. But that's not why I stayed. I fell in love—with Elijah, with you, with our family. I wanted to tell you a thousand times." Silent tears tracked down his cheeks, mingling with the blood from the wound on his forehead as he dropped his head again.

"Who sent you?" she asked, barely breathing. The world tilted sideways. Nothing in her life was what it seemed. She'd spent holidays, birthdays—Father's Days—with this man. He'd helped her survive the worst moments. Had been her uncle's best friend, then husband. He'd been family. A guide. A light.

Sebastian raised his eyes to hers once more. "It's complicated," he said, and offered nothing else. Ophelia grew slack, and she would have fallen if Gabriel had not been holding her. Although her heart was shattered and physically ached, she refused to allow tears to fall.

"Now, what to do with this interloper?" Durante asked, one of his long fingernails digging into Sebastian's arm, bringing a drop of crimson to the surface. Durante scooped the blood with his finger and then flicked it onto his tongue.

Ophelia suppressed a gag as she said, "You promised." She looked at all three members of the Council. She was angry at Sebastian and beyond hurt, but she still would not allow him to be harmed. She had so many questions. "You will let them go. This is the only reason I came here voluntarily," Ophelia said. As much as she ached from Sebastian's betrayal, he was still a father to her.

"My child, there is so much you do not understand. Your mother deprived you of a proper supernatural upbringing," Leander said, lips pursed in disapproval. "The empusae have no quarrel with Sebastian. But he broke witch law by spying on you for years without reporting your existence to the High Priestess. He must be handed over to her. She will decide his punishment," he added, flat and disinterested.

Ophelia felt stuck, anesthetized, unable to move or do anything to help her family. "You will let Alex go. Immediately. There is no reason for you to hold her." Her friend stood in the corner of the room, transfixed, no longer crying as she watched the scene in front of her.

"Of course," Zeon said in a slow drawl, dragging out his words. "As promised. But only after we have the Lunula Amulet. We need to ensure that you uphold your end of the bargain. We can't let the amulet fall into the wrong hands."

"That wasn't the deal," Ophelia said, heat prickling under

her skin. She clenched her fists, forcing the flames to stay buried.

"We agreed to release Alex and Sebastian in exchange for your help finding the Lunula Amulet," Zeon said. "Sebastian will be handed over to the High Priestess. Alex will be released once we locate the amulet, after we've used it to wipe her memory, of course. We can't allow a human to retain that kind of knowledge."

Ophelia opened her mouth to protest, heat flaring in her fingertips. But a sudden commotion behind them cut her off. A loud bang echoed through the chamber, followed by frantic shouting.

Gabriel's hands slid from her waist to her hands, pressing down to smother the fire as sparks bloomed in her palms. Smoke curled between their fingers, but he didn't let go.

"What are you doing?" she hissed, trying to wrench her hands free. She needed her magic. She needed to get her family out of this nightmare.

But Gabriel held tight, even as the flames seared his skin.

"Let me go," she begged, twisting to face him.

He bent low, lips brushing her ear, breath uneven with pain. "I'm trying to help you, you stubborn witch. Stop letting the magic rise. I can smell it on you."

The commotion around them swelled, voices dissolving into a blur of sound. Gabriel finally let her go, and her heart dropped as she turned, meeting Luka's green gaze across the chamber. Several vampires held him back, struggling to restrain him as he fought to reach her.

Gabriel exhaled sharply and muttered, "Showoff."

Ophelia glanced down and flinched. His palms were scorched, seared red and blistered.

"Enough. Bring him forward," Leander ordered, his words slicing cleanly through the din.

Luka shrugged off the guards and strode to the front of the chamber. His posture was proud, chin lifted, though he offered the Council a curt bow as he reached her. "Leander. Durante. Zeon," he said, each name edged with tension. Then he faced her. Fury still simmered in his eyes, but he took her hand and brushed a kiss across her knuckles before bowing low, offering her more deference than anyone in the room had dared.

He straightened and drew her close, sliding an arm around her waist and pulling her away from Gabriel. His gaze met Gabriel's, steady and deliberate. "Thank you for keeping *mea promissa* safe," he said.

Ophelia didn't understand the phrase—but the expression on Gabriel's face said everything. She was missing something important.

Finally, Luka turned back to the Council, ignoring her except for the hand wrapped around her, his jaw set and his lips pressed to a thin line. His breathing was labored, heavier than usual, and she wondered whether he had transformed to get here so quickly.

"You would dare show more respect to a witch than your own Council?" Zeon asked.

"She is more than a witch to me," Luka said, not bothering to offer an explanation.

"Right, she's also a whore you are sleeping with. I can smell you on her from here," Durante said, a smirk on his face.

"You will not speak of her that way," Luka said. His voice was calm and quiet, but lethality laced his words. Durante glared at him in challenge.

"It is good that you are here," Leander said. "You must answer for your crimes against the empusae in Trieste."

Ophelia stilled and narrowed her eyes at Leander. "That man tried to kill me. On neutral territory. Luka was defending me," she said.

"That may be. You are a witch, though, and Luka had no right to kill one of his own kind to save you. He could have delivered the vampire to the Council for punishment," Leander said. "Isn't that right, *Gatto Nero*?"

Ophelia glanced at Luka, then back at the Council. She had to save him. But how could she save all three of them?

"Luka's talents are also unique," Leander said to the other Council members as they deliberated. "We can't punish him with true death. But his skills may serve us in the future. What say you?" he asked Zeon and Durante.

Durante furrowed his brow and tilted his head toward the ceiling, feigning contemplation. Then he clapped his hands together and turned toward Ophelia and Luka, that infuriating smirk curling across his face.

"In exchange for the life he took, he should be kept in the dungeons of San Marino for fifty years."

Luka stiffened next to her, but he didn't speak.

"Zeon? What do you propose?" Leander asked.

Zeon was silent. Ophelia knew he was probing their minds for an answer, so she kept her thoughts blank. "Perhaps there is more to the story that we should know," he said after several painfully long moments.

"Luka, what do you say for yourself?" Leander asked.

"She is my promised under the law of the empusae. She willingly gave her blood to me. Another vampire tasted her and tried to rape her. Surely, you would not deny me that right to protect her."

Ophelia whipped her head to gaze at Luka. *Promised?* What did that mean, and when did that happen? She tried not to let Zeon detect her confusion.

"A witch cannot be promised to you! Your claim is punishable by death," Durante said, his face contorted in anger.

"Luka, even you cannot escape punishment for claiming a supernatural not of your kind," Zeon said. "Explain yourself."

Durante stalked toward Luka and Ophelia, unsheathing a long sword hanging at his side. "Do I have the Council's agreement that Loukas Angelos should be punished with the true death?" Durante directed his question to Leander and Zeon.

Ophelia brought her hand to Luka's arm wrapped around her waist, squeezing it, as Leander and Zeon hesitated.

"What is your explanation, Luka?" Leander asked.

He met Ophelia's eyes, regret etched across his face. In that moment, she knew. He was about to reveal her bloodline. And he wasn't asking permission. But she wouldn't let the truth come from him.

"I am more than a witch," she said quickly, cutting him off.

"What game are you playing?" Zeon asked, tilting his head as if trying to puzzle her out.

"It means I'm not just a witch," she repeated, louder now. "I have vampire blood in my veins, too."

Gasps rippled through the chamber, the air crackling with the buzz of stunned vampires.

"Silence!" Leander said.

"An abomination!" Durante followed.

Luka ignored them. "I discovered that Ophelia was part empusae when she was attacked. The empusae who attacked her could taste it and decided that gave him the right to violate her. I killed him to prevent harm to her," Luka said. "As she is part empusae, that is my right." After a brief silence, Luka continued. "She is promised to me because she gave me her blood willingly. It is my right to claim her as my own, and I demand that she be allowed to leave, with her family, and that no harm come to her. She must be entitled to protection by this Council."

The Council stared at her now with open curiosity. "Who is your father?" Leander asked.

"I don't know," Ophelia said through clenched teeth, not wanting to answer him. "I didn't even know about witches and vampires and supernaturals until a few months ago."

"Do you drink blood to survive the curse of Empusa?" Leander asked.

"No," she said.

"Do you heal yourself?" Leander asked again.

"She heals faster than humans and witches, but not as fast as an empusae," Luka interjected.

"I have never heard of a hybrid vampire-witch," Zeon said.

"We have," Leander said slowly, touching his fingertips to his chin. "A child was born to a witch and a vampire centuries ago. Long before most here drew breath."

"But her existence violates the Alliance," Durante said. "That cannot stand. She must be executed."

"*She* did not violate the Alliance," Leander said. "Her mother and father did."

"Why was the hybrid killed centuries ago?" Zeon asked, his gaze sharpening with calculation.

"Because he was bloodthirsty and mad. He couldn't be controlled. So he was killed," Leander said in his deliberate tone. "It is curious that this witch does not require blood to survive."

Durante's seraphic face was twisted in an ugly rage. "She must die for the sins of her parents. What prevents her from going mad and exposing us all?"

"But she doesn't require blood," Leander said again. "I do not believe she should die tonight. Perhaps another night. Zeon?"

Zeon remained silent for several moments. "I think we need more information. We should wait." His gaze flicked toward Leander, then back to Ophelia. In that brief exchange, she understood; they were aligned. And their support wouldn't come without strings.

Durante was fuming, his fist tightening around the sword he still held. "You know my vote. Death."

"We have rules for a reason," Leander said calmly, "but the punishment is not for Ophelia. Her parents should be brought before the Council, not her. She shall live."

TWENTY-THREE

Ophelia exhaled, a flicker of relief threading through her. They'd voted to let her live, for now. But her reprieve was short-lived. Her body thrummed with warning. This wasn't over. Not even close.

"Will you submit to vampire or witch law?" Leander asked.

"Neither," she said, drawing more gasps and whispers from the crowd. "But I'll help you find the amulet, as I promised. As long as you let my family go."

Durante's dark mood lifted as his lips once again twisted into that maniacal smirk. "As part vampire, the Council is required to protect you, even if you do not wish to have that protection." Slowly, he began walking toward Sebastian.

Ophelia's body went rigid, cold sweeping through her. "Don't you dare touch him."

"Ophelia, he has betrayed you. Lived in your home. Seduced your uncle. All to spy on you. Don't you want him to be punished for his betrayal?" Durante asked, raising his sword toward Sebastian.

"Don't you touch him." Ophelia started forward, but

Gabriel and Luka caged her, each grabbing an arm to restrain her.

"Are you so certain?" Durante asked.

"Of course I am." Her feelings were complicated. But her fury at Sebastian would have to wait. Not here. Not now. Not in front of the Council.

She glanced between Sebastian and Alex, no longer listening to Durante, her mind working to figure out how to save them both. Alex's eyes were wide, red-rimmed from tears. Sebastian, meanwhile, gave Ophelia a look of quiet resignation, a sad smile forming on his lips.

Durante addressed the other Council members. "I propose we punish Sebastian for the betrayal of an empusae, even if she's a half-breed. He violated the Alliance by infiltrating her home. His deceit was egregious. And we are well within our rights to punish a witch this way, especially one with so little value."

"I have no position on punishment of the witch," Leander said, his distaste evident. "I leave it to you."

Ophelia's heart started to beat rapidly as her hands erupted in flames. But Luka and Gabriel didn't break, holding her in place. Struggling against them, she let the flames lick up their arms. This couldn't be happening. She couldn't lose another parent. Not again. Tears stained Sebastian's cheeks as he spoke only to her. "You and Elijah have made me the happiest man. I wouldn't change a thing. Not a thing. I love you both. Never stop looking within yourself for answers."

Zeon finally gave his answer. "We cannot allow such a violation, even if we aren't sure how to handle the half-breed." His voice was thoughtful as he watched Ophelia, apparently waiting to see what she would do. "Punishment must be swift, and I leave it to Durante to decide what that is."

"No, no, no," Ophelia said, her voice rising an octave with

each word, begging as she bucked her body against Luka and Gabriel, trying to break free. But it was useless. The vampires holding her were too powerful, even with her newfound magic. She screamed and screamed as the flames licked up and down her arms, burning the two ancient vampires holding her back. Sweat steamed on them as their skin bubbled. Still, they didn't let her go.

She pleaded with Luka. "Let me go. Please, Luka. Let me get to him." But he wouldn't meet her gaze. She knew he wouldn't move, not if it meant putting her in danger. She shifted to Gabriel instead, locking eyes with his deep brown stare. "Let me go." But he only shook his head, something like regret softening the line of his mouth.

Desperate now, her eyes snapped back to Sebastian. Panic surged.

"Ophelia, don't look," Luka said. "Turn your head."

She didn't. She wouldn't. She needed to see.

Durante dragged the long sword across Sebastian's throat. In a final cruelty, he didn't finish the job. He just cut deep enough to prolong the suffering. Sebastian gasped, blood choking his lungs. Then, after an unbearable stretch of silence, he dropped hard to his knees, then collapsed forward, his hands still bound behind him.

A wail escaped Ophelia as a gush of anger and grief ripped through her. The room started to shake and sway as the air built and stirred around them, whipping her hair around her face and causing the candle flames to stutter.

"Ophelia, stop," Luka said. "Take a deep breath, or the power will overtake you." The vampires around them started to back away as the floor splintered. With a burst of power, she blasted Luka and Gabriel off her. They landed several feet away. Gabriel grunted as he hit the floor, landing on his back. Luka landed on his feet, ready to chase after her.

Durante stalked toward her, the sword raised, but she pinned him against the wall with a torrent of wind.

Zeon made his way to Alex, grabbing her before Ophelia could stop him. "If you don't stop this, you will lose both of them," Zeon said, his words cold and calculated as he pressed a dagger to Alex's throat. Alex tried to jerk out of his hands, causing the knife to slip and slice her skin. Zeon's nostrils flared, and he let his tongue dip to her throat, licking the droplets of blood. His eyes widened, and he pushed her away, causing her to stumble forward. "Fae," he said.

With Alex away from him, Ophelia sent fire toward Zeon, encircling him with a cage of flames.

Luka and Gabriel had reached her again. As Luka reached for her, she twisted out of his grasp. Turning to Gabriel, ready to send flames into his sculpted face, he held up his hands and stepped away from her. "I'm sorry for your loss," he said, bowing his head.

Confused, she didn't have time to ponder his actions. Instead, she ran to Sebastian, ripped the ties from his hands, and rolled him over. Blood pooled under his body, his face already gray. His eyes were wide open with the whites fully visible, now beginning to yellow. He was gone.

"No, Sebastian. No. No. No." Ophelia's heart shattered open as she pulled him to her, weeping onto his chest. Blood smeared in her hair and on her face, but she didn't care. No matter what he'd done, he had been a father to her. He couldn't be gone. She held him close to her, sprawled across him, wanting to slip into her grief. The room around them quaked and rumbled in time with her as the unbearable pain hit her in waves.

Feeling someone next to her, she sensed no danger and forced her eyes to open to find Alex. Her best friend was kneeling beside her, blood soaking her bare knees.

"He's gone. We have to go." She held Ophelia's hand, pleading, "Ophelia, help us leave. I believe you. I believe in you."

Something splintered in Ophelia as she bent to kiss Sebastian on his forehead one last time. Reaching over to squeeze her friend's hand, she drew strength from Alex. Taking a deep breath, she felt her magic stirring, calling the element of water to course through the old pipes of the stone castle. Suddenly, the walls around them started to buckle as the pipes broke open, spilling water through the stone. She used the combination of earth and air to force open the doors around them and to shatter the windows.

Luka reached them, and she found his eyes. "Get us out of here. With Sebastian," she pleaded.

"Ophelia, I don't know if I can get all of you—"

"Luka, you didn't let me save him. Help me with this, at least." She was so angry at him. For revealing her secret. For allowing this to happen. He should have known what would happen.

Luka's eyes dropped, stricken. "Of course," he said, not wasting another minute and transforming his body. But instead of the typical black jaguar, large green scaly skin appeared, filling the room with wings, a barbed tail, four legs, and a horned head. His new body was massive, breaking through the roof above them, revealing the dark sky dotted with stars.

As he morphed, Ophelia used her power to force the other vampires back. No one could get near them as fire and air swirled around them, water shooting throughout the room as it raced through the pipes. Straining, Alex dragged Sebastian to Luka, clambered up the dragon's broad, scaly back, and hoisted the body behind her.

Ophelia felt her rage building. She wanted to destroy this

place and the vampires inside it. Alex seemed to understand. "No, Ophelia. We need to go. Let's get him out of here," she said, yelling over the crushing sounds in the room and pointing to his body.

Her words knocked some sense into Ophelia and jerked her from the haze of revenge. Climbing on behind Alex, she used one hand to hold on tight as she used air to force the other vampires away from the dragon.

Luka pushed off with his reptilian claws, beating his massive, bat-like wings as he took flight. The barbs in his tail hit several vampires on the way up, impaling them. The force of his body and Ophelia's power caused stone to crumble all around them. The disintegrating tower would sink into the rest of the castle, trapping them if they didn't leave immediately.

"Luka, we need to get higher," Ophelia screamed over the wind that raged around them. As he climbed higher in the sky, she felt the magic roil through him. The tower crumbled around the remaining vampires.

Ophelia didn't know how long they were in the air. Luka kept them over the sea and above the clouds to avoid detection. By the time they landed at his estate, her thighs and hands were throbbing from holding on to him and Sebastian. She and Alex slid off Luka's back, landing with a thud on their knees.

At the sound of the commotion, Mo and Brisa ran down the stairs. Bewildered, they looked from Luka's dragon body to Sebastian and then to Ophelia.

"Get him inside," Ophelia said, her voice hoarse and legs quivering as she stood.

Wordlessly, they stepped forward and gently lifted Sebastian, disappearing into the house. Luka shifted back to his vampire form, curled naked in a fetal position on the gravel. He stumbled to his feet, pale and shaking. Ophelia knew it must have taken a great deal of power and magic for him to change into such a form and maintain it while carrying three people. But she turned her back to him and faced Alex.

"Are you hurt?" she asked, her voice barely audible.

Alex was shaking, her teeth chattering, but she pulled Ophelia into a hug, squeezing her friend. "I'm so sorry, Ophy. About Sebastian."

At first, Ophelia stood still, her arms at her side. But then she returned her friend's hug, finally allowing her tears to fall as her entire body shook with grief.

Distantly, she heard her best friend ask Luka where to go. As Alex released her, he stepped forward and lifted Ophelia into his arms, holding her against his chest. She beat her fists against him, trying to break free, but he held on, unflinching as grief tore through her. "You made me tell them. It killed him. How could you? How could you?" she cried, her voice splintering. "And you knew about Sebastian. I know you did." She remembered the look he'd exchanged with Mo when she had mentioned Sebastian. They both knew. And they hadn't told her.

He didn't deny it. He just held her tight to his chest, letting her hit him, as he whispered, "Just let me get you inside." The fight finally left her, and she went limp in his arms. He carried her to the room they had shared and placed her in the bed, pulling the blankets over her body. Alex followed them and climbed into the bed with her, and they wrapped their arms around each other, letting the tears fall until they fell asleep.

Ophelia woke from a nightmare, sweat covering her body, and she felt dampness around her eyelashes. She had dreamed that everyone she ever loved died because of her. Because of what she was. When she opened her eyes fully, she realized it wasn't a nightmare at all. Sebastian was really dead. Her mother was gone, probably dead, as well. Reaching across the bed, she felt for her friend. Alex was breathing deeply and softly, still asleep.

As her eyes adjusted, she spotted Luka in a chair beside the fire, a book resting in his hands. His skin no longer looked pale, and his body held more strength than before—he had fed. He closed the book gently, watching her in silence.

She slipped out of bed and lowered herself to the floor in front of the hearth, leaning her back against his chair. He stroked her hair, winding the long strands around his fingers, waiting. "Why didn't you let me save him?" she asked quietly, her gaze fixed on the fire, voice cracking. "Why didn't you tell me about him?"

"There was no saving him, Ophelia. Durante would have killed him no matter what. Or he would have tried to kill you." Luka's voice was soft, filled with regret. "And I didn't tell you about him because I couldn't be the one to break your heart."

Ophelia squeezed her eyes shut, blocking the tears from falling. "They didn't have to know about the vampire blood."

"There is no hiding that, Ophelia. They were going to find out one way or the other. I'm sorry about Sebastian. I really am, but he made his choice long ago. Saving you was my priority."

"I could have tried to save him. You held me back."

"Forgive me." He scooted out of the chair and sat next to her, their legs touching. Placing one arm around her shoulders, he used the other to mess up his hair. "I didn't want to lose you."

"You should have given me that choice," she said.

"Please understand," he said, lifting his gaze to her and pleading with her.

"Why did you tell them that I'm your *mea promissa*? What does that even mean?" she asked.

"Ancient laws of the empusae. I knew I could protect you if I said you are my promised. It was believable because you voluntarily gave me your blood. They could smell it on me. In me," he said.

"I can't believe he's gone," she said, whispering because it felt like saying the words louder would make it too real. "What will I tell Elijah?" Her voice cracked again as tears welled.

"I can help with that. We have resources to inform Elijah of Sebastian's death, without him having to know how," he said.

"I want Elijah to stay away from this supernatural world. I wanted the same for Alex. Do you think she will ever forgive me?" she asked.

"Forgive you for what, Ophelia? For your true nature?"

"For dragging her into this," she said.

"There's one more thing," he said. "Zeon confirmed it. Alex is part fae. Just a trace, but it's there. She probably doesn't even know. It might explain her skill with medicine...and that calming presence. The fae are known for it."

Ophelia's eyes flicked toward the bed. Alex was still asleep, her breathing soft and steady. "Can we keep it from her?"

Luka's response was gentle but firm. "What would you want? For people to keep it from you? Or to tell you the truth?"

Ophelia let out a slow sigh. "You're right. We all deserve the truth. I'll talk to her."

TWENTY-FOUR

Ophelia and Alex barely spoke on the long flight to New York. Luka had arranged a private plane for them—one that could carry Sebastian's body discreetly. He'd offered to join, but Ophelia had refused. She needed to be alone with Elijah when he found out about Sebastian. It was nearly Christmas, and she needed to be with her father, to wrap herself in the illusion of normalcy, even if it had never truly existed and never would. Luka promised to keep searching for clues about the amulet. Privately, she hoped the trail would go cold forever.

"Alex, I know this is a lot and that you must be confused." She tried one more time to talk to her friend, handling her gently. "I was, too, but honestly, it was a relief to learn about supernaturals," Ophelia said. She crossed and uncrossed her legs, squirming in her seat, unable to sit still. "I'm—I'm trying to give you space, but I want you to know what I know. I don't want this supernatural world to be hidden from you like it was from me. Especially because you have fae blood—"

Alex held up her hand. "I don't want to talk about it. I don't want to learn more. I just want to go home. Pretend this never happened."

Ophelia opened her mouth, then shut it again, the words dying on her tongue. The rejection stung. Where Ophelia had craved understanding, Alex was choosing denial. She let out a slow breath. "Fine. I'll be here when you're ready." But the words felt hollow. It hurt—deeply—that her best friend didn't want to understand the world that had shaped her, or the pain she'd carried alone for so long.

The rest of the flight passed in silence. Ophelia pretended to read, but her eyes kept glazing over, her thoughts spiraling back to Sebastian. Across from her, Alex had curled into herself —knees tucked to her chest, arms wound tight, head resting on her knees. As if she could fold small enough to vanish and make it all go away.

After they landed, Alex hugged Ophelia briefly, her movements rigid, like someone holding back an avalanche with a single breath. "I'm sorry about Sebastian. But I need space. And time. Please understand," she said. Releasing her, Alex disappeared into a cab.

When Ophelia walked into the foyer of her home, she was greeted by Elijah's familiar crushing hug. "This house has been so empty without you." He pulled back to look at her with a huge smile on his face. "Have you been running more? Something seems different. You look stronger. Wait until Sebastian sees you."

That crushed her heart all over again, but she followed the script Luka had given her. "Where is Sebastian?" The lie felt gross and gritty on her lips.

"He had a work trip. Very last minute. He'll be home tomorrow." Elijah frowned. "I haven't heard from him in a day or so, but I'm sure he's just busy exploring." Elijah forced a smile back onto his face, trying to mask his worry. "What do you want to do today? Need rest?"

Ophelia knew the truth would arrive by nightfall. That was how Luka had planned it—discreet, efficient, cruel in its precision. And until then, she intended to give Elijah one last day untouched by grief. One final sliver of joy before the world broke around him like it already had around her.

She smiled, forcing it to reach her eyes even though it strained her bones to do so. "Let's do brunch. With mimosas."

She wiggled her eyebrows, and Elijah's booming laugh filled the foyer, as bright and familiar as ever. It echoed off the walls like it was trying to hold the house together by sheer force of love. "Now you're talking!"

Bundled in scarves and heavy coats, they walked the familiar blocks to their favorite French bistro. The windows were fogged from the warmth inside, and Ophelia watched her father's reflection in the glass as he told the hostess how long it had been since his daughter came home. Inside, they sat at their usual table, tucked near the window, and ordered baked Parmesan eggs and bottomless cocktails.

Elijah wanted to know every detail of her trip. She gave him only the curated memories. The ones with sunlight and laughter. Hiking to the castle in Trieste. Running along crumbling cliffs in Southern Italy. Climbing a mountain in Slovenia where the air was so clean it felt like drinking stars. She swallowed her guilt with every sip, letting the lies burn softer with champagne.

"So," Elijah said, tilting his head, "you met someone."

Ophelia hesitated, her fork suspended in the air. Her cheeks flushed from the drinks, or maybe from the effort of keeping the smile on her face. She dropped her gaze and nudged a bite of egg across her plate. "How did you know?" she asked.

He gave a slow, amused shrug. "A father's intuition." He sipped his mimosa again, watching her over the rim. "Do you love him?"

She glanced up, locking eyes with him for a heartbeat before looking away. "I think so," she whispered.

Elijah studied her a moment longer, his expression softening. "And does he treat you well?"

Ophelia's throat tightened. "He spoils me," she said, her voice cracking around the words. "A lot like Sebastian, actually." She watched his face closely, but Elijah only smiled, misreading the emotion rising in her voice.

"Good. That's all I want for you. To find someone who makes you laugh like Sebastian makes me laugh. Someone who sees how strong you are, but still wants to take care of you."

Ophelia stabbed her fork into the eggs and took a mechanical bite, desperate to swallow the sob clawing up her throat. She nodded through it, trying to hold back the flood pressing against her ribs. Sebastian had been so much more than the lie he left behind. He was family. And now he was gone.

"When do I get to meet this mystery man?" Elijah asked, a teasing glint in his eye.

She toyed with her napkin, pretending to think. "I'm not sure. He lives in Italy...most of the time. It's complicated. Lots of logistics, you know?"

"Most of the time?" Elijah raised a brow.

Ophelia gave him a noncommittal laugh and took another sip of her drink. She didn't trust herself to say more.

Elijah leaned back, his face brightening. "You know what we should do? Something we haven't done since you were little?"

She tilted her head at him, wary. "What?"

"Ice-skating."

Ophelia laughed, genuinely this time, and nodded. "You're on."

They walked arm in arm through Central Park, the snow packed tight along the sidewalks and trees standing bare and stark against the sky. The air was sharp with cold, reddening their cheeks, but it felt like a gift—one perfect winter afternoon, suspended in time.

At the rink, they laced up their skates and wobbled onto the ice like amateurs. They held hands, laughed until their stomachs hurt, and nearly toppled more times than they stayed upright. For a little while, the ache in Ophelia's chest receded beneath the sound of Elijah's laughter and the scrape of blades on ice.

She clung to the moment, knowing the hours were numbered. The knock would come soon. And everything would change.

When they finally made their way back to the townhouse, Ophelia made them hot chocolate. She'd noticed Elijah checking his phone over and over, becoming more worried throughout the day. Finally, after night had fallen, a loud knock broke the silence.

"I'll get it," Elijah said in his cheerful voice, heading toward the door.

Ophelia watched, stricken, a lump in her throat as she swallowed hard. Two men dressed in police uniforms stood on the front stoop. She could tell they were vampires, but Elijah would never know.

"Mr. Chandler?" one of the vampires asked.

"Yes?" Elijah's face twisted in concern, his mouth and eyebrows furrowed down.

"May we come in? I'm afraid we have some bad news."

"Of course." Elijah's voice started to quiver. He opened the door wider and stepped back, giving the officers space to step into the foyer.

As they stepped into the small room, they both removed their police hats, nodding their heads at Ophelia. They knew who she was, as well.

"Mr. Chandler, your husband, Sebastian, was involved in an accident this afternoon." Elijah brought his hand up to his mouth, which was already slightly ajar with shock. "I'm so sorry to tell you this," the second vampire added gently, "but he died at the scene." They were solemn and gentle, and Ophelia was grateful for that.

At first, Elijah's face showed no emotion, then panic bloomed. "This must be a mistake," Elijah said, looking back and forth from the officers to Ophelia.

"There is no mistake, sir. We made a positive ID." The second officer was firm as he held Elijah's gaze.

"No, no, no," Elijah said, over and over as he brought his hands to cover his face and leaned against the wall, sliding down until he was sitting on the floor of the foyer. Ophelia rushed forward, finally able to grieve with her uncle. She knelt down and wrapped her arms around him. They stayed that way for a long time, sitting on the floor, holding each other as they cried.

THE NEXT FEW days were a blur as they made arrangements for Sebastian's memorial. Elijah was holding up better than she'd expected, but his sad eyes made her chest ache. She kept her magic dormant, pretending it didn't exist. The guilt that she couldn't save Sebastian weighed on her like a heavy blanket.

Sebastian's service took place at a dive bar decorated in palm trees, disco balls, and a leopard-print pool table. They rented the entire space and made it a party, just like he would have wanted. As a rule, guests were required to take a shot of liquor after each memorial toast.

About an hour into the night, Ophelia's heart skipped a beat as Alex walked through the door, looking uncertain until her eyes landed on Elijah. Embracing him, they spoke briefly until Alex's eyes landed on Ophelia, and they crossed the room to embrace.

"Are you okay?" Alex asked in a whisper.

Ophelia shrugged. "As expected." Tears threatened to fall down her cheeks, but she forced them back, tired of crying. "And you?"

"Want to take a bottle to the roof so we can talk?" Alex asked.

"That's the best idea I've heard all day," Ophelia said.

They grabbed a fifth of Grey Goose and made their way up black metal interior stairs and found two discarded lawn chairs on the roof. Taking a seat, they looked out over the lights of the city. Alex took a deep drink straight from the bottle before handing it to Ophelia, who took her own. Her eyes watered as the liquor stung her throat.

"Look—" Ophelia said.

"No, let me," Alex interrupted her friend. "All these years. It must have been so hard for you. You kept trying to tell us that you saw things others didn't. The feelings. The episodes. And I loved you, but I didn't believe you. I'm sorry."

Ophelia turned to look at her friend, surprised. "Why are you apologizing? Who would believe that?" she asked, passing the bottle back to Alex.

"I should have. It must've been lonely, keeping all of that to yourself," Alex said, taking another swig of the vodka, still staring out at the city as she handed the bottle to Ophelia.

It was Ophelia's turn to apologize. "I'm sorry that you were kidnapped because of me. I'm sorry that I'm such a selfish friend that I didn't realize what was going on. I'm sorry you saw Sebastian—" Ophelia stopped herself, blinking rapidly to hold back fresh tears. She took another pull from the bottle, embracing the sting that tore down her throat. "Thank you for not telling Elijah. I want to keep this world from him, if I can."

"I wish it had been kept from me." Alex's voice was low as she stood and crossed to the edge of the roof, placing her hands on the concrete ledge just above her waist. "But now I know."

Ophelia joined her, leaning on the barrier and steadying the bottle so it didn't tip over the side. "Do you want to talk about any of it?" She didn't want to push Alex about her fae blood.

"Mo gave me a book before I left Italy. It talks about the legends of the fae—many of whom are natural healers," Alex said, her tone weighted with reluctant acceptance. "It's probably why I've always loved medicine. If I'm honest, I felt drawn to it in a way I never understood. Like I was meant to go to medical school. Like it was in my blood," she added, snatching the bottle from Ophelia and taking a long drink that made her eyes water.

"They are also known as warriors," Ophelia said, nudging her friend gently with her shoulder.

Alex scoffed, a sharp snort escaping her lips. "I'm not much of a warrior."

Ophelia changed the subject. "Thank you for helping us leave San Marino. I could have been consumed by my rage, but you brought me through it."

Alex turned to face her friend. "Of course. I'll always be

there for you. And it was also for Sebastian, no matter what he did."

Ophelia took the bottle and raised it, meeting Alex's eyes. "For Sebastian." She took another long pull. Her eyes burned, not from the vodka, but from the ache she'd carried since San Marino.

CHAPTER

TWENTY-FIVE

The days following Sebastian's memorial blurred together. Ophelia and Elijah sorted through his belongings, read in silence, and took long walks around Central Park—even in the frigid cold, dirty snow crunching under their boots. When her magic began to feel restless beneath her skin, she ran through the park at night, slipping into the woods and letting her power rise. After so many years of wishing she could strip away what made her different, the absence of it now made her feel caged.

A week before Christmas, she returned home from a chilly run, flushed and giddy. She'd just practiced all four elements in the park. But her smile vanished as she bounded up the stairs to the front door. Someone—another supernatural—was inside with Elijah.

Panic surged. Her power flared instinctively as she took the steps two at a time. Elijah's voice floated toward her as she neared the entry, calm and cheerful. Still, she flung open the door, stepping into the foyer. Fire licked at her fingertips, eager for release.

"Ophelia, you have a visitor," Elijah called, his voice lighter than it had been in weeks.

Confused, she passed through the second doorway and froze in the living room.

Luka stood by the fireplace, a glass of amber liquid in hand.

His lips curved when he saw her, one brow lifting as he glanced toward her extinguished flames. He wore dark, tailored pants and a deep green shirt that made his eyes seem impossibly bright, a casual blazer thrown over the top.

She stared, pulse skittering. Sweat slicked her back, her shirt clinging to her skin. She reached up to smooth her hair—wild and frizzy from the run—suddenly aware of every inch of herself.

Elijah's grin stretched wider as he looked back and forth between them. "Is this the *friend* you made in Trieste?" He put emphasis on friend, and Ophelia wanted to punch him in the arm.

"One of them," Ophelia said.

"One?" Luka asked.

Elijah cleared his throat. "Why don't I give you two some privacy?" With a final squeeze of Ophelia's arm, he retreated up the stairs, humming to himself like he hadn't just dropped a bomb. As soon as the noise faded, Luka closed the distance between them in a blur, his eyes locked on hers. The air crackled, electric, as they stood inches apart.

"Miss me?" he asked, almost purring the words.

"Never," she said. Of course, she hadn't been able to stop thinking about him.

Luka traced one hand along her jaw and then down the vein running along her neck. "I think you did," he said.

Ophelia didn't want to pretend anymore. She wrapped her arms around his neck, pulling him close. "Kiss me," she said.

He didn't hesitate. Their mouths met, tongues tangling as

they devoured each other. Luka backed her into the wall, hands gliding down her body to grip her waist.

Before it could go any further, he pulled back, resting his forehead against hers. "I hope you don't mind me showing up like this."

"Well, I know you're a few centuries old, but we do have phones now. A heads-up would've been nice," she said, smiling.

"And miss that surprised face? Dressed like this?" His gaze drifted down, darkening. "Not a chance."

She rose onto her tiptoes and nibbled his neck. Luka groaned, biting his lip. "I want to bend you over this chair right now."

She didn't disagree. But his expression shifted. "We need to talk," he said.

Ophelia groaned. "Can't it wait? Just one normal night? Maybe a date?" she asked.

His lips curled. "A date?" He seemed to weigh the idea, threading his fingers through hers. "What would you want to do on this 'normal night?'"

Beaming, Ophelia nearly squealed. "Let me shower first. Then I'll show you my favorite places."

She was halfway up the stairs when he called after her, "Need a hand?"

She paused on the stairs, her gaze lingering on him. "Tempted," she said with a wink. "But I think I can handle it."

Racing up the stairs, she showered quickly and chose an outfit she knew Luka would both love—and be tortured by. Dressing in a long-sleeved scoop-neck bodysuit that hugged every curve, she paired it with a black leather miniskirt, tights, and thigh-high boots that made her several inches taller. She added a bright red lipstick to complement the outfit. Of course, she wore her mother's bracelet.

On her way down the stairs, Elijah called her name from his study on the second floor. It had been her room when she was a child. When she moved to the third floor, he had transformed the small space into an office piled high with books. She spotted some of his old books on paranormal activity and ignored them, not wanting those memories to spoil her night.

As she stepped into the room, he let out a low whistle. "As your father, I should tell you that I don't think you have enough clothes on. But as a person with eyes, you look amazing."

Ophelia smiled, feeling a slight blush tinging her cheeks. "Will you be okay while I'm gone?" she asked.

"I want you to live your life. And I especially want you to have what I had with Sebastian."

She crossed the room and gave her father a deep hug. "I love you," she whispered in his ear.

"I love you, too. Now go have some fun." He patted her on the back.

Walking down the stairs slowly, she felt Luka's eyes scorching a path down her body. He met her at the landing, holding his hand out, palm turned up. When she accepted, he pulled her to him. "Gorgeous, what are you doing to me?" He bent to kiss her on the neck before pulling back. "Before I rip these clothes off, let's go be boyfriend and girlfriend."

Giggling at the fact that her centuries-old lover had just called her his girlfriend, Ophelia laced her fingers through his and led him to one of her favorite Upper West Side pubs. The bar was narrow and intimate, owned by her former high school English teacher. Exposed brick walls and low lighting gave it a cozy, conspiratorial feel. Framed quotes from famous books and plays lined the walls, and the cocktail menu paid homage to literary classics.

They squeezed past the crowded bar and settled at a dimly

lit table in the corner. Ophelia ordered The Hamlet—vodka with muddled lime—and let herself sink into the illusion of normalcy. For the first time in months, she felt relaxed. Happy. Almost human. As if the past few months hadn't torn her apart and stitched her back together again with magic and grief.

Later, they wandered through Central Park, ending up in the very place where they'd first met—where Luka had shifted to a jaguar to protect her.

"Almost a full moon," Ophelia murmured, tilting her head back to take in the sky. Her breath came out in clouds as she inhaled deeply, the crisp air sobering and sharp.

Behind her, Luka slipped his arms around her waist, pulling her flush against him. His warmth anchored her. She leaned into him, tipping her head back. And his mouth was there, meeting hers in a kiss that felt urgent, like it might be their last.

She twisted in his arms to face him fully, moaning into his mouth as her hand slid down to press against the hard length straining beneath his pants. But it wasn't enough. She needed more—skin, heat, connection. Breaking the kiss, she reached for his belt.

"Maybe this isn't the right—" he began, catching her wrist.

"I need you inside me," she whispered, breathless. "Here." She kissed him again, pulling him closer, her body already yielding to his.

Luka pulled back, scanning the empty path. At this hour, the park was deserted. Apparently satisfied, he led her into the shadows. "You have to be quiet," he murmured, lips brushing her ear before he found the sensitive spot just below it and nibbled. She gasped. "Much, much quieter than that."

He pushed her against a tree, lifting her skirt and slipping his hand beneath her tights. With practiced ease, he shifted her bodysuit aside, parting her before plunging two fingers inside. Then he slid up to circle her clit. Ophelia rocked against his hand, her breath catching in his mouth as he kissed her—deep, devouring—while she came hard, clinging to him.

As her body trembled with aftershocks, Luka spun her to face the tree. He yanked her skirt higher, peeled her tights down, and tore the bodysuit with a sound that made her shiver. The zipper of his pants rasped open. A second later, she felt the hot press of him against her ass.

She arched her back in invitation.

He slid into her with a low groan, each thrust rough and relentless. One hand braced against the bark, the other wrapped tightly around her waist, his thumb still circling her clit. The pressure was unbearable.

Ophelia bit her lip to keep from crying out, the taste of blood blooming on her tongue. Still, a moan escaped, loud and helpless. Luka clamped a hand over her mouth, muffling the sound as they both reached the edge and fell over it together.

When it was over, she slumped against the tree, panting, her cheek pressed to the rough bark. Luka pulled out and zipped up, then crouched to tug her tights back into place and smooth her skirt. Turning her gently, he grinned.

"You have bark in your hair," he said, plucking a piece free and holding it up like a trophy.

She laughed, breathless, and he joined her. Still chuckling, they left the park hand in hand.

Later, when he bent to kiss her goodnight on the steps of her townhouse, she leaned back with a teasing smile. "Stay," she said.

"I'm not sure it would be proper," he said, nervously eyeing her home and scanning the windows—clearly checking for Elijah.

She rolled her eyes. "You're so old-fashioned. But considering you just fucked me against a tree, I think we can handle a sleepover." She grinned, already knowing she'd win this round.

"What will your uncle think?" Luka asked.

"That I'm spending the night with the man I love. He won't care," she said.

Luka followed her inside, silent and sure-footed. In her bedroom, he paused to take it all in, curiosity softening his expression.

"This place feels like you," he said, eyes lingering on the photo of Ophelia and her mom. "I like seeing a snapshot of your life."

She dropped onto the bed and patted the spot beside her. After a beat, he joined her, sitting stiffly. She rose again, stepping between his knees, her thighs brushing the edge of the bed as she ran her hand along his back. When she began unbuttoning his shirt, he stopped her.

"I don't—"

"He can't hear us, I promise," Ophelia said, smiling. Luka's hesitation surprised her.

She stepped back, unzipped her skirt, and let it fall, the ruined bodysuit soon following. Standing in just her boots and tights, she raised an eyebrow. "Would you help me with these?"

Luka looked heavenward. "Gods," he muttered. Then he knelt, unzipping her boots and sliding them off one at a time.

Ophelia peeled off her tights and strolled naked to the bathroom. "Join me?" she called over her shoulder. She heard him curse softly behind her, but soon the shower door opened, and he stepped in.

"Let me," he said, reaching for the shampoo. He massaged it into her scalp, gentle but thorough, fingers working out the bits of bark tangled in her hair.

Afterward, he carried her to bed.

"Now, let me do this right," he murmured.

They made love again, this time slow and reverent, as if he were trying to memorize every inch of her. It had been the perfect night.

TWENTY-SIX

The next morning, Ophelia slipped out of bed and dressed quickly in black yoga pants and a white tank top. She left a note for Luka, letting him know she'd gone to the yoga studio.

Mira greeted her with a warm hug as she walked in. Almost immediately, Ophelia felt the unmistakable presence of another supernatural.

"Is someone else here?" she asked, scanning the quiet space.

"Just me."

Luka had been right. Mira was supernatural, something other. As Ophelia unfurled her mat and sank to the floor, she studied her longtime instructor with open curiosity. Had Mira been planted in her life all these years, like Sebastian?

"What are you?" Ophelia asked, the question slipping out before she could stop it.

Mira didn't flinch. Instead, she reached forward and took Ophelia's hands. "I'm still the same Mira you've known for years. Helping you manage what once threatened to consume you, sometimes at a cost to myself. There are those of us who choose to stay hidden, who want nothing to do with supernatural politics. Do you understand?" Her gaze locked onto Ophelia's, calm but unflinching.

Ophelia nodded slowly. She didn't get to hide anymore. But she had, for over twenty years. And only now did she recognize it for what it had been: a gift.

"I hope you'll let me keep being that Mira," Mira continued. "I knew what you were, but it wasn't my secret to tell. Sebastian kept mine all these years. I hope you'll do the same for me."

At the mention of Sebastian, Ophelia sat up straighter. "What do you know about him?"

"I'm sorry about his death," Mira said gently. "I knew he was a witch. I knew someone had used a cloaking spell to hide the two of you. I don't know exactly what he was caught up in, but I believe he truly wanted to make the world better. And he loved Elijah. And you. I think he kept going all those years because of you."

"Thank you," Ophelia said softly. "He really was a light for us."

A quiet beat passed between them before Mira spoke again. "I sense something in you, Ophelia. A need. How can I help?"

"I don't—I don't know what to do," Ophelia admitted. "I feel lost. I've been trying to unravel a riddle, obsessing over it again and again. And I still can't make sense of it. I was hoping yoga might bring some kind of revelation."

"I think I can help," Mira said, rising. She crossed the room to her sanctuary and returned a moment later with a large, vibrant stone that shimmered in shades of blue and white. She sat beside Ophelia, holding it between them.

"What is that?" Ophelia asked, leaning forward.

"Moonstone," Mira said. "It symbolizes wisdom and new

beginnings. If you meditate with it as your focal point, it can help guide you."

"All right," Ophelia said. It couldn't hurt.

"Good." Mira placed the moonstone on the floor between them, then gently took Ophelia's hands again. At once, a calm settled over Ophelia, her breath slowing and deepening.

"Look at the moonstone," Mira instructed, her voice soft. "Invite knowledge and expansiveness. Breathe deeply. That's it. Breathe in, breathe out. Let your path reveal itself."

A heaviness washed over Ophelia. Her eyelids fluttered shut as she slipped into a meditative state. When she blinked them open again, the yoga studio was gone.

In its place stood Galla and a man—Alaric, she realized—aboard a large wooden ship in the middle of the sea, no land in sight. Alaric rested one hand on Galla's swollen belly as he kissed her cheek.

For a moment, Galla looked blissfully content. Then her head snapped up, eyes narrowing. She had sensed Ophelia. Darkness swept across the sky, and the wind began to howl.

"I did not call you," Galla snarled, her face twisted with rage. "How are you here? How dare a moira help you contact me."

Ophelia's heart pounded. "I didn't," she said. "I don't know what you mean."

"Are you ready for more loss?" Galla asked.

"I have nothing left to lose," Ophelia said.

"You know nothing," Galla spat. "You're not ready to answer the riddle. When you are, regardless of the cost, you'll be ready to find the amulet." She lifted her hands, and the wind rose around her like a storm gathering strength. "Now, be gone."

With a flick of her wrist, Galla hurled Ophelia from the

vision. When Ophelia opened her eyes, she was back in the small yoga studio, seated in front of Mira.

"Close your eyes and bring your palms to your heart," Mira said gently, her own eyes shut. "In a gesture of gratitude, bow your head and place your thumbs to the space between your brows. Lift your gaze when you're ready."

Ophelia bowed deeply and held the pose, finally lifting her head to meet Mira's gaze. "Thank you for trusting me, and for letting me see."

"It will always be my pleasure, Ophelia," Mira said softly.

They embraced, a deep, lingering hug, before Ophelia stepped back into the world—unsure when, or if, they would ever meet again.

As she walked home, the air felt stifling. She already knew what the riddle meant, and she wasn't ready to face that truth. She found Luka in her bed, reading, and climbed on top of him, knocking the book aside as she rested her head on his chest. He rubbed her back in slow, soothing strokes until his body suddenly tensed.

"Your father is coming upstairs," he whispered.

In a blur, Luka vanished into the bathroom. She rolled her eyes. Apparently, there was something Luka feared: her human dad. From the top of the stairs, Elijah knocked on the outside of the study door, not quite entering the bedroom. He definitely knew Luka was there.

"I'm making breakfast," he called, voice raised. "Do you want anything?"

Luka peeked out of the bathroom, eyes wide, his expression tight with panic. She half expected him to dive out the window. Flipping on her most sugary voice, she called back, "That sounds great! We'll be down in a few minutes."

Luka groaned and looked to the ceiling, muttering something under his breath before disappearing again. Once Elijah's footsteps receded, Ophelia slid out of bed and joined Luka in the bathroom. He stood at the sink, bracing himself with both hands on the vanity. She wrapped her arms around his waist and rested her head on his back.

"How can you be hundreds of years old and still afraid of my dad?"

"A good impression matters, no matter your age," he said, turning to face her. His hands settled on her waist.

"We have to go back," he added, more serious now. "Mo found something about the Lunula Amulet's location. I wanted to give you one more night, but it can't wait."

Ophelia sighed. "That's what I was afraid of. Can it wait until after Christmas?"

"I'm afraid not. It's tied to the Winter Solstice."

"I don't want to leave Elijah. Sebastian loved the holidays." Her voice softened. The supernatural world had already taken so much from him. She didn't want to add to the loss.

"I know. We'll have someone here watching him. And I'll try to get you back by Christmas morning," Luka said.

She appreciated that he didn't make promises he couldn't keep. He simply said he'd try.

"Good morning," Elijah called cheerfully as they descended the stairs, hand in hand.

"Good morning," Luka replied, adopting his most formal tone. "May I help you with anything, Mr. Chandler?"

Ophelia stifled a laugh and dropped Luka's hand. Walking over to Elijah, she kissed him on the cheek. "Morning," she said. "It smells amazing."

She knew Elijah needed to feel useful, so she didn't offer to help. Instead, she stole a piece of bacon behind his back and popped it into her mouth.

"Yes, you can help me by calling me Elijah," he said with a pointed smile. "And please, have a seat. We love having meals as a family." A shadow passed over his face, and she knew he was thinking of Sebastian.

"Coffee? Bloody Mary?" Elijah asked.

"Coffee, black," Luka said.

"Just coffee for me, too," Ophelia said as she slid into the seat beside Luka. She realized she was used to sitting across from Sebastian and Elijah. It felt strange to have Luka at her side, and stranger still for Sebastian to be missing entirely.

Elijah handed them both steaming cups of coffee and plates piled high with eggs, bacon, and biscuits. Lost in thought, Ophelia kept circling back to the vision she'd had at Mira's. Instinctively, she knew Galla wouldn't reveal the amulet's location if she told Luka.

"Are you okay?" Luka asked, squeezing her thigh beneath the table once Elijah left to refill his coffee.

She forced a smile. "Fine. Just worried about Elijah."

Luka squeezed her leg again, like he'd made a decision. "Elijah," he said, turning toward her uncle. "I have business in Trieste and plan to spend the holidays at my home in southern Italy. I've invited Ophelia to join me. Would you consider joining us? My company's already chartered a plane, so it's no trouble for both of you to come along."

Ophelia blinked in surprise, but quickly masked it. It was a good solution. The estate was secure, and she'd be able to return with Elijah in time for Christmas. More importantly, it would get him out of the house and away from all the memories it held.

Elijah's expression shifted through several emotions. He looked ready to decline, but then turned to her for silent permission.

"If Ophelia wants me to go, I'd be honored," he said.

"I'd love that," she replied without hesitation. She wanted him close and protected.

"Excellent. If you'll excuse me, I'll contact my team," Luka said, already rising with his phone in hand.

"A *team*?" Elijah mouthed at her once Luka stepped away. "A change of scenery would be good for us," he added more seriously. "It would be hard to be here for Christmas...without him. A spontaneous trip to Italy is exactly the kind of thing Sebastian would've wanted for us."

Ophelia didn't know what to say to that. Thankfully, Luka returned and spared her the effort.

"Can you be ready to leave this afternoon?" he asked.

If Elijah was surprised, he didn't show it. "I'll start packing."

TWENTY-SEVEN

They landed in the middle of the night and took a car to Luka's estate. Ophelia watched Elijah's face as he gawked at Luka's house, his wide eyes finding hers. *"What the hell?"* he mouthed. Ophelia stifled a laugh, remembering a similar reaction a few months ago. Mo and Brisa were introduced as friends, but Ophelia caught Elijah looking at them, shaking his head, as if he couldn't quite place them. Once he was settled into a room for the night, the four supernaturals met in the courtyard to talk about Mo's discovery.

Mo didn't waste time once they were seated around the table. "I found an ancient Akkadian text."

"Akkadian?" Ophelia asked.

"It's the oldest known language, from Mesopotamian times, long thought to be extinct. I had never read anything in that language, and it took me a long time to decipher it. The language is lost to humans, but there is still enough magic in the earth that I was eventually able to interpret it."

"What does it say?" Luka asked, standing to lean over the table, impatient.

"The text describes how a witch can contact her ancestors to speak with them," Mo answered.

"You mean," Ophelia said, hope filling her, "I could contact Galla again? Without her summoning me?" She leaned forward in her chair, reaching up to pull Luka back to a sitting position.

"Or Alaric?" Luka asked, eyebrows arched. He sat, one knee tapping up and down.

"You can only call a fellow witch in your maternal lineage," Mo explained. "And it must be done during the winter solstice, on a full moon, which is rare." A beat of silence stretched as they waited. "That's tomorrow night. After tomorrow, it won't happen again until the 2090s."

For a moment, Ophelia thought of calling her mother, to finally get the answers she'd wanted her entire life. But she forced herself to focus on the bigger picture—to focus on the greater good and destroying the amulet. "I can contact Galla, then. I think she'll tell me how to locate the amulet now," Ophelia said.

Brisa stared at her, clearly prying into her mind, but Ophelia kept it blank.

"There's a catch," Mo said. "The ritual must be performed at the Witch's Cave on Mount Slivnica."

While Ophelia thought about that, Brisa said, with her typical sarcasm, "And there's one more *tiny* issue."

"There's always more," Ophelia said, suppressing a groan.

"The Winter Solstice—Yule—is sacred to witches," Brisa said. "Thousands of witches will descend upon Mount Slivnica tomorrow for the gathering. They can't prevent you from entering the cave, but you'll be surrounded when you try to leave. Unlike when Galla called you to the cave, you would be going on your own. No safe passage is required under our Covenants. It will be almost impossible to get off the mountain without capture."

Ophelia didn't even try to suppress a groan at this point. The last time she'd encountered Sofija had not gone well. She couldn't imagine facing her again with thousands of witches against her, even if they didn't have use of their powers.

"Ophelia, you can do this," Brisa said, finally speaking. "I've been hard on you with training, but you are strong. Stronger than almost any witch I've ever met. And I know you'll figure this out."

Ophelia met her cousin's gaze, sitting taller in her seat. "I can do it," she said, the words steadier than the tremor in her gut.

"I know you can," Brisa said again, nodding at her.

Ophelia thought for a moment before speaking again. "None of you can come with me. It would be too dangerous."

Luka started to object, but he closed his mouth before words came out. He knew the wards would keep him away anyway, and he couldn't break the Alliance. And Brisa and Mo would only be used against her.

"Okay," Luka murmured, staring down at his clasped hands like they held something he couldn't bear to drop. She could hear the reluctance in his voice.

"What else do I need to know?" she asked Brisa and Mo.

Mo answered, "Well, as you know, magic is prevented on the mountain. The wards won't allow you to summon your power. You will be able to say the spell to call Galla. The good thing is, the other witches won't be able to use magic either."

"Anything else?" Ophelia was tired of asking, but she needed to know.

"Sofija is surrounded by neophytes—witches who are vying to be High Priestess one day," Brisa said. "Each of the neophytes has unique talents. Ingrid is one of the most powerful neophytes and can call on ancient spells, including one to see your memories." Brisa paused, looking Ophelia in the eyes and addressing her only. "You won't be able to hide your memories from her. If they can get you away from the wards, Ingrid will try to perform the spell on you. They'll do anything to find the amulet. The witches want to control it just as much as the vamps."

Averting her eyes, Ophelia realized that Brisa knew she was hiding something, and she was warning her to keep her secrets hidden. "Okay. Let's see if I've got this right. Get up the mountain in one piece. Get off the mountain without being kidnapped. With thousands of witches gathered for the Winter Solstice. Without being able to use my own magic. Without your help. Got it. Anything else?" Ophelia asked.

"That should do it," Brisa said as she winked at her cousin.

With nothing more to say, they broke to rest before Ophelia needed to leave for Mount Slivnica. Luka and Ophelia climbed into his large bed. She tried to close her eyes, to conserve the energy she would need, but her mind kept spinning. She turned from one side to the other, then onto her back, fluffing the pillow beneath her head.

"Can't sleep?" Luka asked, scooting closer to her and resting his arm across her stomach as she stared at the ceiling.

"I can't shut my mind off. I'm forgetting something. Something important," she said.

"What can I do to help?" He circled his hand around her stomach, touching her lightly in a soothing gesture.

She sat up abruptly. "I need air."

"I know just the place," Luka said, rolling out of the bed. Neither one of them would get any sleep tonight.

Fifteen minutes later, they were sitting in the sand on the same hidden beach where Luka had told her about the vampire blood. He pulled her close, his arm snug around her waist as they watched dawn erupt from the sky in shades of violet and blue that turned to angry hues of yellow, orange, and red.

"Everything in me wants to protect you. To not let you go alone. But you don't need me. You never have," he said, his voice soft as the horizon began to burn with light.

"Will you be here when I get back?" she asked, her voice barely above a whisper.

"I will always be here for you, as long as I can be," he said, reaching for her and gently cupping her face before drawing her in for a kiss.

TWENTY-EIGHT

The next night, Ophelia stood alone at the base of Mount Slivnica. Though magic couldn't be summoned on the mountain, she still felt the charged hum of power pulsing from the thousands of witches gathered above. Faint strains of music and laughter drifted down the slope as she stepped into the snow-blanketed forest and began her climb to the cabin.

Two witches stood sentinel at the entrance. "The High Priestess is expecting you," one said, pulling open the heavy wooden door to reveal a hall now vast enough to contain several hundred witches. They all faced forward, their gazes fixed on the dais.

"Come forward, girl," Sofija commanded. She sat enthroned in an oversized chair carved with lunar phases and ancient sigils of the witches' elemental powers. Each symbol was etched deep into the dark wood. Six neophytes flanked her —three on either side—like a ceremonial guard. As Ophelia made her way down the center aisle carved by the shifting crowd, she refused to bow. Her spine stayed straight, her expression unreadable. This woman was not her High Priestess.

A low murmur rippled through the gathered witches. Sofija raised a single hand and clapped, the sharp sound cracking through the room. "Silence!"

Then, eyes locked on Ophelia, she asked, "Why have you returned? Ready to swear allegiance to our coven and the sacred Covenants?" Her face twisted into a grotesque grin, already anticipating the answer.

"I need access to Coprniška Jama," Ophelia said.

"For what purpose?" Sofija asked, head tilted to the side in an unnatural angle.

Ophelia met Sofija's gaze without flinching. "To summon an ancient witch."

"Which one?" Sofija leaned forward, her brow furrowing, anticipation flickering into something darker. Several of her teeth were missing; the rest were blackened with decay.

"Galla Placidia."

A collective gasp swelled in the room. Sofija's expression faltered. Her eyes widened—momentarily stunned—but her gift for sensing lies told her that Ophelia spoke the truth.

"That's impossible. She's been dead for more than two millennia," she said, voice tight.

"She came to me in a vision, the last time I stood in the Cave," Ophelia said, her voice steady.

Sofija's eyes narrowed. "And why should we believe you?" she asked.

"You'd already know if I were lying." Ophelia shrugged, defiant. "I've got nothing to gain by deceiving you."

A murmur spread through the hall, low and electric. Shock, suspicion, maybe even fear rippled like a current among the witches.

"We all have something to hide, girl," Sofija snapped, fixing her with a glare.

"I didn't choose this," Ophelia shot back. Her gaze swept the crowd, shoulders squaring. "I didn't even know I was a witch until a few months ago. Since then, I've lost everything—my mother, my uncle, the only family I had."

"Loss is the price of life," Sofija replied coolly. "What makes you think your grief is unique?"

"It's not," Ophelia said softly, locking eyes with her. "I'm not special. I'm just trying to do what's right."

Sofija tilted her head, assessing. "What if we could help you find her? Your mother." Her voice softened, oily with false sympathy. "We have resources. Power. There are some who believe she still walks this earth."

Ophelia's heart gave a painful lurch. It was all she had ever wanted. She'd hoped the amulet might lead her to the truth. And now, Sofija was dangling that hope like bait. She shut her eyes. A warning hum thrummed through her bones. The temptation was strong. But it wasn't the path. "If you could've found her," she said quietly, "you would have."

Sofija's lips curled. "We had no reason to search. But with your blood, a locator spell would be simple."

"And what would that cost me?" Ophelia asked.

"Your loyalty," Sofija replied, lifting one gnarled shoulder in a mockery of nonchalance.

Ophelia didn't flinch. "You want more than loyalty. You want the amulet."

"Don't be insolent, you little fool," hissed the woman beside Sofija, spittle clinging to her jaw. Her dark hair was cropped short, framing a face carved in angles and fury.

Sofija silenced her with a raised hand. "You'll forgive Ingrid," she said, tone dismissive. "She's...protective. Of course, if you pledge yourself to the coven, we would expect your help in safeguarding it. That includes retrieving the Lunula Amulet —so no one can use it against us."

"All I care about is making sure it can't be used at all," Ophelia replied, her voice clear.

"Then give it to the witches," Sofija pressed. "Let us keep it safe."

"No." The word landed like a stone dropped in water, small, but rippling outward. Several witches gasped; others stiffened.

"Then who?" Sofija demanded. "Who would you trust with such power?"

"No one. I mean to destroy it," Ophelia said.

The room erupted in whispers, a wave of unease and disbelief rising like steam.

"Silence!" Sofija barked. Red blotches bloomed across her pale cheeks as she stared Ophelia down. "You'd waste that power? Turn your back on what you are?"

"I don't want power," Ophelia said. "I want a quiet life. But it seems no one's willing to let me live one, not until this is over."

Sofija studied her, that grotesque smile curling once more. "If you intend to call Galla, I won't stop you from entering the cave. Ingrid will accompany you, along with a few of my neophytes. For your protection, of course." Her grin turned serpentine. "We're all eager to understand why she summoned you...and why you must summon her again."

The threat shimmered beneath her words. Sofija had no intention of letting Ophelia leave the mountain unstripped of every secret.

"Come," Ingrid said, eyes locked on Ophelia like a predator marking prey.

Ophelia stepped forward, but Sofija lunged, seizing her

wrist. Her grip was shockingly strong for someone who'd seen two centuries of winters.

"You burn with untapped power," she whispered, just loud enough for Ingrid to hear. "You'll find resistance useless. Our blood is your blood. You will belong to this coven, one way or another."

Ophelia yanked her arm free. "You'll find I don't submit," she said coldly. "And if you're half as perceptive as you claim, you already know I'm telling the truth."

She turned her back on the High Priestess. A beat passed. Then Sofija gave Ingrid a slight nod, permission granted. As the heavy door shut behind them, Ophelia heard Sofija's voice ring out, sickly sweet. "Let us all return to the Yule celebrations!"

The climb to the cave was easier than last time. The full moon bathed the path in silver, and Ophelia suspected her first trek had been muddied by enchantment. As they neared the clearing, the tree line thinned and the hidden meadow emerged, glowing faintly in the moonlight.

Ingrid turned and smirked. "Stay put." She and the other neophytes fanned out, forming a loose semicircle around the cave mouth.

Ophelia didn't spare them a glance. She parted the ivy curtain with steady fingers and slipped through the narrow stone gap. Inside, she sat cross-legged on the cold floor and inhaled deeply, centering herself. Then, she whispered the invocation Mo had taught her.

Power thrummed through her like a struck chord. And then—

"*Nipotina*," came a familiar huff behind her, dry as dust. "You're always disturbing my rest. What is it this time?"

Ophelia scrambled to her feet and turned to face the ghostly figure. "I know what I have to do."

Galla's eyes gleamed with interest. "Ah. So you've solved my riddle?"

"I have."

"Did you share the answer?" Galla asked.

Ophelia shook her head. "I kept it to myself."

"Not even with your vampire lover?"

"Especially not with him," Ophelia said.

Galla's mouth quirked, but her tone stayed crisp. "Then tell me...what is the answer?"

"My blood," Ophelia said, measured, "and the blood of a fae. Together, they can destroy the Lunula Amulet."

"And why yours?" Galla asked, the cadence turning didactic, a teacher nudging her pupil forward.

"Because the essence of all witch magic flows through me. And vampire blood, too."

"And the fae?" Galla prompted, brow arched.

Ophelia nodded once. "Their blood completes the original triad. With both, we mirror the elements that created the amulet. And that's the only way to break it."

"And who is that fae?" Galla asked, her voice low.

Ophelia stared at her hands, twisting her fingers in her lap. "Alex," she whispered.

Galla's expression didn't change. "And do you understand what that means?"

"One of us will die."

"Have you accepted that fate?" she pressed.

"I want it to be me," Ophelia choked out, her voice catching like splinters in her throat. "Not her."

"We don't get to choose, *nipotina*." Galla's tone was neither cruel nor kind. It rang with an air of inevitability. "Are you willing to gamble your best friend's life? To risk everything, just to destroy the Lunula Amulet?"

Ophelia lifted her gaze, shame and sorrow rippling behind

her eyes. But beneath the ache, she knew. She would take the risk. She would die for it, if it came to that. Her mother had made the same sacrifice once. Ophelia could do no less.

"Then tell me," she said, voice quiet but resolute, "where the amulet is. I've done everything you asked of me."

Galla scoffed and flicked her hand through the air, as though swatting away smoke. "You think you've done so much? I killed the man I loved. I sent my daughter into exile. And I've waited centuries for someone worthy to find me, someone who could finish what I began. Are you that person?"

Ophelia didn't flinch. "I will destroy the amulet. No one will ever use it again. You have my word."

Galla watched her for a long moment, as if trying to see through the layers of her soul. Then she nodded, slow and grave. "I believe you. You mean what you say. But the path ahead won't bend for your belief. It will break you, *nipotina*. I can't see where it ends, only that the testing has just begun."

And at last, she gave Ophelia the answer she'd come for—details of where the Lunula Amulet had been hidden, buried so deeply in time and secrecy that no ordinary spell could have revealed it. But as the words left Galla's mouth, something strange happened: Ophelia didn't need them. The moment Galla spoke, the knowledge flared to life inside her. Like the map had always been etched into her blood, waiting to be unlocked.

When Galla finished, her eyes shimmered—not with power, but relief. The ancient hardness in her face softened for the first time.

"You are not alone," she said, her voice barely more than breath. "Your twin flame will meet you at the Eye of the Earth. Let him help you."

Before Ophelia could respond, Galla vanished, her presence flickering out like candlelight.

"Rest easy, Galla," Ophelia whispered into the silence, hoping her ancestor had finally found peace.

She sat back down on the cold stone floor, letting the echoes of the moment settle. When she finally rose, her breath was controlled, her shoulders squared. She was ready for what came next.

She crept to the mouth of the cave and peered out. Ingrid and the other neophytes had drifted toward the tree line, just beyond the enchanted meadow. They hadn't noticed her yet, but they would, any second.

Without hesitation, Ophelia slipped from the cave and sprinted in the opposite direction, up the jagged face of Mount Slivnica. The slope steepened, forcing her to dig her fingers into narrow crevices, hauling herself upward with muscle memory drilled in from training with Luka. She just had to reach the summit. If she did, the rest of their plan would fall into place.

A sudden burst of movement sounded behind her, shouting and boots scraping rock.

They'd seen her. Wards meant no magic, but that didn't stop witches from using fists, blades, or worse. She didn't dare slow down.

Near the top, she felt it: power coiling inside her, returning with every upward claw of movement. Sitting on the beach that morning, the truth had clicked into place. The wards didn't fully suppress her magic. They dampened it, but couldn't erase it. Not with blood like hers. Luka had suspected her hybrid nature—half vampire, half witch—confused the mountain's defenses. If she reached the summit, she'd be at full strength again. She was nearly there.

Then a hand closed around her ankle and yanked.

She fell hard onto a flat outcrop, rocks biting into her palms and knees. Pain flared, but she twisted with the momentum, flipping to her back and kicking out.

Her boot cracked against a jaw—Ingrid's. The neophyte staggered, snarling.

Ophelia scrambled upright. She didn't want to use magic yet—not unless she had to. Not when she needed every drop of it for escape.

Ingrid lunged.

Ophelia met her with a right hook to the mouth. Blood sprayed as two teeth flew from Ingrid's lips. The neophyte let out a guttural sound and doubled over, but not for long. She snapped back up and slammed a fist into Ophelia's side, then delivered a brutal uppercut beneath her chin.

Ophelia reeled. The impact rocked her vision, her balance. She skidded back, heels scraping near the cliff's edge.

One more step and she'd tumble all the way to the cave. And if that happened, she'd never get off this mountain. She snatched a jagged rock from the ground and hurled it like a fastball. It struck Ingrid squarely in the temple with a sickening crack. The neophyte clutched her head.

Ophelia didn't hesitate. She launched a brutal kick that dropped Ingrid to her knees, then snapped her leg out again, driving her boot into Ingrid's chest. The woman tumbled backward, catching herself just in time, now dangling by her fingertips over the ledge.

Ophelia didn't stay to watch her fall or climb back up. As much as she wanted to keep fighting, she could see the others closing in.

She turned and ran.

The slope grew steeper, harsher. Her thighs burned. Her hands scraped raw as she scrambled up the final stretch, breath ragged and sharp in her throat. But with every foot gained, the air changed. Thicker. Wilder. Familiar.

Her magic returned in a rush. At first, it was a flicker, then a flood.

At the peak, she swayed, chest heaving and light-headed. Below, Ingrid had hauled herself back over the ledge, blood trailing from her mouth. The other neophytes surged forward behind her.

Ophelia flung her arms wide. A spiral of flame erupted at the ridge, encircling the witches in a twisting wall of heat. They skidded to a stop, eyes wide, faces illuminated by the inferno.

She raised her hands again, calling on the mountain. The earth shuddered beneath her boots. Wind roared in from every direction, swirling into a column of air and dust. Her hair whipped around her face as the updraft lifted her, toes leaving the ground, then ankles, then knees. Ophelia hovered above the summit, her silhouette framed by fire and moonlight.

She looked down at the witches below and shouted through the wind's howl. "Tell Sofija the Lunula Amulet will be destroyed!"

Then she pushed upward—drawing on air and stone, on will and fury—and rose beyond the wards.

Mo's voice echoed in her mind. *"Centuries ago, witches could fly. Maybe you can too, with your command of more than one element."*

She hadn't believed him. Not really.

But now she was above Mount Slivnica, soaring through the Slovenian sky, the full moon blazing above her like a spotlight from the gods. At first, she dipped and lurched, her body struggling to balance the push and pull of flight. But slowly, instinct kicked in. Earth grounded her. Air carried her.

When the wind turned cold, she summoned a pulse of fire to her skin.

Below, the witches gaped in stunned silence. Except Ingrid,

who stood with her arms crossed, blood on her chin and hatred in her eyes.

Ophelia didn't look back again.

The last of her magic leeched from her bones as she flew, each second heavier than the last. Her body trembled from the inside out. She'd never pushed this far, never drawn this deeply from the well inside her, and it showed. Every gust of wind scraped against raw nerves. Every heartbeat felt stolen.

She wasn't going to last long.

Though the flight was short, she focused on reaching neutral territory—somewhere safe—before she lost control entirely. If she passed out midair, the witches wouldn't have to capture her. Gravity would finish the job.

Finally, the familiar shimmer of Trieste's coastline rose to meet her, the sea glinting like dark glass. She angled downward, barely managing to slow herself before she crashed onto Luka's terrace in a graceless heap—flat on her back, limbs trembling, lungs burning, vision swimming.

For a moment, she couldn't move. Couldn't even breathe.

Then Luka was there.

Strong hands wrapped around her neck, squeezing before instinct gave way to recognition. "Who the—?" he started, then froze. His eyes widened in horror. "Gods, love. I'm so sorry—I didn't know it was you—I didn't think you'd be back so soon—"

The words died in his throat as he took in the sight of her: her blue-tinged lips, the violent shivers racking her body, her eyes barely able to focus.

"Shit," he breathed. Without another word, he scooped her up and carried her inside, cradling her against his chest like something fragile. The fire flared to life a heartbeat later, flames snapping as he moved with blinding speed to wrap her in a thick blanket, brew a scalding cup of tea, and return to her side.

She was upright on the couch, but slumped and shaking, unable to grasp the mug he pressed into her hands.

"It's okay," he murmured, kneeling in front of her. "You used too much power. We'll work on your recovery when we train again."

He gently brought the cup to her lips. She turned her face away.

Her voice, when it came, was raw. Barely more than a breath. "I need a phone."

Luka hesitated, confused, but didn't argue. He retrieved his cell and placed it in her trembling hands.

She could hardly hold it steady. But her fingers, numb and stiff, somehow managed to tap the digits. The number she knew by heart. The one she'd called more times than she could count since childhood.

It rang.

Once. Twice.

Then a voice.

Ophelia closed her eyes. "I need your help."

CHAPTER

TWENTY-NINE

Alex landed at the Trieste airport the next day on a private plane Luka had chartered. He'd offered to come with Ophelia to meet her, but she needed this moment to be just the two of them. Still, Luka had insisted she take his black SUV with the dark-tinted windows. Trieste might be a neutral zone, but that hadn't stopped violence before. Driving the hulking vehicle through the quiet city streets felt less like transportation and more like preparing for battle.

Once Alex was buckled beside her and the doors were locked, Ophelia swept her gaze across the snowy parking lot. It appeared deserted.

"What's going on?" Alex asked, twisting in her seat to study Ophelia.

She hadn't explained much on the phone. Just that she needed help. And Alex, bless her reckless, loyal heart, had gotten on a plane within hours.

"Want to help me save the world?" Ophelia said with a wry smile, still scanning the perimeter.

Alex snorted. "I've never known you to be so dramatic." Her tone was teasing, but there was tension beneath the joke.

Ophelia could hear it. She met her friend's gaze, searching for the truth behind the smile. "I'm not," she replied.

They both knew that wasn't true. The tension broke with a shared laugh, brittle but real.

Alex's smile faded as she angled toward the window, watching the snowfall mute the colors of the city into ghostly pastels. "I just wish you weren't in the middle of all this."

"Me too," Ophelia said softly. "But I can't walk away. Not after what happened to Sebastian. And to you."

A long pause. Then: "What do you need?" Alex didn't meet her eyes this time. Her arms crossed over her chest, her gaze fixed on the empty stretch of asphalt ahead.

"I need your help to destroy an amulet."

And so Ophelia told her everything. About Galla and Alaric. About how madness had twisted Alaric's ambition, and how Galla had killed him to keep the world safe. About the child she spared and the stories she scattered to mislead those who might go hunting for the truth.

"Where did she hide it?" Alex asked, her tone sharper now, curious and engaged.

Ophelia's smile held a flicker of admiration. "She was brilliant. Everyone assumed Alaric had gone west, maybe to Spain. That's what the legends say. But Galla planted those stories. In reality, they crossed the Adriatic and went east, to what we now call Croatia."

She paused to let Alex catch up.

"The Cetina River empties into the sea at Omiš. They followed it inland, all the way to the Eye of the Earth, where the river begins. That's where she buried the amulet. She killed Alaric and his men, burned their bodies, and used powerful magic to seal the site. No one's ever found it. Not even with spells."

Alex exhaled slowly, her breath fogging the cold glass. When Ophelia finished recounting Galla's story, Alex let out a low whistle. "Anything else?"

"I wish I could say no." Ophelia hesitated, then reached across the console to squeeze Alex's arm. "We need to destroy the amulet together. Because between us, we carry the blood of the three supernaturals who created it."

Alex raised an eyebrow. "And?"

"And one of us will probably die," Ophelia admitted, her voice barely above a whisper. She'd considered keeping that part to herself, but of course she couldn't. Not with Alex.

Silence stretched between them. Long enough that doubt crept in. Maybe Alex would say no. Maybe she should.

But then Alex finally spoke. "Thank you for telling me the truth." Her tone was steady. "When do we leave?"

"Are you sure?" Ophelia asked.

"No," Alex said without hesitation.

"You don't have to—" Ophelia began.

"They'll come for me either way," Alex interrupted. "If I don't help, they'll use me against you. Because we're like sisters. And I don't want to live like that, always looking over my shoulder. I want my life back. Med school, marriage, maybe kids. But I can't have any of that if I leave you to face this alone. If you're willing to die to stop this, I can't stand by and do nothing."

Ophelia's chest tightened. She hated that Alex was right. If they failed, her friend would never be safe again.

"Okay," she said quietly. "Let's go get Luka."

Alex made a face. "Do we have to?"

Ophelia let out a surprised laugh at her tone. "Yes. What's that about?"

"Nothing," Alex said too quickly. "I just...don't think he's the one for you."

Ophelia blinked. "And how would you know?"

"It's a gut thing. Sure, he's gorgeous and obviously cares about you. But something feels off. I can't explain it." Alex shrugged, her posture tight with discomfort.

"A few months ago, you were pushing me to find someone. Now that I have, you're warning me off him?"

"Ophy, come on. We're about to risk our lives for the fate of the world. I'm allowed one moment of best-friend meddling."

Ophelia exhaled a laugh, the tension between them dissolving. "You're right. That's what friends are for."

She reached over and gave Alex's hand a squeeze, then shifted the SUV into reverse. "Let's go make sure an ancient supernatural relic doesn't mind-control every army on the planet," she muttered.

Alex snorted. "Totally normal Tuesday."

They both laughed, the sound small and bright against the weight of what lay ahead.

THIRTY MINUTES LATER, they'd collected Luka, and now he was driving like the devil was on their heels, eyes locked on the winding road as the SUV tore through the borderlands toward Croatia. The air inside the vehicle was taut with unspoken questions. They could've flown and rented a car closer to their destination, but discretion mattered more than speed. Even a private jet left a trail. This had to stay off every radar, magical or human. Not even Mo or Brisa knew where they were going.

The hours passed in a blur of snow-dusted fields and dense, leafless forests. Winter had stripped the landscape bare, revealing the bones of the countryside: gnarled branches, jagged cliffs, the occasional farmhouse watching their passing with shuttered eyes. Luka kept them off main highways, veering instead onto country roads so narrow they sometimes felt more like whispers through the land than proper paths.

As dusk bled across the sky in streaks of violet and rust, Luka turned off onto a dirt road. The SUV groaned as it climbed higher, tires crunching over frostbitten gravel. Every bend seemed tighter than the last, the forest pressing in like it wanted to swallow them whole. When they crested the final rise, a stone chapel came into view—small, ancient, and leaning slightly with age. Moss coated its sides like a second skin, and half the roof had caved in. The surrounding silence was uncanny.

"This is it," Ophelia whispered, more to herself than to the others.

Magic pressed against her skin the moment she stepped out. It was ancient, layered and intricate, like a thousand whispers woven into the earth. The air shimmered with it. Galla's wards. No wonder this place had remained hidden for so long.

They stepped out into the brisk mountain air, and a chill raced up Ophelia's spine. She was vibrating with nerves. Alex reached for her hand and squeezed. Her palm was cold but steady.

Behind the church, they found a narrow trail framed by bleached stones and brittle, lifeless brush. The wind picked up, whistling through the barren trees like a warning. From the crest of the path, the source of the Cetina River came into view.

Ophelia's breath caught.

The Eye of the Earth looked exactly as Galla had described: a swirling pool carved into the limestone, impossibly clear and unnaturally deep. Its shape was unmistakable: a dragon's eye, iridescent and watching. Shimmering shades of turquoise and sapphire churned below, hiding a dark abyss that seemed to pulse with ancient intent.

They descended slowly, boots crunching on loose dirt, until they stood at the shore. The water lapped gently at the rocks, but the magic here was anything but gentle. It climbed up her legs like vines, seeking a home in her skin. Ophelia stood between Alex and Luka and took their hands. The connection grounded her. Alex's grip was tight, while Luka's thumb stroked small circles along her palm.

"What now?" Alex asked, her voice quiet.

Ophelia hesitated. "I don't know," she said, though something deep in her bones said otherwise. She didn't know the spell. But she knew what to do.

She released their hands and pointed to the base of the path. "Luka, can you stand there?"

Before stepping away, Luka turned and gently took her by the shoulders. "You've got this, love," he murmured. He kissed her—firm and fleeting—then stepped back, eyes locked on her as he moved to the edge of the clearing.

Ophelia exhaled and raised her arms.

"Alex, you might want to step back," she said, already feeling the shift in the wind. Air coiled around them, swirling faster, pulling leaves and dust into a chaotic dance. The pressure in the air thickened, humming against her skin. Her magic stirred, the water below beginning to churn, calling her home.

Ophelia closed her eyes and reached down—deep, deep—into the bones of the earth. She pictured the silt and gravel, the centuries of stone layered over secrets. Her magic unspooled with force, pulling the wind into a vortex as the ground beneath them began to tremble. The last threads of sunlight vanished behind a cyclone of air and dust. The sky turned a bruised gray-black, clouds dragging low like an omen.

Alex stumbled as the ground shook harder, her voice rising above the roar. "Ophelia!"

Magic poured off Ophelia in waves, furious and unstoppable. Even Luka, usually unshakeable, braced himself, eyes narrowed as he watched the growing storm. They stood untouched at the eye of it, but the land around them heaved like it was alive.

The waters of the Eye erupted. A churning, muddy surge spilled over the rock-lined shore as Ophelia called on the earth to stir the depths. Sediment swirled to the surface, thick as smoke. And beneath it, something responded. Ancient, powerful, waiting.

The Lunula Amulet.

Ophelia dug deeper, summoning more magic from within. The wind howled, a living spiral, and the water shot upward like a geyser, jets arcing into the darkening sky. The pressure built and then broke. Earth and stone burst upward in a violent upheaval. The Eye vomited treasure. Gold coins, necklaces, and fist-sized jewels exploded from the depths like shrapnel, raining down with sharp, metallic clinks. The air was thick with glittering fragments of history.

Alex gasped. Luka took a step back, stunned. But Ophelia's focus tunneled to one object singing to her across time.

The amulet.

It spun upward in the current, the magic inside it thrumming like a heartbeat. Ophelia raised one hand, fingers trembling, and beckoned it toward her. The wind obeyed, cradling the amulet in invisible arms until it floated gently into her palm.

It was exquisite.

A solid gold crescent moon, inverted and impossibly smooth, strung on a thick chain that pulsed faintly with energy. Embedded in its surface were three stones: a gleaming black diamond, a blood-colored gem dark as garnet, and a diamond so clear it caught even the failing light. Smaller diamonds circled its edge like a constellation frozen in gold. It looked untouched by time, no corrosion or age. Magic had kept it whole.

Ophelia barely had a moment to register its weight before she felt it.

Luka.

He stepped forward, and she didn't need to see him to sense the change. His breath had quickened. Magic crackled in the air between them.

She glanced over. His fangs were out, his hands twitching, reshaping. Fur bloomed across his skin as jaguar claws replaced fingers.

"Fuck," she muttered, backing up.

The amulet's pull had already taken hold. Galla had warned her. Few could resist it, but this fast.

Then—shouts. Car doors. The slam of boots on gravel. Ophelia snapped her head toward the church. A line of vampires was cresting the ridge—twenty at least—fanning out with predatory precision.

Gabriel was at the front. When their gazes met, he gave her a crooked, knowing smile.

"Fuck. Fuck. *Fuck.*" She staggered back, eyes darting between Luka and the approaching threat. The amulet pulsed in her hand like it was alive. How the hell had they found her?

She'd already expended a massive surge of magic to unearth the amulet. And she would need even more to destroy it. But she was too far in to hesitate now. With a grim breath, Ophelia summoned what strength remained and conjured a ring of fire around herself and Alex. Flames erupted in a sudden arc, crackling and fierce, casting dancing shadows across the stone shore.

It wouldn't hold the vampires off forever, but it might buy them enough time to finish what they came for. Luka was closing in again, his steps heavy with intent. "Luka, don't," she called, her voice trembling with urgency. "Please, listen to me."

She raised a hand and sent a blast of wind toward him. It slammed into his chest, halting his advance just outside the fire's edge. Dirt kicked up around his feet as he skidded to a stop. "Please," she shouted, her voice raw now, fraying at the edges. "If you love me, help me. Luka!"

For a breathless moment, he hovered there, torn between desire and devotion. Then something in his expression shifted. He blinked, shaking his head as though surfacing from deep underwater. His gaze dropped to his clawed hands, then up to her face. His fangs were still bared, but the hunger in his eyes was dimming.

"I'm sorry, my love," he said, breath ragged. "I don't know what came over me." He staggered backward, putting distance between himself and the ring of fire, his eyes locked on the amulet like it was tearing him apart.

"You have to destroy it," he said, voice rough with regret.

Ophelia wasn't sure how long he could resist its pull.

"Then stop them," she said, flicking her chin toward the vampires descending the path. Their footsteps were closer now.

Luka growled low in his throat, the sound feral. "With pleasure," he snarled.

And then he was gone, his form blurring as he shifted. Black fur overtook his skin, claws gouging the earth. The jaguar burst forward with a roar that echoed off the cliffs, a living shadow racing up the slope toward the oncoming threat.

Ophelia turned back just in time to see Alex staring at the amulet, her pupils blown wide. "Oh, fuck me," Ophelia muttered. "Not you, too."

Alex didn't blink. "Just let me touch it," she whispered, hand drifting toward the gold.

Panic surged through Ophelia. She reached out and slapped Alex hard across the cheek.

"Wake up," she snapped. "We have to destroy it."

Alex stumbled back a step, blinking fast, her breath catching. She raised a hand to her stinging cheek, then nodded like she'd just shaken loose a trance. "Tell me what to do," she said, her voice steadier now, jaw clenched.

THIRTY

Raising her pant leg, Ophelia drew a dagger from her boot and sliced clean lines across both of Alex's palms, then her own. Blood welled and dripped, warm and bright. She clasped her right hand to Alex's left, their mingled blood sealing the connection.

"Now, take the amulet with your left hand."

Ophelia didn't wait. She pressed the amulet into their joined hands, streaking its flawless surface with blood. Then she began to chant.

> ***Ammar dandannu šaluštu banû aban***
> ***lamassi,***
> ***Apālu lū šaluštu abātu.***

The words, spoken in ancient Akkadian, echoed the riddle Galla had once whispered into her mind:

> *The power of three created thee,*
> *So, too, shall three destroy.*

Magic surged through Ophelia, raw and wild. Vampire blood mingled with her elemental power—earth, air, fire, water—intertwining with the fae magic pulsing through Alex. The amulet flared with light, unleashing a stream that circled them before shooting skyward, binding them in radiant threads of energy.

She chanted the incantation again. And again. Each repetition was a plea that the amulet would shatter before it claimed Luka. Or Alex. Or both.

Sensing danger pressing in, she shifted her focus to the flickering ring of fire encircling them. Beyond the flames, Luka —still in jaguar form—fought off five vampires. His claws slashed, his jaws snapped. Just when it seemed they'd overwhelmed him, he sprang back to his feet in a frenzy of fang and fury. But he was flagging, each breath labored.

And then, impossibly, Gabriel appeared. Sword in hand, he moved like something out of legend, cutting through the vampires with ruthless grace.

A fresh vibration ripped through the ground, stronger and darker than before. Ophelia's gaze snapped up the hill. Durante was descending the dirt path with dozens of vampires in his wake. Her heart plummeted. Luka and Gabriel would never survive that onslaught alone.

She tried to lift her hand, to call fire or wind to their defense. But her palms were sealed to Alex's and the amulet, bound by magic and blood. She was trapped, forced to continue the incantation as the battle raged beyond her reach.

Movement at the top of the ridge caught her eye. Brisa. Mo. Ingrid.

What the hell?

Even as the question formed, she saw them spring into action. Brisa summoned gusts of air to send vampires tumbling back. Mo split the ground beneath their feet. And

Ingrid lunged into the fray with vicious precision. They were here. They were fighting for her. Even Ingrid.

The magic inside Ophelia burned, hot and relentless. She wasn't sure how much longer she could endure it. She looked at Alex and nearly choked. Her friend's skin had gone ashen, her features slack with exhaustion.

"No, no, no," Ophelia breathed. This was it, what Galla had meant when she said there would be no turning back. The magic had taken over, pouring through her like a tidal wave. And still, she couldn't stop.

Beyond the dying fire, she saw movement. Durante was nearly at the edge of the ring. The flames still held, just barely, flickering wildly as her strength waned. She wouldn't let him reach the amulet. She forced the incantation faster, her voice rising with urgency. Again. Again.

A vampire at Durante's side passed him a dagger. Smirking, he drew back his arm and hurled it straight through the fire, aimed at Alex. Ophelia strained to move, but the binding held her fast. She couldn't even scream. The dagger struck the glowing shield of light that surrounded them and ricocheted to the ground, harmless.

Durante's face contorted, lips thinning with fury. "Ophelia," he snarled, "stop this madness, or I'll kill your lover."

Her eyes flew to Luka. He was no longer in jaguar form, too drained to hold the shape. Now he fought in his vampire body, blades in each hand, battling back-to-back with Gabriel. But he was fading fast.

Up the hill, Brisa hurled wind like a blade, felling two more attackers. Mo tore great cracks in the earth beneath their feet. Ingrid was locked in brutal combat with a snarling vampire. All of them bloodied. All of them relentless.

And Ophelia—still bound, still helpless—could only chant.

"Last chance, Ophelia," Durante warned, his voice a knife at her throat.

Ophelia's stomach churned as Durante drew a long silver sword. It was the same blade that had ended Sebastian's life. She opened her mouth to cry out, to warn Luka, but the incantation still held her lips captive. No scream came. Only the relentless chant.

Durante struck fast. Two savage slashes across Luka's back sent him crashing forward to the ground. But Luka rose again, twisting to face his enemy. They began to circle, two predators pushed past their limits. Luka's arms trembled from exertion. His legs wobbled with each step. The grace that once defined him had given way to staggering exhaustion.

The sword came down. Luka blocked it with crossed daggers, but Durante didn't let up. He advanced again and again, each strike harder, more brutal. Their weapons clashed, the rhythm of battle a blur of motion and steel. But Luka was losing ground. When he faltered, stumbling just a fraction too long, Durante drove the blade into his gut.

Blood spilled down Luka's front as he dropped to his knees. Durante turned to Ophelia, gloating. "Is this what you want?" He lifted the sword to Luka's neck.

Ophelia's body was paralyzed by the spell. Her voice, bound to the incantation. Her power, locked into the amulet. She couldn't cry out or save him. Tears streamed down her cheeks, helpless and hot.

Then—Alex. Ophelia's gaze snapped to her friend. Alex's body remained upright only by the amulet's magic. Her skin had turned a sickly gray, and her eyes had rolled back into her head. She might already be gone.

I won't lose them both.

Rage and desperation surged through her. She funneled the last of her strength into the ritual, chanting louder, pushing every ounce of magic she had into the amulet. Her palms burned. Her limbs trembled. She didn't care.

The amulet shuddered. A crack split through its surface.

She roared the incantation one final time. And the jewel shattered. It exploded in a blinding burst of light, flinging Ophelia and Alex apart. They hit the ground with a bone-rattling thud. Ophelia lay sprawled on her back, blinking up at a sky now glittering with fragments of gold and diamond, suspended like stars.

The fire ring was gone.

And Durante was standing over her, sword poised at her throat. Her thoughts flew to Alex. Was she breathing? Was she alive?

Ophelia met his eyes. "Do it," she rasped. "You'll never have the amulet. Or me." His mouth curled. "As you wish."

He raised the sword with both hands.

And Luka slammed into him from the side.

The two bodies crashed to the ground. Luka pinned Durante, fangs bared, inches from his throat. But then he stopped.

Durante shoved him off.

And that's when Ophelia saw it. A knife, buried deep in Luka's chest. Straight into the heart. Her scream tore from her throat at last. "Luka! Get up!" But the magic had vanished. Her limbs refused to obey.

Panic surged as she locked eyes with the monster who had taken everything. What had been done was already unraveling the world around her. Luka lay dying. Alex remained out of reach. The chain of horrors she'd set in motion showed no signs of stopping. Durante's twisted smirk was etched into his face like a brand. Slowly, deliberately, he raised his boot and slammed it down on the hilt of the blade lodged in Luka's chest.

The knife drove deeper. Even from where she knelt, she heard the crunch of bone. A scream tore free. Luka's heart shattered. A true death.

Her body convulsed with grief. No air filled her lungs. No thoughts could form. Only that smile—Durante's cruel, mocking satisfaction—held her in place. Something snapped.

She reached out, calling the dagger that had fallen during the ritual. It obeyed instantly, slicing through the air and into her waiting grip. The same blade she'd used to bleed her palm. To bind her friend. To destroy an ancient evil.

Now she would use it for something simpler. Vengeance.

As Durante closed in, his pace confident and unhurried, Ophelia stood her ground, silent and still. Letting him come. Letting him believe she was broken. And then she struck.

With the last of her strength, she launched forward. Her body collided with his, and she drove the dagger into his chest, straight through the heart. His eyes widened in shock, but she didn't stop. She twisted—once, twice, a third time—until he dropped to his knees, gasping.

She met his stare, holding it.

Then, with one clean motion, she drew the blade across his throat, severing it. His head fell. His body collapsed beside it.

This time, there would be no coming back.

She shoved Durante's body away and collapsed to her knees, the ground unforgiving beneath her. Every muscle trembled. Her lungs burned. She didn't know how much more she had to give.

Alex lay crumpled ahead. Luka, motionless behind. Her heart fractured at the sight of them: both broken, both hers.

She screamed in raw frustration, the sound scraped from the depths of her. She could only get to one. And she might only be able to save one. *Please forgive me,* she begged silently, casting one last glance at Luka. Then she began to crawl, dragging her body across the dirt and ash toward Alex. Her best friend. Her sister in all but blood. Her chosen family. She couldn't let her die.

When she reached Alex, her chest wasn't rising.

"No," Ophelia whispered.

She tried to push herself upright but collapsed again, her arms limp. Her hand still gripped the bloodied dagger, but it felt like stone in her grasp. As she spotted movement from the corner of her eye, she twisted protectively over Alex's body, raising the blade with trembling hands.

Gabriel.

He stopped a few feet away, both hands raised. "Ophelia. It's me. I'm not here to hurt you. The fight's over. The witches—Mo, Brisa—they've got the rest. You're safe. Let me help."

The dagger clattered to the ground.

Ophelia leaned forward and began chest compressions, sobbing as she pressed down on Alex's sternum, her hands slipping from weakness. "Come on, please. Please, don't do this. I need you. I need you." She sealed her lips to Alex's and breathed.

Nothing.

Gabriel knelt beside her, his voice soft. "CPR won't be enough. Not this time."

"Then what?" she choked out. "Tell me. I'll do anything." Her face was streaked with blood, dirt, and tears. "Please. I can't lose both of them."

He hesitated, then said, "Your blood. You could try giving her some. The magic might be enough to pull her back."

Ophelia blinked. "Could it kill her?"

"I don't know," Gabriel admitted. "I don't think any fae has ever taken blood like yours."

Still, there was no choice. She reached for the dagger, but

her blistered hands slipped against the hilt, too weak and wrecked.

"Please," she whispered, holding her arm toward him.

Gabriel didn't hesitate. He took the dagger and gently sliced a line across her wrist. "Now, hold it to her mouth."

With his help, she pressed the bleeding cut against Alex's lips. Her body curled instinctively around her friend, shielding her with what little strength she had left.

"Please don't die. Please come back," she murmured against Alex's hair. "You're my sister. I can't do this without you. I won't."

"Not too much," Gabriel warned, trying to pull her away. "You could hurt her."

"I don't care if it kills me."

"But it might kill *her*," he countered. Then, reluctantly, he brought his own wrist to his mouth, opened a vein with his fangs, and offered it to Ophelia. "Please. It'll help you heal."

She turned her face away. Gabriel sighed but didn't press further.

Ophelia reached down, took Alex's hand, and gasped. A burn sparked along her skin, a familiar echo of the amulet's magic. But then...warmth. Color crept back into Alex's cheeks. Her lips, once pale, were pink again. Her chest began to rise, slow and shallow, but steady.

"She's breathing," Ophelia said, the words a prayer. "She's going to live."

She looked up at Gabriel, eyes glassy with relief. "Can you carry her to my car?"

"Of course," he said gently. He bent and lifted Alex into his arms as if she were weightless.

As he climbed the path with her friend, Ophelia sat back on her heels, blood dripping from her wrist, the world still spinning. But hope flickered.

She had saved one.

As Gabriel disappeared up the path with Alex, Ophelia began crawling toward Luka. Her limbs shook with each movement, her hands blistered and raw, her muscles screaming in protest. But she didn't stop. If she could just reach him, maybe she could still save him.

When she finally reached his body, hope crumbled. His skin had lost all color, drawn tight over his bones. His frame, once so strong and vital, had begun to shrink in on itself. She collapsed across his chest, pressing her cheek to him, and let out a broken sob.

"Luka," she whispered. "Why are you leaving me, my love?" Her voice cracked. "Why would Galla send you with me, only to take you back? Why now?"

She stayed like that for a long time, unmoving, willing his chest to rise, his heart to restart, her magic to reignite. Nothing came. Shadows gathered around her. She didn't have to look to know Brisa, Mo, and Gabriel had joined her.

"Ingrid stayed with Alex," Brisa said quietly, quieter than Ophelia had ever heard her.

Ophelia didn't lift her head. "Will you help me with him?" Her voice was barely audible, the question scattered into the dirt.

"Tell me what you need," Mo said gently.

She didn't answer right away. Just let the silence settle around them, thick with smoke and grief. Finally, she spoke, her words ragged. "Why?"

"Why what?" Mo asked.

She raised her head toward the circle of people who had fought beside her. They looked as wrecked as she felt—smeared with ash and blood, their eyes hollowed by loss.

"All of it," she whispered. "Why any of this?"

Gabriel was the one who answered. "Luka and I didn't

always see eye to eye. But we wanted the same thing. We fought for the same world."

There were no answers that would satisfy her, and she knew it.

She tried to rise, to lift herself from Luka's body. Her arms buckled. Again, she tried. No one moved to help her, and she was grateful for it. This was something she needed to do on her own. On the third try, she made it to her feet.

"Help me take him to the water," she said. Her voice was steadier now, threaded with resolve. Luka deserved to rest beside Alaric, in the sacred place where this had all begun, where Galla's sacrifice had bought them time. Their stories would echo together.

Gabriel bent and lifted Luka's body with reverent care. Ophelia followed, limping in his wake. Brisa and Mo came behind, silent.

At the edge of the Eye, its waters once again a brilliant turquoise, Gabriel knelt and laid Luka gently down.

He glanced at Ophelia. "May I?"

She nodded. Gabriel bowed his head, both hands placed over Luka's heart. "Thank you, brother," he said softly. "For your strength, your sharp tongue, your loyalty—even when it cost you everything." He whispered something more that Ophelia couldn't hear, then pressed his forehead to Luka's and stepped away.

Brisa knelt next. She touched Luka's shoulder, her expression crumpling. "You'll be missed, vamp," she said, her voice thick. "Even your brooding."

Mo placed a palm over Luka's chest. "Goodbye, old friend. You did right in the end."

Then they stepped back, giving Ophelia the space she needed. She dropped to her knees beside Luka, taking his hand in hers. His fingers were already stiff with death. She brushed his hair from his brow and leaned close, her lips near his ear.

"Thank you," she whispered, "for finding me in the dark. For showing me what I could be. For loving me even when I didn't know how to love myself." Her throat closed. She unclasped her mother's bracelet—her last true heirloom—and wrapped it around his finger. A single tear rolled down her cheek and fell onto his, the last piece of herself she could give.

She kissed him once, soft and final, before she stood.

Summoning the air around her, she shaped it with trembling hands. The wind rose in a spiral and lifted Luka's body, carrying it to the surface of the Eye. As he touched the water, the ripples expanded outward. Then, gently, he began to sink.

The water swallowed him slowly, reverently, until nothing remained but stillness and sky.

"Goodbye, my love," she whispered.

THIRTY-ONE

Ophelia stood beside the tree in her New York townhouse on Christmas morning, the twinkle of lights casting soft reflections across the hardwood floor. Most of her bruises had faded. Her scars had nearly vanished, except for the thin line carved into her palm. That one would remain. It was a permanent reminder that destroying the amulet had left deeper wounds than magic could heal.

She and Elijah had agreed to make an effort this year, to conjure something resembling festive cheer. Sebastian had adored the holidays. He had loved baking elaborate cookies and handpicking gifts with uncanny precision. Now, it was their turn to carry the torch, even if the fire flickered low.

Ophelia crouched to retrieve a brightly wrapped package from beneath the tree. "Alex, this one's for you." Her best friend, still fragile, sat swaddled in blankets. Silver streaked her golden-blonde hair. But she was alive and breathing. And that was all that mattered. She, too, bore the amulet's mark on her palm, a scar that would follow her through every season yet to come. She and her parents were staying at the town-house, nominally for the holidays. In truth, they all understood the real reason: safety.

Ophelia reached for another gift. "Cousin, your turn." She handed the larger, heavier box to Brisa.

"This better be the daggers I've been coveting," Brisa said with dry amusement. Across the room, Alex's parents stiffened. Mo gently reprimanded her for the comment, and Ophelia laughed, a raw, unexpected sound that startled even herself. She clamped down on it. Joy felt misplaced with Sebastian and Luka gone.

"Elijah, where are you? I have something for you, too," she said.

"Coming, dear," he called, stepping into the living room with a tray of mimosas, coffee, and buttery biscuits—their Christmas breakfast ritual. "Help yourselves," he added, setting it down amid the pile of opened boxes and crumpled paper.

He was trying. Ophelia could see that. This was usually Sebastian's domain. Even the apron he wore, soft pink with faded embroidery, had once been Sebastian's. She crossed the room and wrapped her arms around Elijah, holding him quietly before stepping back and pressing her hand to his chest, right over the heart and the apron.

"Is it okay?" he asked, his voice tinged with hesitation. "Wearing this, I mean."

"It's more than okay." She managed a smile, though it trembled at the edges. "Here, your present." She offered him a small box.

"Thank you, daughter." He folded her into another hug, this one lasting longer.

Ophelia hadn't told him the truth about Luka, not really. She'd let Elijah believe the relationship had ended on its own, not that Luka had died to protect them all. But she couldn't shield him from this world forever. For now, they had this morning, this ritual. And that would have to be enough.

When the threat of tears surged, she reached for a mimosa and a biscuit, chewing dutifully despite the chalky taste. The bubbles went down easier than the food.

She settled onto the floor in front of Alex, legs folded beneath her, and watched as the rest of the gifts were opened. She couldn't help but laugh—truly laugh—when Brisa let out a delighted squeal over the silver daggers she'd been eyeing for weeks. The laugh grew louder when Alex's parents exchanged a horrified glance as Brisa began spinning them, effortlessly twirling the blades like batons.

"There's one more," Mo said quietly, handing her a small box wrapped in black-and-silver paper. He sat cross-legged on the floor nearby. "Luka asked me to give this to you, if he couldn't."

The weight of the gift in her hands nearly undid her. She inhaled deeply, bracing herself. Pressing the box to her face, she caught his scent—night-blooming jasmine—and nearly lost her composure. With slow, reverent fingers, she loosened the lace and peeled back the wrapping. Inside, resting atop velvet, was an envelope addressed in Luka's sweeping, elegant script.

To My Love,

If you're reading this, then I am no longer with you.

Our lives did not remain bound as I had hoped, but the time we shared was the brightest of my many centuries. I was given a vision long ago, one that foretold my end. I always knew our days would be fleeting, a single breath in the span of eternity.

But even so, I would not trade a moment.

Watching you rise into your power filled me with something I had not felt in lifetimes—hope. And to love you...to be loved by you...that has been one of my life's greatest honors.

This gift reminded me of the fire that lives inside you. Not just the magic, but the brilliance of your mind and the purity of your heart. Keep following both.

And for me, my love, my final request is simple: Live. Don't just survive, but live with joy. And choose happiness when you can.

With all my love,

Luka

Ophelia buried her face in her hands as silent sobs overtook her. She hadn't meant to cry, especially not today, but the ache of his absence shattered what little composure she had left. He'd known. He'd seen his own death and still walked willingly toward it to help her. She was furious that he hadn't told her. And she missed him so fiercely, the grief pressed into her bones.

Alex shifted closer, rubbing slow circles into her back. "It's okay," she murmured. "You're allowed to fall apart."

Ophelia nodded into her hands, trying to steady her breath. "I wanted this to be a happy morning."

"You don't have to apologize," Elijah said gently from across the room. "It's okay to grieve."

She wiped her face with trembling fingers and reached back into the box. Nestled beneath the letter was an old, ornate key and a set of legal documents. He'd passed his entire estate to her. The house in Italy. Everything.

Her throat constricted with guilt, but she swallowed the fresh wave of tears. There was one more item. She lifted the jewelry box from the velvet lining and opened it with reverent care.

Inside lay a necklace unlike anything she'd ever owned. A delicate platinum triangle framed a teardrop emerald, the same color as Luka's eyes. The stone hung from the triangle's apex, centered like a heartbeat. Tiny diamonds traced the lines, leading to a single, larger diamond at the base, and just above that, a small ruby. The chain itself was platinum, studded with bezel-set diamonds that glinted like stars.

Elijah crouched in front of her. "Let me," he said softly. His hands reached behind her neck, fastening the clasp. The necklace settled against her chest with a comforting weight. As he gently brushed her hair aside to make sure it lay flat, she pressed the emerald pendant to her sternum and closed her eyes. A silent promise formed in her chest: she would wear it and remember him.

After breakfast and the final round of presents, Ophelia's skin felt too tight, her thoughts too loud. She needed movement. She changed into warm running leggings and a long-sleeved athletic shirt, pulling her hair into a long, efficient ponytail. Her fingers lingered on the necklace one last time before she stepped outside.

Ophelia stepped onto the stoop and drew a slow breath. The air held that strange winter contradiction of crisp, yet warm. It smelled faintly of pine and city soot. She bounded down the townhouse steps, spotting the black SUV parked half a block away. Two vampires sat inside, watching but not intruding. She gave a short wave. Gabriel's men. He'd insisted on providing protection around the clock.

She still didn't understand him. Why he'd helped at the Eye of the Earth. Why he remained, hovering at the edge of her life like smoke refusing to dissipate. Whatever his reasons, he hadn't posed a threat. And her family needed guarding. So she allowed it, for now.

The illusion of safety had shattered with the destruction of the amulet. The supernatural world had seen what she was capable of, and that kind of power didn't vanish without consequences. Someone would want it. Someone always did. She'd been naive to think freedom would follow.

But she would not be used. And when they came, she'd be ready. But for now, she ran. She crossed into Central Park and angled toward the North Woods, where the city gave way to something older, quieter. The ground softened beneath her feet, and she let her magic take over, pushing her faster with every breath. Wind clawed at her limbs, trying to keep up.

As the air cooled, she pulled warmth from her core, kindling it like a small fire in her bloodstream to keep her pace steady. The stream nearby murmured its eternal lullaby, syncing with the rhythm of her steps and pulse.

Then something shifted, subtle but unmistakable. A prickle moved along her spine with the press of a presence. Someone was near. That familiar thrumming gathered in her chest, spreading like a warning flare across her skin. She slowed to a stop, every sense on high alert. Another witch was nearby.

She summoned flame to her fingertips and turned toward the thickest part of the woods. This wasn't the first time something—or someone—had followed her. But she wasn't the same girl who had fled from the jaguar in the woods. She was ready now.

A twig snapped behind her. She spun, flames launching from her hands.

"That won't be necessary," came a calm voice as the stranger neatly sidestepped the blast.

Ophelia didn't lower her hands right away. Her chest heaved, heart hammering against her ribs. The fire still burned in her palms.

The woman stood a few feet away. She was older, but unmistakable. Streaks of silver threaded through brown curls. Time had carved lines into the skin beside deep, familiar eyes. But the face hadn't changed.

She stared, breath frozen. "Mom?"

EPILOGUE

The witch stood at the edge of the spring, the turquoise-blue water swirling gently near her feet. Its shape had returned to resemble the eye of a dragon. The earth around her had settled shortly after the other witch left. The dust and dirt returned to their resting place, while the sky had shed its angry black, yielding to vivid hues of blue and white. All was calm now. Exactly as the moira had foretold in the vision gifted to her all those years ago.

Raising her hands, she parted the surface and used the force of the water in the spring's depths to bring the body to the surface. The magic in the waters had restored the deathlike pallor of his skin to its natural hue. As he broke through, his eyelids fluttered open slightly, revealing emerald orbs.

A pained moan escaped his lips, his breath catching. He whispered, "Oph—," his throat scratchy, the rest of the word inaudible. He kept babbling, but she ignored him, guiding his heavy body to rest on the shore atop a large canvas. She pulled the fabric around him, leaving enough to grip in both hands.

This was going to hurt.

Grasping the ends of the canvas, she dragged his body across the rocky ground, leaving a trail of wet dirt behind. Huffing as sweat shimmered on her skin, she glanced at him, certain he'd passed out from the pain. But his chest still rose, sporadic and uneven. Glancing up the hill, she wiped her brow and rubbed the dull ache in her lower back.

Just a little farther. She could do this. She would do this.

By the time they reached her car, parked near the church, the night air had closed in again. She wrestled him into the back seat, bracing both feet on either side of him as she hauled with all her strength. Once he was in, she found herself trapped beneath his weight. Gasping from the effort, she paused to catch her breath. Finally, she wiggled free, landing on the floorboard, then crawling out of the car and collapsing onto the gravel, hands and knees scraping against the ground.

She stood, gravel clinging to her skin and digging into her palms. One last glance at the spring made her shudder—the force of magic here pulsed, ancient and alive. Then she turned, climbed into the driver's seat, and headed down the gravel road.

Away from the Eye of the Earth.

ORDER BOOK 2 of the Wildes Witch Trilogy: Out of Ashes

ALSO BY CARRIE VIXENHART

THE WILDES WITCH TRILOGY

Eye of Fire, Book 1

Out of Ashes, Book 2

Flames of Fury, Book 3

PRAISE FOR VIXENHART

"This is an incredible debut! Vixenhart sucks you right in with intriguing characters and an enthralling world. I was swept up with the fast pace and witty writing. Prepare to read through without stopping once you start, as you'll be flipping pages to get answers. I cannot wait for the next one in this trilogy!!"

Ali Dean, USA Today Bestselling Author

AUTHOR'S NOTE

Thank you for diving into Ophelia's world of magic, mystery, and untamed passion. If you enjoyed this journey, I'd love to stay connected.

JOIN MY NEWSLETTER

 Want exclusive sneak peeks, updates on future books, blog posts, and behind-the-scenes content? Please visit my website and sign up for my newsletter! www.vixenhart.com

SOCIAL MEDIA

Let's keep the conversation going! Follow me on social media for updates and a glimpse into my writing life. @carrievixenhart

Acknowledgments

No one lives in a vacuum. Some might say, "You think you just fell out of a coconut tree!" I certainly couldn't claim that. This book would not have been possible without the support and encouragement of so many incredible people.

First and foremost, to my brilliant and beautiful daughters, Adison and Alanis: you are the root of everything I do. An accidental pregnancy at 20 was the best thing that ever happened to me. Adison, your passion for life lights my fire. Thanks for growing up with me and being one of my biggest cheerleaders. Alanis, your vibrant spirit gives me courage. Naming my books? Absolute genius. I can't wait to see you both flourish in your own creative journeys.

To my family, thank you for providing endless content since day one. Having raunchy and rambunctious sisters (and a mother!) will fuel my writing forever. To my sisters, there is no bond quite like ours. To my mom, I will probably always write complicated mother figures. But as a mom, I understand we're all a mix of beautiful layers, and I'm really proud of yours. To my dad, I'm so glad you get to sit back, listen to our banter, and smirk. Being surrounded by so many brilliant and beautiful women is no easy feat, but you've risen to the challenge.

Alison, having a sister-in-love like you has been the greatest gift. This book and my journey over the last few years would not have been possible without your selflessness and support. I don't know how we hit the jackpot with you, but our modern family is all the better for it.

Maw-Maw, your bravery in being the first person in our family to go to college—in your forties and with four children, no less—will forever inspire me. Because of that one step, you changed the course of future generations. I hope you're proud of what you started—I sure am.

To all my other family members and friends, I love you dearly. I can't list every name, but please know that your support means the world to me. A very special shoutout to Alex, Chris, Craig, Dash (& Heather), Elayna, Kelly, Keri, Lara, Melissa, and Shelby. I could keep listing names forever, but eventually, I have to stop. Thank you especially to the brave souls who volunteered to read sex scenes and provide feedback. That was truly selfless of you.

To my yoga community, thank you for keeping me grounded. Amy & Alex: you've created a magical and sacred place.

To my Writing Friends, it's been wild taking this journey with you! Special thanks to Lara, Lynn, and Brigette for years of laughter and camaraderie. Now, can we please schedule a meeting just to brainstorm synonyms for "limp"? And a very special thank you to Alex—who knew getting laid off could lead to this?

This book wouldn't exist without all the incredible feedback I've received from so many people, including (but probably not limited to): Mary, Toni, Rebekah (& Bunner), Kelly, Keri, Alison, Alex, Deb, and numerous writing friends over the years (Lara, Lynn, Brigette, Susan, and Virginia, to name a few).

To my two Smut Lover book clubs, thank you for being my people. Nothing beats bonding over spicy stories with fellow filthy fiction fans who truly understand the art of a well-written...scene.

Huge thanks to my editors, Andrea Hurst, Leanne Rabesa, Jamie Ryter, and Noah Sky, for helping shape this book. For my beautiful cover art, thanks to Sarah Hansen of Okay Creations. And to Samantha Randolph at Sam's Creative Cure, your work is stunning, and watching your journey has been inspiring.

Books—even the ones about witches and vampires—are born from shared experiences. Thank you for being part of mine. I wouldn't change a single step of this crazy, beautiful journey.

ABOUT THE AUTHOR

A free spirit at heart, Carrie Vixenhart's passion for life has carried her across the globe. She delights in sharing new wonders with her daughters, both through travel and the magic of books. Carrie is perpetually drawn to the ocean, where she feels most at peace. A dedicated yogi and aspiring sailor, she dreams of one day exploring the world by water. Fueled by a bottomless coffee cup, she weaves high-suspense urban fantasy packed with steamy romance and supernatural drama.

instagram.com/carrievixenhart

tiktok.com/@carrievixenhart

amazon.com/author/carrievixenhart

www.ingramcontent.com/pod-product-compliance
Lightning Source LLC
Chambersburg PA
CBHW022025310726
48972CB00006B/1804